What readers say about Robert Chazz Chute's work

Chute sucks you in from word one and pulls you down his post apocalyptic rabbit hole! You will sleep with the lights on, covers pulled over your head and dust off the old teddy bear for comfort. Horrifically well written and engaging. There are other popular books in this genre, but after reading this there is nothing else that climbs to the heights of Chute's caliber. Chazz ranks among the top tier of our generation's storytellers. ~ Alex Kimmell, Author of *The Key to Everything*

Robert Chazz Chute is such a skilled spinner of tales that the reader is more than willing to suspend any possible disbelief to go along for the ride. ~ David Pandolfe, author of *Jump When Ready*

It's not very often one finds a writer with such a dark side that has such a great sense of humor. ~ Glenn Roberts, Amazon reviewer

* * *

The author has a definite talent with words and ideas. ~ Love to Read!, Amazon reviewer

His words lift and dance off the page, bringing the story to life. ~ Kindle Customer, Amazon reviewer

The world building is horrifically well done with twists and turns and deceit around every corner. ~ Wanda, Amazon reviewer

Nothing but sheer exhaustion could tear my eyes from the captivating dance of words choreographed by Robert Chazz Chute. ~ Halph Staph, Amazon reviewer

Wonderful action constantly holds your interest. ~ Sharon Finn, Amazon reviewer

The complexity and attention to detail throughout absolutely blow me away. ~ Kindle customer, Amazon Reviewer

* * *

Very few authors impress me with the their actual writing style, it's usually always about the story. But this author paints such beautiful vivid pictures with words that I found myself not only enjoying the story but enjoying the way the words created images in my mind. I know that sounds corny, but it is true. ~ B.H., Amazon reviewer

Chute gives us story worthy of Stephen King. A read both thoughtful and fun. ~ Linda Beer Johnson, Amazon reviewer

The author does an excellent job building the characters and getting you invested and involved. ~ Michele L. Hebert, Amazon reviewer

I just can't say in words what a powerful author this is! ~ Delinda L. Calkins, Amazon reviewer

Robert Chazz Chute writes so skillfully as to make the supernatural seem perfectly logical - and terrifying! There are twists, turns and surprises galore. You will be glad you bought this book - until you lose sleep because you can't put it down. ~ johligo, Amazon reviewer

When I want to read apocalyptic books or zombie stories, those books have to also be extremely well-written and something that I could recommend with zeal and confidence to everyone I know. Robert Chazz Chute's books are exactly that. ~ Mazie Lane, Amazon reviewer

He makes the stuff that is obviously fiction, believable. ~ W. Nickels, Amazon reviewer

I am a lover of paranormal, dystopian novels and depth of story as well as intelligence in writing style, and Robert has it all. Humor, wit, depth, intelligence and an awesome way with words/writing. ~ Amazon Customer, Amazon reviewer

WALLFLOWER

Robert Chazz Chute
Published by Ex Parte Press
First Edition January 2016
ISBN 978-1-927-607-37-4
Cover art: *Cyrano in the Garden at Midnight* by the author.

Published by Ex Parte Press
For inquiries, email expartepress@gmail.com.

DEDICATION

**To Kurt Vonnegut, raise a glass.
And dedicated to you, the Reader, and the
lives you might have lived.
To the life you might yet live.
~ RCC
*December, 2056***

*As many rivers to a dark sea,
we follow twisted skeins of streets,
ranging far and rarely straight.
In wonder and fear, we face one fate.*

"The universe is full of magical things
patiently waiting for our wits to grow
sharper."
~ Eden Phillpotts

Ray Bradley tried to kill himself. He steered his Honda Civic into a thick palm tree. In that one fleeting moment, he had lost sight of any possibility that he could change his life for the better.

Suicide is a bromide, a reflexive impulse often reconsidered, sometimes too late. If the perpetrator doesn't die before one hopeful thought can percolate through his brain, he'll wish he hadn't thrown himself into the path of the oncoming subway. We are all in that race between thinking and impulse, unconscious instinct versus conscious intent.

But philosophizing prattles our way to a dead end. Consider the case of that past and future time traveler, Ray Bradley.

Ray's boss at the studio was a bright young woman named Taren Fugelstein. Taren's birth name was Karen, but she moved from St. Paul to Los Angeles and wanted to work in the entertainment business. The flight to California does that to a lot of people.

Taren nee Karen told Ray he had to produce more pages each day. When that order didn't take, Taren insisted Ray visit her psychologist, Dr. Circe Papua.

"Dr. Papua really helped me get over my cramps, Ray. You've got to go."

"I don't have cramps."

"I think you do," Taren said, "but they're in your head. Hypnosis can help lots of problems," Her gaze seemed fixed on his protruding gut. Was she trying to be mean or was she trying to help? Ray wasn't sure. He reddened with embarrassment. "Um...I don't want to tell all my problems to a stranger, Taren."

"Gonna have to tell her, Ray. You've exhausted all your friends."

"Joe still thinks I'm The Man, capital T, capital M," Ray said.

Joseph Grenwell, his best friend since college, wrote scripts with him. Ray called his friend Grins Well because Joe was always his best and most appreciative audience. Joe had recommended Ray for the game show job.

Ray wrote jokes for *What's My Rhyme?* The show was in its second season and it was only half of a game show. The other half was reality TV.

"Altered reality," Grins Well called it. The premise was simple: young rappers competed to win $250,000. The twist was that the competitors had to collaborate with team members from their family.

Taren preferred elderly grandparents for the role. "America wants to see shirtless, muscled young men and sexy young women rapping with their grandmothers. There's nothing funnier than watching an old lady scold her grandson as he searches for a new rhyme for the words, 'bitches and hos.'"

Ray would still be delivering barbecue ribs if not for Grins Well. Before the game show job, a couple of nights a week, Ray would put his name in a hat hoping to win the raffle for stage time at the Comedy Store. If his name was pulled from the hat, he'd get to practice his stand up skills at two in the morning for a couple of heckling drunks.

One of the older comics took Ray aside after he kept coming back for more punishment. "You've got something, kid, but maybe there's a cure for it. Ease back on the stick and write more before you come back. Stand up comedy is hard on-the-job training. It's the only job where you're guaranteed to fail publicly and embarrass yourself for at least the first few years."

Ray was a funny guy, but impatient. He didn't want to wait to get better. Besides, he was more of a storyteller than a joke writer. He built a narrative and invited the audience to go on a journey with him, finding the funny along the way.

Guys who weren't as funny as Ray got more stage time because they delivered punchlines faster. Even if most jokes failed to land, those comics got more laughs because they were firing faster per minute.

Despite his persistence going to open mic nights, Ray never got invited back to be a regular.

"Openers start shows big," one club owner told Ray. "Headliners finish big. You're a middle. Solid filler, but too serious and chewy by half."

"I'm doing something different," Ray told them.

"That's your problem," the club owner said. "I'm trying to sell drinks here. The more the audience laughs, the thirstier they get. It's business. Do the math."

"I suck at math."

"So you can't be a comic or an accountant. Maybe you're a florist and don't know it yet. Or join the army or something."

Ray stuck to his guns, convinced his brand of storytelling would catch on. In the meantime, he was grateful to be paid so well to write jokes, even if it was for *What's My Rhyme?*

Except he wasn't writing many jokes.

"Our game show is a reality show," Taren told him. "To get picked up for a third season, we need a lot more witty stuff, especially for the grandmas to say. That's cute. The network will eat that up."

"If I can write enough unreal stuff for our reality game show." As Ray's boss stared back at him over her desk, Ray prepared to fight the decree that he see her therapist.

Then Taren said, "It was Joe who asked me to talk to you."

"You're funny," Ray said.

"I am rather funny," Taren said, "but nobody's laughing so this must be my serious boss face. We're not laughing at what you've turned in lately, Ray. It's too dark and mean. This is a fun show and you're missing the spirit of WMR."

The spirit of WMR? Ray thought. *Well, la-di-da! Where does she get off telling me to go to therapy? Or calling this stupid show WMR?*

Discovering that Joe Grins Well had talked to Taren behind his back about his problems was the first betrayal. Worse? They were right. Ray wasn't funny. Not anymore. Since funny was what he was paid to be and do, he could add unfunny to his list of problems.

"That's a long list," Ray muttered to himself.

"A good cooperative employee who wants to keep his cushy writing job says what?" Taren said.

"What?"

That's how Ray began visiting Dr. Circe Papua once a week on the eighth floor of a shabby old office building in Hollywood, off Lebrea.

Dr. Papua didn't try hypnosis on him once. His therapist, Ray decided, had attended the Cheerleading School of Psychology: No pills, talk it out, use affirmations, cope like a grown-up, forgive your inner brat and call your soul back. Papua's approach was very chewy granola and birkenstocks. Her office wall was decorated with photos of herself beaming smiles with Dr. Deepak Chopra, Dr. Drew and Anthony Robbins.

Despite how trite her advice sometimes seemed, Ray became less focused on his regrets. He pretended to be more optimistic about the future. He never actually *felt* more optimistic. However, Dr. Papua's policy was, "Fake it until you make it."

Though her academic diplomas hung over the toilet, he somctimes wondered if Dr. Papua was faking being a therapist. He could have gotten her advice — slogans disguised as wisdom — from a sad afternoon of eating Baskin Robbins in front of the TV while watching Dr. Phil.

However, reporting to Dr. Papua seemed to be the driving force of his improvement. He felt he had to be better at something before his next appointment.

Besides, his insurance paid most of her huge hourly fee and the time away from the office was a welcome escape from the pressure cooker.

The most immediate problem (one day pre-pothole) was that Ray's wife of six years, Marla, left him. She'd talked of working on the relationship. Then she suggested a trial separation. She talked most about how Ray had to work on himself. "You're so damn lazy!"

"I'm not lazy. I'm moody. I'm brooding. Like Batman."

"You sleep on the couch when you get home and play *Call of Duty* when I'm ready to go to bed. You sure *look* lazy."

"I'm tired."

"You need to get more exercise."

"I would, but I'm awfully tired."

"Excuses!"

"Look, I'm having a hard time at work and...okay, maybe I'm a bit depressed and when I get like that, I just want to retreat into sleep."

"You're retreating from me," Marla said. "You're supposed to retreat *to* me."

Ray thought, *why would I want to do that?*

Ray said, "We're a team against the dark forces of the world. We're Team Bradley! Go, us!...yay."

From the sour look on Marla's face, it was apparent Dr. Papua was the better cheerleader.

Ray's solution was to stay later at work. He slept on the cot off the writing room. He told himself that every marriage had its ups and downs. Ray thought he had more time to turn things around. Then Marla packed a bag.

Ray was under the impression she'd gone to Cuba

to "sort things out." She hadn't asked for a ride to LAX. When Marla left him, her kiss goodbye was an airy peck on the cheek. The kiss had all the passion of an aunt kissing a nephew goodbye, if the nephew's face was a ball of volcanic, eruptive acne.

Ray shouldn't have been surprised when a friendly young Hispanic woman approached him as he was getting into his Honda.

"Mr. Ray Bradley?" (Huge smile with a big gap between her front teeth. When she said, "mister" it sounded like she said, "*me-tar*.")

"Hi. That's me. I'm Ray." He put out a hand and she slipped the divorce papers into his palm.

"You've been served." Not so friendly now.

"Nice job you've got," he said. The process server spun on her heel and climbed into a rusty old red Ford. He watched her rumble off to go ruin someone else's life. Once she'd disappeared from sight, he allowed the first tear to fall.

But the process server hadn't ruined his life. Ray had managed that on his own. Taren wouldn't keep him on for the next season of the game show. Marla was out and away, flying free of his dark cage. He'd weighed himself that morning. Ray weighed 270 pounds. Despite encouragement from fat acceptance websites, he felt awful. "I'm visiting fat acceptance websites," he said aloud to no one.

Ray needed pills. Dr. Papua didn't prescribe pills, but Ray figured he'd need a lot of pills before nightfall if he was going to solve his problems, once and forever.

He was driving fast when he hit the pothole. It was a solid *ka-chunk* and he wondered briefly if he'd damaged the car. Then he thought, *I don't have to worry about bills anymore. That's over. The trying is over. Game called on account of despair.*

Ray hadn't given suicide much thought since he was a teenager. Cutting had assuaged the impulse when he was fifteen. Cutting up as the class clown pushed the idea away when he was sixteen. At seventeen, sex put suicidal ideation at the back of his head in some forgotten neural closet. Sex on Earth was too good to leave, so he had no suicidal impulses.

Suicidal intentions were suddenly back in season. What Ray hadn't expected was the euphoria that accompanied surrender to Death. As soon as he committed to the idea of killing himself, he felt so much better. Marla would be sad. Better, she might even blame herself, at least a little. Marla was cold, but, like most women, she'd take more than her share of the responsibility for his desperate act.

Ray fantasized that Taren would feel bad, too. No reason she should, just...he wanted to be missed. Joe would no doubt deliver his eulogy. Ray hoped Joe would fail to make it funny. He hoped Grins Well would only get a few laughs by recounting Ray's best material. He hoped Joe would use their spec movie scripts to show off his best stuff, not the silly puns from *What's My Rhyme?*

A few seconds post-pothole, Ray's smile faded. He could already feel his resolve ebbing as the euphoria drained away with it. Before the good feeling could disappear completely, he stomped on the gas and screamed in rage as he pointed his Honda Civic at a thick palm tree.

That could have been the end of his story. He almost succeeded. If Ray Bradley had killed himself, he would have missed out on saving the world from itself and possibly changing the universe.

Makes you think, doesn't it? But only time travelers jump to the end. Here's what happened with Ray, failed comic, depressive, and once and future time traveler.

2

Dark.

Light.

Dark.

"Hey! His eyes fluttered for a second! Hello?"

Nothing.

"Can you tell me your name?"

Nothing.

"Mr. Bradley? Mr. Ray Bradley?"

"Mm?"

"Do you know what day it is?"

"Someday."

"Er...okay. Who is the president?"

Ray cleared his throat. Something tasted awful and he wanted to spit it out. However, the bitter thing was his tongue. "Of what?"

"What?"

"The president. Do you want to know the president of the United States or the Elks Club?"

"The United States. Can you tell me, sir?"

"Uh...lemme sleep. Turn down the music."

"Do you know where you are, Mr. Bradley?"

"Who?"

Dark.

Light.

Dark.

Somewhere in the dark, someone screamed and kept screaming. They were angry about something. It started with a diatribe about pain and ended with a rant about being fed stewed tomatoes.

It was the complaint about stewed tomatoes that made Ray think he was in a hospital. Where else do they force feed people stewed tomatoes?

But why, Ray wondered, would he be in a hospital?

Oh.

Right.

Tree.

Ray's first thought before he dared to open his eyes was that he could smell urine and he worried it belonged to him. He tried wiggling his torso a little bit, but that hurt too much. He had to open his eyes to assess the situation and his eyelids were heavy.

Somewhere nearby, two women laughed. He wondered if they were laughing at him. He tried to sneak a peek. He thought at first that his head was covered in gauze but it was simply that his eyelids were stuck together.

The laughers were dressed in white. *Nurses,* he decided. He wished they'd be quiet. They laughed too loud. To Ray, they sounded like two barking seals getting slowly ground up in assembly line gears at a microphone factory.

Behind the nurses, he heard music, far off, but distinctive and sweet. He heard a violin and a cello doing battle with a bass sax. He tried to remember if he'd heard that song before. He decided he had not. He wanted to hear more, but the laughter drowned it out.

"Sh," he pleaded.

The laughing stopped abruptly. "He's awake."

"Mm."

"How are you feeling today?"

"Gotta pee. And I want to hear the music. Turn it up."

"You have a catheter in, sir, so go ahead. Shelly, call Dr. Evans."

"Do you know where you are, sir?"

"I'm cold," Ray said.

"We'll get you a heated blanket in a few minutes, honey."

Honey. Ray liked that. He hadn't been called honey in a long time.

"Could you turn up the music, please?"

"There is no music here, Ray."

"But...but I can hear it." The more he listened, the louder the music became. Someone had turned up the volume. The tension across Ray's shoulders and chest eased.

One of the nurses left and the one who called him honey took his pulse. "Do you know where you are, sir?"

He opened his eyes and the room came into focus. He was on a hospital ward surrounded by old men in hospital beds. The light seemed too bright and his head hurt. He looked at the nurse. He guessed she was Brazilian.

"Brazil," he said.

"No. You are not in Brazil. Care for another guess?"

The nurse's hair was a cloud of tight, black ringlets. "Some of the most beautiful women in the world come from Brazil," Ray said. "I don't think they allow anyone less than gorgeous to leave the country, just to keep up the country's reputation for beautiful people. You're Brazilian, right?"

His throat was dry. He wanted to sound smooth, but instead he croaked like a frog as he spoke.

She laughed. "Nice try. I'm from Honduras."

"Dammit. Well, that's good, too."

"What's the last thing you remember, Mr. Bradley?"

"I remember you called me, 'honey.' Now you're calling me, 'Mr. Bradley.'"

"I couldn't very well call you by your name and then ask you if you knew what your name was, could I?"

So that's how it was. Her withdrawal disappointed him. It wasn't a sexual thing he was trying (certainly not with a catheter jammed up his johnson). It was her friendliness he craved. The nurse seemed so nice. He *craved* Nice. He hadn't had enough of capital *N*, Nice.

"Sir?"

Oh, no! Sir? It felt like she was running away from him, just like...just like.... *Hm.* Ray was sure he had a wife. He was sure she'd run away. The knowledge pained him, but what worried him more was that he couldn't remember her name.

An eon or two passed while Ray searched for something he couldn't find. The name was in a cupboard of his brain...and yet....which one?

"Mr. Bradley?"

Ray startled. It was the nurse again, still here after so many civilizations must have risen and fallen. *Time is so...elastic,* he thought. "Y-yes?"

"Do you know where you are?"

"You just asked me that."

"Actually," — she checked her watch — "it's been about twenty minutes since I asked where you are and your answer wasn't very accurate. You drifted off."

"Oh."

Twenty minutes? How could that be?

His nose itched. Ray raised his hand to scratch the itch and found his right hand was restrained at his wrist. After a year or so passed, he hurried to try to free his left hand. Different hand, same problem. "Could I have some drugs?"

"Why do you feel you need drugs, sir?"

Ray sighed. He'd liked the nurse, but she was exhausting. "Headache."

"The doctor will be along to talk to you soon."

"The pain is getting worse."

But the doctor did not arrive soon. A doctor did eventually appear, but only after Ray began to cry. His head felt like it might come apart at the seams. A giant, rusty screw seemed to be twisting into the back of his skull.

Giant rusty screw. Unlikely, he thought, *but certainly far from impossible.*

The doctor was a woman with a thick, Slavic nose whose blonde dye-job was growing out to reveal black roots. Ray didn't trust her because of those roots. She looked too sloppy to be a capable specialist carrying an iPad. Without a word, she looked at his chart and made notes.

"Hello? Are you the doctor?"

"Yes, of course. I'm Dr. Rose." Her voice was harsh, like she had gravel instead of tonsils.

"Rose. First name or last?"

"Last, of course."

"Ah. Of course, of course. But a rose by any other name would...something."

"I'm told you don't know where you are."

"I've got a catheter in me and I'm hooked up to machines I don't understand. This better be a hospital...I just don't know which one. Either that or I'm a high roller with a medical fetish in a very weird Vegas casino with a medical theme."

"Ha." She did not laugh or smile, though she did say, "Humor. A good sign. Do you remember what happened, Mr. Bradley?"

"No. Not really. I assume I hit my head."

Dr. Rose did not look up from the chart. "And why do you assume that?"

"It hurts."

"Good!"

"Good?"

"You have some deductive reasoning."

"Some."

Without warning, the doctor reached out and pulled his upper eyelid back and shone a light into his eye. It felt to Ray like she'd stabbed him in the eye with an icicle. Ray let out a shriek and squirmed. Squirming hurt his ribs.

"Just one more moment, Mr. Bradley." Then she did it again with his other eye and he shrieked again, loud enough that the sound hurt his own ears almost as much as the bright beam of light.

"You're oriented to place," she said. "Do you know what time it is?"

Time for you to get a watch. That was one of the first jokes he ever told. It was from a kid's joke book from the school library. He remembered that, but his wife's name was...?

Ray shrugged and looked out of the windows at the end of the room. "I dunno. It's night."

"Good enough. Please count backwards by sevens, starting at ninety-nine."

"Ninety-two...um...my head hurts a lot."

"What's ninety-two minus seven, Mr. Bradley?"

"Eh...a bunny rabbit ridden by the little Monopoly Game character in a top hat."

"Are you joking?"

"Thought I was. I guess not."

"So the number...?"

"I dunno. Head hurts too much to care."

"Don't worry about it, Mr. Bradley." She still hadn't looked him in the eyes since cruelly shining a flashlight into his pupils.

Ray tried to raise his hands and pulled weakly at his restraints. "Why these?"

"The police thought it would be a good idea. Don't worry. We'll try to have you up and around tomorrow, with assistance. Rest for now. Close your eyes and try to think of nothing."

"Impossible. The music is too nice."

"What music?"

"You don't hear that?" He hummed a few bars and his headache receded a little.

"I don't hear that, though...that sounds nice."

"How can I sleep when that's playing?"

"Try not thinking. The music is in your head. Auditory hallucinations. They are likely to pass. You've had a serious TBI. If the music doesn't go away, tell us. We'll give it some time. Too early to worry about that. Any questions?"

"You can't hear that symphony?"

"No."

"Are you sure?"

"Certainly."

"What's a TB.... What?"

"TBI. Traumatic Brain Injury."

"Oh. Shit. My brain is where I keep my stuff."

"It'll be fine, Mr. Bradley. The pain and the music will probably go away with some more healing time."

At the thought of the music going away, Ray thought he might cry. He sucked back the impulse. If the nice nurse were here, she might hold his hand or give him a gentle pat on the shoulder. The doctor would not be so merciful.

"I don't want to take the music away. I want to stay in the music."

"Very well, for now."

In that instant, Ray resolved to never tell anyone about the music playing in his head. They might try something, like electro-convulsive therapy, to take it away.

"Why am I restrained?"

"You were served divorce papers three days ago."

Three days? *Three. Days!*

"The papers were found in your car. The police suspect you did not have an accident."

"Uh...I've been asleep for three days?"

"A coma, yes."

"Has my wife come to see me?"

"I don't know."

"Am I going to be okay?"

"Bruises. Lacerations. Apparently, you crashed into a tree at high speed. Was it your intention to hurt yourself, sir?"

"No!" Ray said.

"Okay. Someone will come around in the morning to talk to you about such things, I'm sure."

"What do I do?"

"Lay still. Think of nothing. You've sustained a trauma. You need time." Dr. Rose delivered this news with all the passion of a waitress reciting the lunch special for the fortieth time. "The treatment for concussion is basically to stare at a blank wall and give your brain a rest. You'll need time. We'll give you more medication for the pain, though you're already close to topping out on the dosage."

"Oh," Ray said, to show he understood. But he didn't understand. The conversation with Dr. Rose was too taxing and her voice hurt him. What terrible black magic was this that a woman in a position to heal vulnerable people could torture them with her awful voice?

Ray stared at the ceiling. He was getting a divorce. That seemed like big news, but he still couldn't remember his wife's name.

He reawakened a moment later and it was morning. *Shit! Shit! Shit! Time,* Ray thought, *is all screwed up.*

The music was still there. It was jazz this time. A lone clarinet and a muted trumpet serenaded him.

Daylight was too harsh. The music turned to a soft lullaby and Ray lost himself, gratefully, to the flow of the music, eager to retreat into sleep again. The music carried him into unconsciousness and he didn't care if he ever woke up.

Sleep is good practice for Death. Each night is a welcome end. Each dream is an afterlife. Perhaps, every time we wake up, we have died in the night and

awoken in a new, very similar dimension.
Ray figured out that puzzle later. In the past.

3

When Ray surfaced from sleep again, Dr. Circe Papua sat next to his bed. Trumpets sounded, like a call to battle. He knew who she was immediately. His wife's name was still hazy.

Hazy...wait...could his wife's name be Hazel?

His rising headache seemed to answer: no.

Dr. Papua wore a blouse of gold lame and she held her high heels by the straps in one hand, bouncing them impatiently.

"Hi," Ray said.

"Taren called me."

"That was nice."

"I am not happy with you, Raymond."

"Okay."

"You did not mean to kill yourself. This was a cry for help."

"How do you know that? I'm not sure that I'm sure."

She stood and pulled his hospital gown away from this shoulder to expose an ugly blue and yellow bruise. "You wore your seatbelt."

"Huh. I guess I must have. Doesn't hurt. Much."

"It will hurt as they titrate the meds down. Then you'll feel it."

"You sound like you want to hurt me."

"I do not want you to kill yourself, or try to. You might have accidentally succeeded. You should have called me instead."

"How do you know for sure it wasn't an accident?"

"The papers in your car. Your car is totaled yet you were on a residential street. You were speeding. The police told Taren that there were no tire marks. You did not touch the brakes."

"That sounds like I was more committed to suicide than you think. The seatbelt must have been an oversight. We all click the buckle out of habit."

"Are you looking for sympathy?"

"Um...something tells me the right answer is no."

"You should have called me."

"I wasn't thinking straight. I'm still not. Could you talk a little quieter? My head hurts."

Dr. Papua nodded, smiled, and then spoke so loud in Ray's ear he recoiled. Other patients turned their heads to look. "Next time you decide you want to kill yourself, *call me first!*"

Ray tried to hold his palms over his ears. His restraints were too short to allow him to put his hands to his head. "*Sh! Sh! Please!*"

When Dr. Papua spoke again, her voice dropped to a whisper. "I do have hope for you, Raymond, but you really have to get over your feelings of entitlement."

Ray was about to speak, but he could tell she was wound up and he would have to let her talk to take the pressure off her spring. He shut up and listened.

"You have problems, Raymond, but not unique

problems."

"Oh," Ray said. The job. The divorce. The memories sifted back in quickly, filling the void. "My life wasn't supposed to work out this way."

"Many people feel as you do. Most everyone at some point."

"Everyone? Really? How do they live?"

"You're lucky. You get a second chance at finding out."

"Yeah? What happens now?"

"You will get counseling here. You'll continue to see me when you get out. You will get past this. It will work out."

"Will it work out well?"

"It will work out okay, at least."

"I want it to work out better than just okay."

"That's the entitlement I was talking about."

"So, lower my expectations."

"Be realistic."

"I'm suddenly feeling suicidal again. Thanks for stopping by, Dr. Papua."

She leaned forward and held Ray's hand. "Have you ever read *Peanuts*? The Charlie Brown comics?"

"I suppose."

"Charlie Brown goes to Lucy and Lucy says, 'You want to know what your problem is?'"

"I don't want to know."

"That's what Charlie says," she said. "But your subtext is a little more complex. As many people believe, you want to think it is a just universe. If you work hard and you are a good person, you think you should be rewarded. If you are not rewarded — and you, Ray, definitely don't feel you are rewarded adequately — you think you must be a bad person.

You are not a bad person, Ray. You are just an emotional animal and a collection of choices. You got to a bad place and now you think you are out of choices. You believe that the past is your destiny. You do not think you can change. You can change."

"How?"

"By doing it."

"Well, gee, why didn't I think of that?"

"Don't deflect."

"It's not deflection. It's not that simple."

"Ray, if you want to be different, live differently. Each choice is a step toward what you think you really are."

Ray sighed. "Psychobabble makes my head hurt more."

She stood. "Then we will speak again in my office when you are feeling more receptive to what I have to say. For now, take your meds, do as you are told and stare at blank walls and ceilings."

Ray looked away. "A wall, a few painkillers and words? That's really all modern medicine has to offer?"

"For now. Your brain bounced around in your skull. You need time. I hear it heals all wounds."

"How long until I can get the restraints off?"

"They will no doubt take them off for breakfast. You get to keep that big tracker in your bracelet until your seventy-two hour hold is over. Then you are free to go home and kill yourself. I suggest pills. Wreck another car and you could put other people in danger."

Ray didn't want to meet her eyes, but he did. "You really don't like me."

"I don't like what you did. You could have made

me look bad."

"Sorry."

"Fine. I would have gotten over it in a day or two. There are legitimate reasons for suicide, but you are not there yet, Ray. Suicide is selfish. It takes away possibilities and choices. You owe the people who care about you more than that. You owe yourself more than that."

"Sorry."

"Don't be sorry. Be a person."

"Okay. Do you have to be so mean about it?"

Papua laughed. "The staff here will treat you well. It will be dignified and caring and respectful. You see me as an authority figure and you are often deferential to the point of obsequiousness. Perhaps, since I can be more honest with you, we will cut through some of your bullshit faster, yes?"

"Oh." Papua had never told him he was cowed by her. Now that she said it, he wanted to do something to demonstrate it wasn't true. It occurred to him he was too intimidated by her to say anything defiant. She might yell in his ear again.

"I hope that when you get out of here, you will make an appointment to come to my office. I hope you can find it in yourself to be honest with me so I can help you."

Oh my god, I've hurt her feelings, Ray thought.

Papua walked away in bare feet carrying her high heels and a little clutch purse. He watched her go. The sway of her hips began the slow beat of a bongo rhythm. It came to him from the air and it became more complex once Dr. Papua had disappeared through the door. A pan flute joined in and all Ray wanted to do for the rest of his life was listen to the music in his head.

He didn't want to visit her office again. *Don't give the bitch the satisfaction,* he thought. *Besides, I have the music.*

But he knew he would see her again. He wanted to believe she was right about making new and better choices. He wanted to believe he could change.

Ray didn't believe yet.

4

Ray was surprised to get out of the hospital after a mere three days. The doctor who discharged him, Dr. Evans, said the hospital needed the bed for someone else.

"But I just tried to kill myself!"

"You gonna take the pills we give you?"

"Yes."

"You gonna take too many pills, try to kill yourself again?"

"No. I don't think so."

"We're good then. You're very lucky, you know."

"I don't feel lucky."

"About the time you enjoy the taste of a pizza or smell a flower, you'll remember why it's good to live. Come back if you change your mind and start thinking about killing yourself. We're a hospital, not a babysitting service."

"Spoken as a true healer."

"Or kill yourself. Up to you." Dr. Evans walked away, writing on his clipboard.

Ray flashed on an early memory. He saw himself as a boy away at summer camp. It was his first time away from home and he had loved it. He hadn't realized then that it would be his last chance at a carefree summer. The following summer he worked in a dark warehouse moving furniture, loading and unloading trucks.

He hadn't wanted to leave the summer camp in Maine back then. He didn't want to leave the hospital now. Ray climbed back into his bed and pulled the thin sheet over his head. He pulled his knees to his chest into the fetal position and listened to a flight of violins sweep in, beautiful and otherworldly.

In the darkness under the covers, he could feel the pounding at the back of his skull recede. Sleep was on its way. The violins slowed to a sweet, soft lullaby.

He was drifting off when a nurse pulled the sheet back and told him it was time to leave the womb. Ray stared at her. It was the pretty, curly haired nurse who wasn't from Brazil. She was from...? Where?

"Don't look at me in that tone of voice," she said.

"Old joke."

"Ah. I forgot. You're the comedian."

"I was a comedian. I'm a television writer now. I write bits for *What's My Rhyme?* You like that show? I can get you tickets."

"Sorry. Never heard of it. But go back to work, take your pills, get counseling. Don't do anything that gets you back here."

"It's easier living here," Ray said. "At work, I have to find the funny."

"Go find the funny, Mr. Bradley."

"Again with the 'Mr. Bradley.' Don't you think if I knew where the funny was, I would be somewhere else?"

27

She shook her head. "Ray, you have a concussion."

"And headaches."

"Yes, and headaches. But one ward over there's a young woman who was in a car accident the same night you came in. Her boyfriend was driving. She had both feet up on the dash. They had a head on collision. When her air bag went off, it drove her knees into her face. She's blind and her boyfriend, who walked away from the crash, just left her. He's not coming back."

"Wow."

"What does that make you think of your situation?"

"That people suck."

"And?"

"I think...I think I don't want to say."

"Why?"

"Because it's the wrong answer."

"What do you mean?"

"Her situation sucks. My situation sucks. Her problems don't make mine look smaller. They make me feel sick about my problems plus pile on guilt."

"You're right."

"I am?"

"Yeah. That was the wrong answer."

Ray looked at the floor. He could not meet the nurse's gaze. He felt like a bug, but he felt he had to say something to defend himself, too. "People are starving in Africa and that's terrible. They're starving, but that doesn't lessen my headache."

"Okay."

"Okay, meaning you understand?"

"Okay, meaning you can go. Bye, Mr. Bradley. Don't end up back here or I'll make you use the bedpans I keep in the freezer."

"That's funny."

"That's not a joke. That's a threat."

* * *

The cabbie reeked of patchouli. He picked up Ray at the front door to the hospital and zig zagged him home. The taxi driver tried to make small talk about the weather, but it was Los Angeles. What could there be to say that was new? The sun shone bright and, despite the sunglasses his doctor had given him, Ray's headache raced back to full force. He'd failed his attempt at suicide, but sunny LA. might kill him yet.

And that was the hell of it. Ray Bradley, the kid who'd once thought himself indomitable, was a man on the way back from the looney ward of the local hospital. The aspiring genius was stuck at *aspiring*. And LA. did not care. That's LA.

Everywhere Ray looked people went on with their lives, oblivious to the fact that he had almost left the world. They'd never feel the loss, or even pause at the mention of his name.

Phillip Seymour Hoffman had killed himself, albeit accidentally, with a massive cocktail of drugs: cocaine, heroin, benzodiazepines and amphetamines. Come to think of it, given the quantities involved, maybe Hoffman's exit was a successful suicide instead of a failed attempt at temporary escape? Everyone missed the brilliant actor.

But his work would last. Hoffman had achieved a degree of immortality Ray would never reach. There were no rapping grandmas in Phillip Seymour Hoffman's film history. Hoffman would stay brilliant and beloved and immortalized on film until nuclear holocaust or cataclysmic disease or the heat death of the universe wiped out everyone who had ever watched and loved a movie.

Who would mourn Ray Bradley? When Ray did succeed at dying, his friend Joe would feel sad, but Grins Well would probably get over it pretty quickly. He was resilient. Ray's parents would be shocked, but would they be surprised? They'd mourn him most, but once they, too, were dead, what legacy did Ray possess? He had no wealth to donate to an honorable charity and no children to carry on his family name.

And now he remembered his wife's name. Marla. The memory was a bitter reproach. He was only thirty, it was true. It wasn't like he could never find anyone new. However, dating again didn't sound like an opportunity for fresh love and adventure. Finding someone new felt like an ordeal in which he would have to tell all his old stories again. "If I can remember any old stories," Ray said aloud.

"What did you say, sir?" the cabbie asked.

"Nothing. Just facing the existential and dating abyss."

The cabbie nodded his understanding and said nothing.

Ray closed his eyes and pictured Marla waiting for him at home. He'd tried to kill himself so, surely, she'd be back, ready to welcome him home. She must be worried sick. Good. Maybe he wouldn't have to tell his life story to someone else.

A plan began to form. If he'd had his laptop in front of him, he'd have written out the speech, polishing it until he'd reached the peak of persuasion. This was too important to screw up. He saw his future and now Marla was back on the Ray train. He'd faced his mortality, somehow survived, and he was appalled at his insignificance to the world. Dr. Papua was right. He'd almost denied himself a new beginning.

The plan hurt his head. Ray swallowed another pill ahead of schedule but, what was one more pill now? He had his life and marriage to save.

He'd sit Marla on the couch and say, "I know things have been bad. I haven't been the best husband. We owe a lot of money and...well, this has been a wake-up call for me, Marla. For all our history and all we've meant to each other, you owe me one more chance and I'm going to do a lot with it. I promise."

He'd hold her hand, the left, because there she wore the wedding ring. He'd hold her hand in both of his and stare into her eyes and swear, "Stay. I'll change and we'll make it work and many years from now, I'll speak your name with my last breath. Your name will be my last word. In love."

The cab's brakes squeaked and the cab pulled to a stop in front of his building. Ray couldn't run from the cab. His head pounded too much. He did manage to pay the pachouli-scented driver and tip him a twenty. Ray walked up the steps to his apartment and buzzed it, eager to give Marla his speech through the intercom, before he forgot it all. He'd stammer and stutter in a rush to get it all out, somewhat

Woody Allen in his delivery. Marla would be charmed and take pity on him. He'd settle for pity at first and someday, when he was on top, Marla's eyes would shine with respect and pride whenever she looked his way.

It could be like a romantic Nora Ephron movie times ten. It sounded like a deleted scene from *When Harry Met Sally*.

Or better, Ray would write a movie. The first scene would be the hook of crashing into the palm tree. The horn would blast on and on.

Cut to the hazy resurrection and the uplifting music in the hospital. The next scene would be this one: Ray returning home to the wife who almost left him. It would be a rags to riches story of failure followed by redemption. Marla would love it. Marla would love him.

The music in Ray's head was something jazzy and uplifting and hopeful. Ray pictured Woody Allen on clarinet and Duke Ellington kicking in high on the ivories.

No one answered the buzzer.

The music stopped.

After a few minutes, a Jamaican man Ray recognized came out of the front door and held it open for him. He didn't know the man's name, but they had nodded to each other at the mailbox and at the front door many times.

"Hey, hey! You okay?" the Jamaican man asked.

Ray smiled. He was shaky but he managed a whispered, "Yes." His head hurt too much to nod now.

"I read the note on your door."

"There's a note on my door?"

"Yeah, that's what I'm saying to you."

"You shouldn't read other people's notes."

"Sorry. You're right." Beat. "But the whole building's read your note."

"Really?"

The man nodded and began to walk away.

"Is it a good note?"

His neighbor shook his head.

The music only Ray could hear was a throng of bagpipes playing a funeral dirge.

5

The note taped to Ray's door was a long list of
Marla's complaints. She'd pressed the tip of the pen
much harder than was necessary.

There wasn't much there that Ray didn't already
know. The list was a reminder of how bad the last
while had been.

How long was 'a while'? Ray wondered. *When a
relationship goes sour, does anyone ever know the
exact moment it starts to turn bad, or is the
bitterness an accumulation of small, intolerable
events?*

Loving couples overlooked minor transgressions
all the time. Where were all the good memories in
Marla's note? The fond remembrances? The grace
and transcendence? He couldn't actually remember
any really nice things himself at that moment. Most
of his marriage was a black hole in time. His
headache was roaring back, blotting out the light.

Inattention. That was first on the list and probably
true. Ray could be distracted with his own thoughts
easily. Or *Call of Duty* and a plethora of other cool
video games. Or he'd bury himself in work, trying to

make more money and always behind on the credit card bills.

Constant fighting. Ray blamed Marla for starting the fights. Or worse, she ended the spats with a slamming door and no resolution was ever reached.

"Marla," Ray once told Grins Well, "does not engage in the soft science of diplomacy."

"You're lucky she doesn't engage in the sweet science." His friend ducked an imaginary punch and threw a few jabs and hooks to underline his meaning.

"Write that down," Ray said. "That's good!"

"Really?"

"No. Shaddup."

Joe barked his strange laugh and broke into his patented, ear to ear grin.

"I'm saying, Joe, that my dear wife does not have an appreciation for nuance and proportionality."

"Ball-buster, you mean."

"I wouldn't say that, Joe. Not where she can hear you. But if, in argument, I say I like blue paint and Marla likes red paint, she gets pissed too easily and says, 'Did you *look* at the hot toothless checkout girl at the grocery store?' And all that time I thought I was arguing about what color to paint a door."

"*Mm*," Joe faked a swoon. "Hot toothless girl."

"And if Marla is affronted for some reason...say you brought home regular milk when she '*specifically*' asked for soy milk, all of a sudden she's all like, 'I'm going to burn down this apartment with you in it!'"

"Sounds serious."

"And if you said something that was meant to be funny...say if *I* called her a ball-buster? What do you

35

think she'd say?"

Ray and Joe chorussed together, "'I'm going to burn down this apartment with you in it!'"

When they stopped laughing, Joe would offer his couch for the night and Ray would accept. Ray had exiled himself from the apartment several times and Joe always had an empty couch waiting.

In the morning, Marla would be doubly angry with him for staying at Joe's place. "You're supposed to go to *our* couch where you can see me giving you the silent treatment. If you leave, how are we going to stay up and fight?"

"I don't want to fight."

"That's the problem. A man stays and fights for his marriage."

"I didn't think screaming would help."

"Leaving is worse."

"How could it be worse than a screaming match?"

"If you stay and scream back, I know you still care."

"When you scream at me, I *do* care less." Ray had meant to toss it off as a joke. Sort of...at the time... maybe it was a joke.... But it didn't fall flat because his delivery was off. That wasn't the funny thing to say. It was the true thing to say.

Deep breath.

"I don't want to fight for our marriage, Marla. If we both love each other, marriage shouldn't be something we have to work so hard at. It's love, not work, right?"

"If it's love on both sides, yeah. I guess you're right, Ray." But she didn't say it like he was right. Her tone was flat. Marla said, "You're right," the same way she told him he was wrong.

36

Maybe that was the moment she knew she was going to leave. Maybe you *can* tell the exact moment a relationship goes sour. Ray had somehow missed that moment and it was too late to get it back and try again.

All that? Ray remembered that. Staring at that itemized list, he realized he should have known that was his wife's deciding moment. Marla had taken a circuitous route through the apartment to slam every door, including the one to the linen closet.

Impatience and *condescension* were also on the list. Yes, Ray could be mean when he was mad. Heckler practice, he called it. Marla had thought mean was funny when they were dating. That had changed in so gradual a process Ray wasn't sure when the ratio of her laughter to grimaces and hard stares had flipped.

Farts were also mentioned on Marla's list. He wondered if that was just showboating for the neighbors, though. It seemed such a nit-picky thing to put on a public notice, grinding in the shame like tossing a salt shaker into a gaping chest wound. Ray was pretty sure he was no better than average or at least no worse than most on farts. Unless...how was such a thing honestly scored? Sound amplitude? Proximity? Pure evil methane deadliness?

Ray pulled the note down from the door and realized she'd stood at the front door to write it. Marla had pressed hard enough that he could see and feel the faint impression of the pen's stylus in the wood's soft, brown lacquer.

There would be no eloquent, romantic speech. There was no Marla to persuade. He'd almost died and his wife wasn't interested in the romantic movie scene that would hail his redemption.

Worse? If he had died, Ray realized now that Marla would have become a tragic figure. Her friends would say, "Poor Marla. We should fix her up with a young Adonis to make her forget that fat slob."

His wife would be a young widow who had married a troubled loser in the game of life. On every date and at every cocktail party and at every opportunity, Marla would affirm that she had won and Ray had lost. His beautiful wife, the woman who used to bring him breakfast in bed and feed him bacon, would say, "I left him so he killed himself. He was always nothing, but without me, he *knew* he was less than nothing."

"Jesus!" Ray said aloud to the empty hallway. "I gotta live!"

He would not live for love. Hope wasn't holding his attention. The future was a far off thing that held too many possibilities to predict. But spite? Spite would keep him alive. He was suddenly determined to lose weight and take better care of himself. It wasn't so much about a makeover for his life then. Ray's only plan was to outlive Marla.

Yes, spite would do nicely.

Far off, Ray heard drums. He could tell they were huge drums. Taiko drums. Ray pictured muscular Japanese men stripped to the waist banging drums taller than the drummers. It was a driving rhythm. War drums.

Perhaps the anger would last long enough for him to figure out what he had to do next. The thought made him want to hurry to his bed and go fetal again. He didn't make it as far as the bed. The couch was closer to the door and his headache chose that moment to crush his skull into the size and shape of a kid's football.

Ray fell to the couch and wept and wept.

The taiko drums disappeared, replaced by weeping cellos. He popped another pain pill. It was a long time before he slipped into a fitful, dreamless sleep.

As angry as he was, his last thought before sleep closed in was of Marla forgiving him everything. He still hoped to wake from this strange nightmare in her arms, or at least to the warm smell and friendly sizzle of frying bacon.

6

When Ray awoke, no Marla and no bacon. He hauled himself to the bathroom, urinated, paused, and threw up. His headache receded an inch when he vomited. Then the pain hammered him in the back of the head again as soon as he stood straight.

Ray decided to give the headache a name: Torment. Soon, he had nothing left in his stomach to sacrifice to the porcelain god.

The physiotherapist at the hospital had given him instructions, written out for later because, Ray was sure, he'd missed most of it in the dizzying few days of therapy. He'd need more physiotherapy exercises, he was told, but for now his main job was to stare at a blank wall, drink lots of water and take his painkillers.

"How long before the pain goes away without medication?"

The physiotherapist shrugged. "High speed crash. Could be a while."

"A while?"

"Uh-huh."

"So there's a science to this?"

"Sure."

"But the best you can say is, 'a while?'"

"You'll know your killer headaches are receding when you start to feel your neck pain more."

"Looking forward to it."

Bent over in the bathroom with the dry heaves, Ray realized he hadn't been drinking enough water. In that moment, he would have drunk from the toilet if he thought it would make a difference.

Instead, he made his way to the kitchen, leaning heavily on walls along the way. LA tap water. Better than toilet water, but not by much.

In books, tough guys swallow pills dry. Ray was no tough guy. The curly-haired nurse had taught him that capsules float. With capsules, he had to tip his head forward to get it to the back of his throat to swallow. Pills don't float. With those, Ray had to tip his head back. Either approach made his head hurt worse. Torment's pain reached around either side of his head and squeezed as misery drilled into his temples.

Ray wondered if he'd been discharged too early. His doctors seemed confident he could cope with the pain and continue his rehabilitation from home, but if he were good at coping, he wouldn't have ended up in a hospital in the first place, would he?

Ray stared at the pill bottle. Before he left the hospital, he'd asked the curly-haired nurse if there was something stronger they could give him for the pain. She'd looked up from his chart for a moment, smiled and shook her head. That seemed a cruel smile.

"How long until the pain medication kicks in?" He'd said it as loudly and as harshly as his headache would allow.

"With the placebo effect, in as little as five minutes."

"What if I don't believe in the placebo effect?"

"Actually, that doesn't matter."

"How long?" Ray asked miserably. "I'm too smart for the placebo effect!"

She nodded. "Okay. Then you get to be right and feel the pain for half an hour before the painkillers kick in for real."

"Oh, sweet Jesus! Why didn't you just tell me five minutes?"

"Because, if the pain didn't lessen in six minutes you'd call me a liar. Just like you, I hate to be wrong, Mr. Bradley."

Ray awoke from the reverie. He looked down. He still stood at the kitchen sink. The pill bottle was to his left. The empty water glass sat on the counter to his right. Ray didn't know how long he'd been standing there and he couldn't recall if he'd swallowed a pill or not.

The aftertaste of LA tap water was a clue. He guessed he'd taken a pill, but he'd have to sit in pain for half an hour to be sure. He was supposed to sit and stare at a blank wall and think of nothing. Instead, he sat on his couch and stared at the one painting on his living room wall.

To rest his concussed brain, Ray was supposed to think of nothing. That seemed impossible. Within seconds, he was thinking about the tap water. He thought of the tap water and all the pipes it had sluiced through to finally arrive at his apartment. Water pipes were old just about everywhere. In many cities, crumbling brick and algae-covered stones and even hollowed tree trunks served as water pipes in the oldest neighborhoods.

No wonder Starbucks coffee and bottled water ruled LA. By law, the city's restaurants had to filter the water they served patrons. Since the drought, water restrictions were heavier. The state of California wasn't watering the highway medians. At restaurants, you had to ask for a glass of water. They couldn't bring water as a matter of course. Would California's drought be over before Ray found a new woman with whom to face life's challenges and ease each night's loneliness?

Ray's mind turned to the painting. He'd painted it himself years ago during an early struggle with writer's block. He'd thought he could open the gates to creativity by coming at the writing sideways. It hadn't worked. Bills and past-due notices gave him inspiration to write when messing around with acrylics failed. Still, it was the only painting Ray had created that he really liked.

It was a colorful, impressionistic picture on a sixteen by twenty-inch canvas. Ray called it *Cyrano in the Garden at Midnight*. Among the many pretty yellow and red flowers, a hidden face with a long nose peered up at a far swirl of stars.

Ray loved that painting. Tragically, it was giving him a headache. Or maybe he hadn't taken that pill after all? Not knowing bothered him almost as much as the fierce pounding that had moved to the center of his skull. He closed his eyes and waited for Torment's onslaught to ebb.

Ray heard the key turn in the lock behind him. And he knew. He *knew!* He'd been too harsh. Marla had thought better of her note. He didn't even have to look to know it was she. His dear wife knew she'd gone too far pinning that nasty public diatribe to their door. She'd heard of his suicide attempt and she was drawn back.

Marla, he was sure, could recall the happy times in their marriage that he, at present, could not. She'd fill him in. He'd be spurred to turn his life around. Confronted with mortality, they'd each be filled with new resolve to be kinder to each other and their marriage would work. They'd make many new, happy memories and they'd do it together. The slate was wiped clean. Forgetting made forgiving easier. It would be as if they were dating for the first time, falling in love all over again. This time for real.

The front door opened. He heard the rattle of her keys and the sound of paper bags being set on the table by the door. She was taking care of him again. He'd forgiven Marla everything, humiliating note and all, even before he opened his eyes.

Joe Grenwell stood before him. His trademark ear to ear grin was missing. "Marla gave me the key." He placed the key to the apartment on the coffee table between a six-pack of Dr. Pepper and Ray's pot of coffee on its hot plate. "I figured you'd show up soon and I should check on you," Joe said.

"They let me out fast."

"Surprisingly fast."

"I'm going to be okay. It was one weird moment, that's all. Now I'm dealing with a concussion, but... you know..."

"Brought some groceries so you don't have to deal with going out. You may want to order your groceries in for a few days, huh? I'll fill up your fridge. Um... how you *really* doin', buddy?"

Ray looked up into his best friend's eyes and began to cry. "She's not coming?"

"No. I'm sorry."

"Not your fault."

"I know."

"It's my fault."

"Okay," Joe said.

"Did Marla say when she'd come by? Later, maybe?"

"She won't."

Ray stared at the floor and sighed. He wiped his tears but they were soon replaced with new, hot tears. When he could be sure his voice wouldn't crack, he asked, "When did you see her last? Where did she go? What's she doing? What do you know?"

Joe put his hands in his pockets and shifted from foot to foot. "It's...it's not great news. I don't think now is the time."

"I'm alright. That's what Marla doesn't understand. That's what I have to make her understand. I have to feel better and I will feel better. The Honda's totaled, but I get it now. Small price to pay, really. I'm ready to make big changes and I'm going to be okay. We're going to be okay. I've decided."

Joe nodded slowly but said nothing.

"Where's Marla?"

"Waiting. In the car."

Ray's shoulders relaxed and his headache eased off another inch. He smiled. "Then everything's going to be okay!"

Joe shook his head. "I don't think so. Not exactly. Short-term, no. Long-term, yeah."

"I got the divorce papers, but we need to give

counseling a real shot. Lots of people go through trouble. When I talk to her — "

"Marla doesn't want to talk, Ray. She says she's sick to death of talking."

"Heh. 'To death.' I know a little something about that."

"Buddy, I don't think — "

"Grins Well, take me to my fair maiden!" Despite his headache, Ray tried his best pirate voice. "Avast! Me bride be waitin'! *Arr!*"

"Not for you, my man."

"What?"

"She's not waiting for you to get your act together. Not anymore. Her words, not mine. Sorry, dude."

"Cold."

"It gets colder. Marla never went to Maine. The day you thought she went to the airport, she moved in with me. I'm sorry but...well, that's the way it is."

Ray stared at him, his eyes glassy. "I'm...she's what? With *you*?"

"That's the way it is, yeah."

Ray took a breath. His first impulse was to leap off the couch and hit Joe. Joe might even let him, but the energy expenditure might kill Ray, or it would feel like a fresh spike through his head. Joe and Ray stared at each other a moment, neither knowing what to say.

Finally, Ray said, "I'll put the groceries away myself."

"Right. Good. Take care of yourself, Ray. Taren says to take all the time you need. Somebody from human resources will call you."

"Whatever."

"You aren't going to do something stupid, are

you?"

Ray waved him away. "No." He took a deep, shaky breath. "I'm going to prove to Marla and to myself, that it's a just universe. I'm going to come out the other end of this like *The Six Million Dollar Man*. Better. Stronger. Faster. Because dated references and high aspirations are what I'm all about. I'm going to prove to her she's wrong about me."

"I believe you, Ray. Just focus on saving yourself first, okay?"

Ray could tell Joe did not believe him. "Good luck, Joe. I think...I don't know. I just think you'll need luck. She's a difficult person."

"Heh. You were right before, Ray."

"What?"

"I'm not going to say it's her fault and certainly none of this is my fault. You want to get past this, see yourself for who you really are, man. Sorry, but a lot of this is on you."

Nodding hurt Ray in lots of ways. Maybe it was the circumstance. Maybe it was mental illness. Maybe it was the sad cellos. Ray could feel the serotonin getting sucked from his body, replaced with misery and self-loathing.

He was sure he'd hate Joe later. At that moment, he was too tired to spare some hate for his best ex-friend. All the hate Ray had at that moment went straight to his own pounding heart and pulsing, painful brain.

7

Ray took down his painting and turned it to the wall. "Stare at nothing with me, Cyrano."

Ray grunted as he lowered himself to the couch. He tore open a couple of cups of apple sauce and spooned it into his mouth mindlessly. Then he worried that, since he enjoyed the taste, maybe he was actually being mindful without realizing it.

"Empty your mind," Dr. Rose had said.

"I'm going through a divorce and I'm probably going to lose my job. How am I *not* going to think about all that?"

"I'm not here to solve all your life's problems, Mr. Bradley. I can tell you that, unless and until you can follow my instructions, you will be in no position to address your non-medical challenges."

"I thought this was the age of holistic medicine. I thought all my er...*challenges*...everything is ultimately medical, right?"

Dr. Rose had sighed heavily. "I'm a doctor, not a life coach."

Ray gritted his teeth. "A blank wall? Really? Shit! Shit! Shit! Witchdoctors with rattles and salves made out of bug guts are higher tech than this!"

"That's the treatment plan for concussion. Check in with your counselor and come back for follow-up tests next week. Your irritability is part of the brain injury. Lack of inhibition."

"I was pretty irritable before."

"Then perhaps your brain problems are part of a pre-existing condition?"

"What condition?"

"The medical jargon translates to 'being an asshole.'"

Before he left the hospital, Dr. Evans asked about the music. "I still hear it in my head," Ray admitted. "It's the only good thing about this."

"Did you have auditory hallucinations previous to the accident?"

"I used to do a funny bit about fudge brownies waking me up and calling me down to the kitchen at three in the morning, but — "

"That's a no. We might be able to quell the music with anti-psychotics."

"Never mind. I told you. The music is the only good part of this. It might be the last good thing I've got now."

"Suit yourself," Evans said.

When Ray concentrated on the music, Torment turned its face to the side. The headache didn't come at him full on. It was as if the music was an invitation for him to take a slow, deep breath in the middle of a race. The cellos were still there, playing a round of something surprisingly sprightly.

He felt something in his chest. It rose, lifting him. As soon as he paid attention to the strange feeling of euphoria, it crashed away and Torment roared back, pounding at his eardrums with each colossal beat of his heart.

From now on, my life will be divided and defined by the palm tree, Ray thought, *pre-collision and post.*

Ray stared at the wall.

8

Wall.

Blank wall.

Wall.

It didn't take long for Ray to feel bored. He wanted to watch television or go to a movie or pay more attention to the music or go scream at Joe and Marla. Instead, he did as his doctors had instructed and stared.

When he realized he was doing as he was told, he began to fidget, crossing and uncrossing his legs and squeezing his hands into fists — tight, relax, tight, relax. He considered pacing in circles around the couch, but Torment might squeeze his head like a pimple about to burst if he moved around too much.

He stared at the wall until he thought he might go insane. He stared at the wall until he began to pluck hair from his forearms for a pleasant distraction.

The boredom made him think of the Sundays his father made him go to church. The minister would drone on. The choir would stand and sing an old, utterly joyless hymn. Ray would pray for an asteroid to wipe out the congregation and end the suffering.

He'd stare at the crucifix and do as he was told. He thought of Jesus dying on the cross. *Probably to get out of church,* Ray thought.

Wall.

Wall.

Wall.

Think of nothing. Just stare at the wall.

A hymn. He heard a sweet, slow hymn start up, better than anything he'd ever heard in church. It didn't sound sad. Instead, the music communicated power, from God to people.

Ray thought again of his old church. Each Sunday, he would imagine violent criminals bursting into the church, demanding money or...something. Ray never thought through what the villains plans could be. Instead, he imagined saving the day. In each outlandish scenario, Ray would save the minister, despite his boring sermons.

Ray imagined himself doing backflips and cartwheels over pews and people. He'd dodge bullets and subdue the bad guys singlehandedly. As a boy, Ray was no more capable of cartwheels than he was now. Still, it was a powerful memory.

Wall.

Wall.

Nose itch.

Wall.

Nose scratch.

Wall.

Ray noticed a crack in the plaster, high up near the ceiling. No, not a crack. A tiny chip of paint. No, not even a tiny chip of paint. Just one inelegant brushstroke. The more Ray stared, the bigger the flaw appeared. How could he have missed it?

Wall.
Wall.
How? It had been in front of him for years, yet he hadn't paid attention.

Inattention: one of the line items from Marla's long list of marital complaints. That thought, of course, led him back to Joe and Marla. Marla and Joe. His Marla was no longer his Marla. She was Joe's Marla and he was hers. How long had that been going on? She was right. He hadn't paid enough attention.

A saxophone started up. It sounded a playful bar or two, followed by...a warning?

The wall moved.

Ray snapped back to attention. His mind had wandered. He was certain. The wall, of course, had not moved. It was a trick of the mind and eye.

A long time ago, he'd visited a yoga studio for several months. It was a free yoga class and the instructor was a cutie named Marla.

He could do downward dog easily then. The name of the yoga position was pretty much all he could remember now. Marla had taught Ray about meditation.

The trick was emptying the mind. Ray could manage that in the odd moment. However, he only knew he had achieved the goal when he wasn't doing it anymore. As soon as he exclaimed, "*Hey, I am meditating! This is it!*" he fell out of the empty state of mind.

He could still picture Marla in a black unitard perched on a yoga mat in full lotus position. "Think of meditation as the space between the words," she told the class. "Concentrate on the space between the words and you'll find peace there. You'll probably begin to read the words, but when you lengthen your spaces between the words, you'll be meditating... until you realize you aren't meditating or until I ring the little bell. Whichever comes first. Let's begin. Space out."

Ray never made it so far into meditating that he reached the ring of the bell. He did not observe his thoughts or fall into the space between thoughts. Mostly, he thought about how vegetarians fart a lot, or that his nose itched or that he was bored. Mostly, his meditation practice consisted of wondering, *When is she going to ring that damn bell?* And, *when am I ever going to get to talk to her without all these weird yoga people around?*

The truth was, Ray was looking for ways to have dates without paying any money for the privilege. That was how he met Marla Biggs, or Marla in Full Lotus, as he came to think of her.

After nine classes, Ray had sweetgrass tea in the yoga studio's little common area. The other students drank tea, too, chatted about Macrobiotic diets, and got in the way of Ray talking with their instructor.

After a while, the other yoga students went home and that left Ray and Marla alone over a cold teapot. Marla asked him how he liked all that sweetgrass tea he was guzzling.

"I hate it. You wanna go out for a latte? Anything, as long as it's loaded with sugar and won't cleanse my liver and optimize the vibration of my chakras. Screw that."

Marla gave him a slow smile. "It's about time. I thought you'd never ball up and ask me out."

Six weeks later, they went to Vegas on a whim. Ray

knelt before her on the Strip outside the Venetian.

"Let's hit every Vegas cliche," he said.

"Here? You're doing this here? Now?"

"It's perfect," Ray said. He kissed her hand. "Everything is a gamble. Let's throw the dice and put all our money on you and me forever."

That was all Marla needed for a proposal. Marla in Full Lotus became Mrs. Marla Bradley. For a while.

The wall moved again. The saxophone sent up a discordant blare of alarm and Ray jumped.

9

Ray reflexively grabbed the arm of the couch, ready to crawl under the coffee table. He'd been through a lot of earthquakes, but experience didn't help with earthquakes. It was just as scary every time Earth heaved and rearranged the furniture.

But this was not an earthquake. Confused, Ray looked around the room. No dishes rattled. Nothing swayed. No car alarms blared outside.

If anything, the apartment seemed quieter than usual. The clock that ticked too loudly in the bathroom was silent. He heard no sirens or shouts. No footsteps fell hard on heels in the hall. No dogs barked.

Ray held his nose and blew to try to pop his ears. Something was...not *wrong*, exactly. Something was off. The sudden quiet reminded him of a winter morning in Boston when he was a kid. Sometimes the snow fell so thick overnight that it deadened all sound and the city was muted.

He heard only one thing clearly: the insistent, Hitchcockian climb of worried violins.

Ray looked to the wall again. It looked different,

but not in a way he could readily identify.

Shifted?

Skewed?

Lurking?

Maybe the pain medication had poisoned his perceptions. He remembered standing at the sink trying to figure out if he had taken a pill. What if he had stood there for a long time, struggling with the same question over and over in a loop of lost time? He had deduced that he had already taken a pill. But what if he was wrong? What if he had rejected a pill once, but had actually taken several? How many pills was too many? How many before his liver shut down?

Ray caught movement in the corner of his eye. He stopped focusing on the details of the paint job. His gaze shifted to soft focus.

At first, all he saw were floaters in his vision. But the floaters slowly multiplied and the wall rippled.

Ray shrieked. Each beat of his heart was a hammer blow to his skull. Unseen ropes tightened around his chest, squeezing and compressing his lungs. He gasped for air and pressed his back into the couch.

Afraid to look and afraid not to look, Ray rubbed his eyes with his fists.

"I'm dying," he said.

He didn't want to die. What a difference a few days makes.

He thought he had forgotten the car crash in a loop of missing time. He could not recall the burn of the seatbelt or the sound of crushing metal or the spray of safety glass crinkling. But now he could remember the feeling he had as he stomped on the accelerator: defiance.

There was no defiance in him now. Only fear. He reached for the phone on the end table, feeling his way, his gaze still riveted to the rippling wall. It looked like a beige pond standing at a ninety degree angle and...aware of him?

He would dial 911.

He would tell the dispatcher he was suicidal.

He would tell them he was in the throes of an accidental overdose and hallucinating.

Rivulets coursed through his vision. Ray froze. At first, he thought he was going blind. However, he soon realized the wall was turning black, stained by streams of thick, black water.

"I took too many painkillers," Ray told the wall. "I'm on a bad trip! Or the asshole up in 5B has a waterbed leak!"

The wall rippled again, but this time its waves were not subtle. The waves stood out from the wall, first six inches, then a foot. Then more.

C'mon in! The water's fine!

The wall leaned his way. It drew closer and filled his vision.

Ray lunged for the phone and knocked it over, into the path of the wall. It was coming for him now, reaching for him with octopus arms.

"Help! Somebody *help!*"

It caught him by the wrist. Ray began to disappear into the black, wet wall. He pissed his pants as he fought to pull away, to run for the door. The wall began to envelop him, each tendril as strong as tar.

Ray Bradley was pulled from his living room screaming.

The music stopped.

10

Ray was still screaming as he tripped over a root and fell into an oak. He hit his head on the trunk and scraped the skin off his forehead on the way down. The front of his pajama pants was wet.

As he fell to the forest floor, he braced himself for the pain he was sure would split his skull. It didn't come.

Ray's forehead hurt and blood dripped into his right eye, but the headache he expected from his concussion did not arrive. He'd left Torment back in his living room.

Ray rolled onto his back and stared at the blue sky through the treetops. He wasn't near his home. The angle of the light seemed wrong, too, though he did enjoy the bright sunlight. Moments ago, each sunbeam would have felt like a knife in the eye. Now, aside from the fresh scrape to his forehead and his wet pajama pants, he felt fine.

As Ray got to his feet, touched his forehead and looked at his fingers. Not much blood, though it occurred to him that a tree had injured him for the second time in a week. He brushed the rust-colored pine needles from his filthy pajamas and looked around. He still wore black socks. The forest floor beneath him was soft with deep green moss.

He saw no landmarks. He was surrounded by trees and they all looked alike. Still, something about this place felt familiar.

"I'm dead," Ray said, testing his voice. He still had one. It sounded louder and stronger than he remembered. "Oh, dear God! I overdosed and went to...?"

Which was this? Heaven? Hell? Purgatory?

He was happy that he wasn't naked, but wished he had died with more clothes on so he could face eternity with a little more dignity. Aside from the spot of urine, his pajamas had pictures of cowboys on them. It was kitschy and nostalgic when he bought them, but this was no way to dress for an afterlife.

Wait. He had pajamas with pictures of cowboys on them when he was a boy. "I'm not dead. I'm having a bad trip. Somebody put acid in my Oxy. Somebody skip the needle. I'm in a loop."

Ray stood still and listened. The far-off whoosh of traffic on a highway to his left slipped through the trees. He walked toward the sounds of rushing automobiles.

Searching for answers felt like searching for lost keys. First people check their pockets and the hook or the bowl by the door. When they don't find those keys, they eventually end up looking in the refrigerator. Ray began to hurry, but toward what, he didn't know.

He reached the crest of a small hill. Far off, he could hear children laughing. He tightened his robe's fuzzy belt around his waist and picked his way through the trees, hoping to spot others before he was seen.

To his right, he spotted something he recognized. It was impossible, but he knew this place, if only vaguely. Through a gap in the trees he spotted a wide, red building that looked like a barn. It resembled Camp Bethany, a Christian children's camp his parents had sent him to the summer he turned twelve. Impossible, but it looked real.

He wondered how deep this hallucination would go. If he walked out of the woods and past Camp Bethany's main building, would he find the campers' cabins, bunking eight kids to a room, far too small and hot on summer nights? Would the old dirt road lead to the wooden gate he remembered? If he walked out of that gate and turned left, could he walk the mile to the general store? Would it be waiting by the little bridge in the center of a village named the Corners? If he hitched a ride, would the illusion of Poeticule Bay, Maine still be waiting at the lip of the Atlantic? Would the double scoop of heavenly hash ice cream taste real, too?

"Ray," Ray told himself, "you are standing in a forest in Maine in your robe and pajamas. A minute or two ago, you were in LA. Your wall got crazy and sucked you all the way across the country, which is a pretty good spin of the globe. Clearly, the answer is..."

He stopped, dumbfounded.

There weren't many possibilities. The most plausible solution was that he was, at this moment, stuck in a coma. Dr. Rose or Dr. Evans had missed something in his X-rays and CT scan. He had a cerebral hemorrhage and his brain was, at this moment, drowning in blood.

He looked around, not knowing what to do. Was he dying on his living room floor or was he still in a hospital bed? If he thought really hard, could he let the doctors know he was self-aware by pinging a beep or two off an EEG monitor?

There was something called Locked In Syndrome. The sufferer of that medical dilemma was trapped with an active mind in a body that no longer worked. Or maybe this was simply how God punished suicides.

Any other, better possibilities?

If it was a prank, it was the most elaborate joke ever. It was possible, though. Joe had brought him groceries. Maybe they'd poisoned him. Maybe... what? Maybe Joe and Marla conspired to kill him, lost their nerve and deposited him in the same woods he'd played in one summer as a boy?

Could this really be an elaborate prank? He did work on a game show and, as a breed, TV writers and comedians were mentally ill. He could have been drugged. Theoretically, he supposed, it was possible to transport someone across the country and keep them unconscious for days. But...he could still taste apple sauce and Dr. Pepper. The piss at his crotch had turned cold.

"That's it. I'm in a coma or dead. Oh, sweet, Jesus! What do I do now?"

Of course! He was back at Camp Bethany. It made perfect sense. Near death, his mind had reached for the last place he'd received religious instruction. The last time he felt sure there even was a God was here in Maine. But his belief wasn't because of a sermon.

That arose from his first kiss. That had occurred in these very woods.

At twelve, he wasn't very chubby yet. He'd been a cute kid with an unfortunate bowl haircut and haystack hair. The girl had been a year older than he. She was...?

Emma. Emma S. Emma Something. Emma Seaforth! Her last name was Seaforth. Seaworthy Emma Seaforth. They'd taken a class at camp together in canoeing. They'd shared a canoe and a kiss.

Ray hadn't suspected Emma liked him until he accidentally turned their canoe over as they tried to pull it onto the shore.

When Ray tipped them in the water, he'd hurried to stand in the shallow water and wade ashore, his cheeks burning with embarrassment. Emma stayed in the water. She lay down in it up to her neck and laughed.

"C'mon in! The water's fine!"

Ray remembered hearing that just as...no, it wouldn't do to buy into this hallucination. He had to think his way out of this somehow. Then he heard the familiar creak of a swinging chain through the trees and Ray finally believed.

On the last day of Christian summer camp, here at Camp Bethany, Emma Seaforth kissed him goodbye. But it wasn't a goodbye kiss. It was a you-should-have-kissed-me-more-when-you-had-the-chance sort of kiss. A grown up kiss, soft and lingering and on the lips. Neither of them wiped their mouths afterwards.

Some black kids at camp, the ones from Louisiana, spoke in tongues when the Spirit moved through them. The kids from staid little Presbyterian churches in Wisconsin who had never heard of a revival looked at those kids with terror.

Ray didn't believe in speaking in tongues. Unlike a real language, those Louisiana kids seemed to babble the same syllables too often. The touch of Seaworthy Emma Seaforth's lips was the closest thing to true divine revelation Ray had encountered that summer.

Ray had flown all the way to Bangor from Boston on his own to come to Camp Bethany. The kids liked his accent. They were easily impressed because he told them he was from Boston's Combat Zone. He didn't really live anywhere near Boston's infamous section of the city, but that summer Ray reinvented himself. He'd become something of an exotic creature to a bunch of hick kids.

He became a little less shy that summer. He even discovered that, when he loosened up, he could make people laugh. Making people laugh (the other boys generally and girls in particular) became his goal.

Ray Bradley didn't find Jesus at Camp Bethany, but he discovered he had a good sense of humor. And Emma Seaforth found him. That was a good start. That was enough to set him on the path to...

Oh. Right.

He was a comedy writer for a brainless TV game show he didn't like. He'd thought he was meant for so much more. He'd become a suicidal guy past his prime whose wife was sleeping with his best friend.

Camp Bethany had put him on a path. Comedy was going to be the way he made his living. Somewhere along the way, Ray had lost his way. Now he'd come back to his beginning.

An accident of birth had made him a human being.

Jokes made Ray a person. He'd never really felt like a man. He'd barely stood on his own two feet. He hadn't become the hero he thought he'd become.

I'm in a loop, Ray thought. *Okay...what now?*

One sad realization of his failure at life and then... Ray was sure that, with this depressing revelation, he was about to die. He hadn't pictured his last moments like this. Who could have? He'd expected a life review, like some people close to death said they experienced. He'd assumed that would be a mercifully quick flash, like a movie on fast forward. Then the screen would go dark and he'd find out of it was a double feature or if life ended after one failed chance.

Through swaying trees, Ray heard the creak of the swinging chain again to his left. A child wept.

The big, red meeting hall stood through the forest to his right. But to the left? Ray strained his memory. A clearing with a rusty yellow swing set and a teeter totter awaited up the path, in the direction of the weeping. The clearing was supposed to be for the younger kids, but that was where Emma Seaforth kissed him. He couldn't get another girl to kiss him for two years after that. It had been the worst dry spell of his life.

Ray turned away from Camp Bethany's meeting hall, guided by the sound of the child's cries. He walked forward on automatic, driven by nostalgia and curiosity.

As he drew closer, Ray knew it was a boy's cry, angry and sad in equal measure. A path he hadn't remembered appeared and Ray took it, quickening his step. He knew who he'd find when he peered around a tree. It was impossible, but he already knew.

Ray took a deep breath and let it out slowly. He'd never felt this way before. He found himself in what could only be called a fascinated panic.

The rusty yellow swing set was still there. A boy in a light blue Camp Bethany t-shirt and matching shorts sat alone on one of the two swings. The kid stared at his feet and wiped his tears with the back of his fists.

"Shit! Shit! Shit!" the boy said in a stage whisper as he pounded his bare knee.

Shit! Shit! Shit! Ray thought. *I know that bowl haircut! And this is 1996!*

11

The boy Ray had been looking up as his grown self crashed out of the woods. Ray realized his mistake as soon as he ran at the kid. Boy and man were equally terrified.

The kid jumped off the swing. "Are you okay, mister?"

Ray slowed, got to the swing set and leaned against it, breathing hard. The feel of flaking yellow paint under his palm seemed like too rich a detail to be a hallucination.

"You're bleeding! I'll go get help."

"Wait! Don't go. I think I'll be okay if I sit for a while. We have to talk."

The kid looked at him warily. He couldn't stop staring at Ray's forehead, where the tree bark had ripped skin away. When Ray crammed his wide butt onto the swing, the kid waited and watched warily.

Unlike modern swing sets with rubber slings for seats, this set had a wide plank of weathered old barn wood held in place by rusty chain. Ray hadn't sat on a swing set since he'd sat on this one.

Yes, Ray thought. *I'm beginning to think this is*

real. Dying of a brain hemorrhage on my living room floor back in LA is more likely, but on the slim chance this is real, I have something to do. It's my only hope.

Ray heard a chuckle. A *knowing* chuckle. It didn't come from him and it wasn't the boy, either.

"C'mon in. The water's fine."

That time, he heard the voice as an earnest, whispered invitation. The voice was that of an old man. Ray twisted left and right and studied the edge of the clearing.

No one there.

Ray looked at the boy's face. He could tell the kid was on the edge of running back to camp and bringing adults. Camp counselors had faith in Jesus but wouldn't believe Ray about...well, whatever this was. Authorities would be called. Questions would be asked that Ray couldn't begin to answer. The Sheriff would have him locked up in the Waterville Asylum. Or in jail in Bangor for hanging out at a kids' summer camp in his pjs.

"Ray...uh...Raymond. I've got to talk to you and fast because this is my first trip and I don't know how long it will last."

The boy crossed his arms and stepped back. "How do you know my name?"

"Look...I know what this looks like. I know you want to run because you always want to run. You're more scared than you ever want to let on. You're scared all the time, even more than you think you are."

The kid turned to walk away. "You hit your head, mister. I'll go find somebody."

"No. Then it might be too late. I dunno..."

The boy didn't look back. Ray fought the urge to run after him and hold him until he could explain. The kid could outrun him and catching hold of him would only make the boy's fear grow.

"How is Emma?"

The boy paused and looked back.

"Who?"

"Emma. Seaworthy Emma Seaforth."

"You're a pervert. You were spying on us!"

"No. That's not true."

The boy glanced down at his wet crotch. "Pervert!"

"No. I can explain." Ray wasn't sure he could explain, but he pulled the robe tighter to cover his wet pajama bottoms. "It's going to sound crazy, but if I talk long enough it might make sense." *At least to one of us,* Ray thought.

"I'm leaving!"

"Stay. Stay out of reach if you're that worried, but you must hear what I have to say."

"Why?"

"Because...because the future depends on it."

That was a little overblown. He'd made it sound like the safety of the human race was at stake. However, Ray knew this: he'd always wanted to be a hero. He hadn't made the big time as a comic, but just as he'd saved his church congregation over and over in his imagination, maybe he could do something noble now.

Even if this is just an elaborate hallucination in the end, Ray thought, *it feels real enough. I could prove something here. Whoever's watching — c'mon in, the water's fine — ...I could prove to them my life wasn't a waste.*

Then inspiration struck. "This is the last day of

summer camp."

"Yeah. So what?"

"So...so Emma Seaforth...where is she?"

The kid looked at his watch. That was another nifty little detail. The kid didn't have a cell phone. Casual use of cell phones for kids was far off in the Yet.

"Emma left for home with her parents about...forty minutes ago."

"And you came back to the place where you got your first kiss. To cry."

Ray had pushed too hard. The boy looked like he'd burst into tears again.

"You *are* just a pervert. Spying on people!"

"No. How would I know it's your *first* kiss? After she kissed you, Emma asked if this was your first kiss and you said it wasn't. You said you used to have a girlfriend, right?"

"Of *course* it wasn't my first kiss. I'm from Boston!"

Bah-ston.

Ray smiled. He'd forgotten how strong his accent used to be. Then — he couldn't help himself — Ray chuckled. "No shame in first kisses, you know. You were worried you did something wrong because she asked if it was your first kiss. Don't worry. You did nothing wrong. You were just so shy around her all summer, that's the only reason she asked. Emma was being sweet. She didn't have a mean bone in her body. Give it time and you'll figure it out. I'm right."

"Who *are* you?"

If Ray had more time to think about it he would have lied. He would have come up with something better than what he blurted. "I'm you."

His twelve-year-old version laughed. Hard.

Ray wiped the blood that had smeared down his face and stared at his gut. "Well...this is humbling."

"How old are you?" the boy asked. "Like...fifty? Fifty-five?"

Ray sighed. "You're twelve and I just turned thirty. And if you don't take care of yourself...if you eat too much and stay out in the California sun too much... well...this is what thirty looks like if you're doing everything wrong. At least with us. Wear sunscreen and a hat more, is what I'm saying."

The kid laughed harder. "I look nothing like you!"

"Our birthday is November 9, same as Carl Sagan and Lou Ferrigno. You've been listening to Toni Braxton all summer. You know all the words to *You're Makin' Me High*. Emma liked her music more than you did...um...do."

Poor Toni Braxton, Ray thought. *Lovely and talented, she still has divorce, a couple of bankruptcies and a diagnosis of lupus ahead of her.*

In 1996, Ray had a lot of life ahead of him, too. Neither he nor Toni saw what life had in store for them.

He looked at the boy. "You can save us, Raymond."

"You are so full of shit!"

Ray remembered buying popcorn and sharing it with Emma. They'd been on a rare field trip with the rest of the camp to the small, one-screen theater in Poeticule Bay.

"On the trip into town, on movie afternoon... remember? You hoped the camp counselors would let the group see *From Dusk Till Dawn*. You said you wanted to see it again, even though you hadn't seen it at all. You were still too young. Well, Dad said so, anyway. You told Emma you loved all of Quentin Tarantino's movies and you said that back in Boston they'd let you watch anything."

The boy stared at him, wavering between sitting and running away. "How could you know that?"

"I am you. I know how it sounds — "

"How could you remember that if you're — " little Raymond shook his head at Big Ray.

"I remember because one of the camp counselors overheard you and scolded you on the bus, in front of Emma and everybody. They said you shouldn't watch a movie with demons in it."

Ray recognized the set of the boy's jaw. He'd seen that look in the mirror after a fight with Marla, angry and thinking of all the things he should have said.

The kid puffed out his chest. "And I said, 'I don't believe in demons!'"

Ray smiled. "But you didn't really say that. That's what you wished you'd said, right?"

The boy looked at the ground. When he looked up, however, he had a sly look. "What was the counselor's name who bitched me out about it?"

"I...uh...I don't remember."

"Then how do you remember the rest? You're a terrible liar!"

"It's been a long time. Wait...M-Mark! It was Mark something."

"Marco."

"Fine! Marco. It was a long time ago for me. I remember the details that mattered most. You remember stuff like first kisses and...and fights and being embarrassed. I don't forget the least knock or insult. Pardon me for forgetting the *o* in Marco!"

The kid sneered. "You've hit your head and it's

scrambled your brains, mister. I'll go get your *friend*, Marco. You tell him his trick didn't work. I'm not stupid and I'm going home to watch every Tarantino movie!"

Ray talked fast, desperate. "You almost kissed her under the fireworks last night but you were too shy and afraid the guys would razz you, especially if she turned you down. Now you wish you'd made the first move. You would have got more kissing in before she had to leave with her parents."

"Did someone from my cabin — "

"They wouldn't know. You'd never tell the boys in your cabin this stuff. You were afraid they would... you *are* afraid they'd make fun of you and you always want to look cool, no matter what. Still do."

Navigating tenses through the time machine was difficult. Watching *Terminator* and *Back to the Future* marathons hadn't prepared Ray for these linguistic nuances.

"How come you don't talk like me?" the kid asked.

"We...you move to California next year. Dad's been out there working this summer, right? You'll move in time for Christmas with palm trees. Mom will tell me — us — years from now that she almost left Dad because she couldn't stand the Boston winters so he was lucky he picked up the job in Santa Monica. You'll move again to LA a couple years after that. Remember what I said when that stuff happens."

"But, the way you talk — "

"I lose the *Bah*-ston accent and start pronouncing my *r*s because kids in high school will make fun of it and think you're stupid, though you'll emphasize your accent and push it really hard when *Good Will Hunting* comes out."

"What the hell are you talking about?"

Oh, right. Raymond probably didn't even know who Matt Damon was. Not quite yet.

"Look, you don't have to believe me, but when Dad gets a job out West, you'll know for sure that I'm for real. This is your chance. Don't blow this."

Raymond stared at Ray for a moment more. Then the boy came closer and sat on the swing next to him. "Okay, psycho. Talk."

12

If the kid had been much older, Ray wouldn't have been able to convince him of anything. Depending on how harsh you were, the minds of twelve-year-olds are either more malleable or they're stupid enough to believe anything.

Once the boy sat on the swing, Ray knew he had a fighting chance to change the boy's future. He hoped to change his life, too. Maybe this was a different timeline unconnected to his reality. When your wall turns into black water and reaches out to suck you back into what appears to be your past, there are no instruction manuals or guarantees.

Ray thought there was still a better than even chance he was dying in his living room. His brain was probably working through this escapist fantasy to make his death easier. If he did change the past, would he return to his present or a new one? Would he be erased? If so, how could he come back here to save himself? He'd read enough sci-fi to understand the problem of time paradoxes. No one had read enough sci-fi to understand and solve those paradoxes.

"What's your job?" the boy asked.

"We're funny for a living."

"You don't seem funny."

"I'm funnier with more advanced notice. It's been a tough day. I've had a lot of tough days lately. I think that's why I'm back here. To fix things."

The boy's eyes narrowed. "What do I do wrong?"

The question stung Ray in a way he did not expect. His parents were critical people. He hadn't understood how ingrained the impulse to find fault had been until he saw himself suffering it.

Ray hadn't become really funny until he let go of the notion that anyone who objected to what he said must, automatically, be right. It had taken him a long time to figure out when to discount the opinions of others. "Comfortable in his own skin," people called it. Comedians called it, "Giving zero fucks."

"Hey!" the kid said. "I asked you, what am I doing wrong?"

"Sorry, Raymond. This is...I'm a bit off. I hit my head and — "

"I can see that."

"No, I mean, before." Ray waved the details away. "I don't know how much time I have so I should be concise."

"What's concise?"

"Fast."

"Then why didn't you say that?"

"Can we start over? Not from the beginning. I mean, from the time you sat down and decided to shut up and listen?"

The boy nodded and Ray immediately felt terrible. "Sorry. I've got a short temper today. I've been through a lot."

"Okay," the boy said in a small voice.

Ray took a deep breath and let it out slowly, hissing through his teeth. "When someone needs advice, it's pretty simple. Usually, you tell them what they want to hear and they go away happy. If that sounds too harsh, you tell them to imagine that they're being asked the same question by a troubled friend."

"How is that supposed to help?"

"People are always clearer on other people's problems than they are on their own. For instance, you know how tough Dad is on you when you're at bat and loses his mind when you get struck out?"

"Yeah."

"He only does that because he always wanted to play in the majors and he wasn't good enough."

"He never told me that."

"He will," Ray said. What Ray didn't add was that, over Thanksgiving dinner, his father, Ken, would mock Ray for gaining weight in his first year of college.

"Looks like you swallowed a pig." Ken reached out and pinched his belly. "That what you call the Freshman Fifteen?"

Ray got pissed off because Ken embarrassed him in front of the girl he brought home for Thanksgiving. Especially after his father added, "Pretty girl like that should expect more from a boyfriend." Ray and Ken argued outside in the yard after dinner. Ken promised to back off about Ray's weight problem, but Ray lost the girl that night, anyway. It wasn't his weight that bothered the girl. It was because Ray scared her. She didn't like how mad he got, yelling at his father.

Ray cleared his throat and tried to clear his mind. This was such a common fantasy, it was a meme on Facebook: if you could tell your younger self one thing, what would it be?

"You'll meet a girl named Marla," Rat said. "She's a yoga instructor. She's bad for you. You're probably not great for her, either. Don't marry her. In fact, just stay away from yoga."

The boy wrinkled his nose. "Why would I ever want to do yoga?"

"For the girls."

"When do I get to see Emma again?"

"You don't."

The boy looked away, fighting back tears.

"I'm sorry," Ray said. He meant it, too. When had he become so callous about feelings? Watching the boy cry over the girl who gave him his first kiss, sadness welled up within Ray, too.

"When your parents...our parents will notice you moping. You'll feel bad for a while. There will be a couple of letters back and forth, but Emma will withdraw. It happens. Often. It doesn't make that kiss any less important or any less real. Mom and Dad will dismiss your feelings. They'll call it puppy love. They won't understand how deep your feelings are. It's not that Emma is the love of your life. It's that you let a chance at first love slip away."

"Uh...thanks." The boy wept silent tears.

"Just tell yourself you did the best you could with what you knew and how you were at the time. You know better now." Ray wasn't sure if he sounded too California granola. Dr. Papua was big on validating feelings. Ray suspected positive self-talk was well-known in 1996, but probably not among twelve-year-old boys.

"Did you bring back lottery numbers for me? For us, I mean?"

Ray laughed. "Heh. I wish! That would have been a great idea!"

"No, duh!"

"I didn't know I was coming here today."

"So...what? You *fell* into a time machine?"

"It's tough to explain. I wouldn't believe me so let's focus on you."

"I'm supposed to stay away from girls named Darla who do yoga," the kid said.

"Marla!"

"Okay, what else?"

"Read more. Get better grades so you can get into a better school. Do some open mic stand up gigs as soon as you can so you'll get better faster."

"Stand up gigs?"

"Stand up comedy, yeah. And learn to type."

"Should I be writing this down?"

"Yeah."

The boy reached into his back pocket and pulled out what looked like a flyer. It was Camp Bethany's closing day program. He had a nub of a pencil, too, from the camp's mini-putt.

"You'll meet a guy named Joe Grenwell. You'll call him Grins Well. He's not a bad guy, but he can't be trusted around your girlfriends."

"Sounds like a bad guy."

Ray considered this. "Maybe, but if things don't go well otherwise, he's the one who will get you a job writing for a game show."

"Writing for a game show is a job?"

Ray laughed. "Believe it or not, yeah. It's a good

gig if you can get it. The pay's not bad and it's easy, but you can do better."

The boy stopped writing. "Shouldn't you be telling me to go get a job at the Jet Propulsion Laboratory instead of doing what you've already done? If it didn't work out the first time — "

"We suck at math."

The boy frowned for a moment and then gave a slow nod. "Word."

Heh. *Word*. He used to say that a lot. Too much *Fresh Prince of Bel-Air* back in the day.

"What about investing in companies? Shouldn't I, like, invest in stock or something?"

"You won't have any money to invest."

"I could change that. Dad does the stock market a little. What about working in...I don't know...cars and stuff?"

"Look, I don't know anything about stocks. Detroit goes under, anyway. Dad doesn't make any money off that. He'll lose the house in 2008. With mortgages and all that, everyone goes underwater."

The boy's eyes shot wide. "Is there...is there a tidal wave or something?"

Ray burst out laughing, which only made the kid mad. The boy hated to feel stupid just as the man he would become hated it.

Young Raymond stood and paced back and forth. "You told me where you came from. That sounds pretty good. But *when* are you from?"

"2014."

"What's it like?"

"There's a black president."

"Wow."

"Not so much. He's too much like the white guy he

80

replaces. I guess you could bet all the money you have that Obama will win in 2008 and 2012. If you stick too close to my timeline...well, you won't have much to bet. Write this down: stop spending so much. Save more. Be frugal."

"The president's name is Obama?"

"Yeah, yeah. Write that down, too."

"Is he Irish?"

"Heh. Yeah. Black Irish."

"What's Black Irish?"

"No. Um...actually, I don't even know what Black Irish is."

"I've never heard that name before. Obama. What else do I need to know?"

Lots of possibilities occurred to Ray. All those great ideas flew out of his head when he looked up and saw his father. Ken Bradley stood at the edge of the clearing, hands on hips.

"What are you doing out here with this man, Raymond?"

The boy was so startled he shook. His eyes were red. His cheeks were still tear-stained.

Slack-jawed, Ray pulled himself up from his seat on the wooden swing. His robe came open as he did so and his penis poked out of the wet flap of his pajamas.

His father stalked forward, "What the hell are you doing out in the woods alone with my son in your goddamn *pajamas*?"

"Wow!" Ray blurted, "You've got *hair!*"

Ken Bradley planted his feet and punched the son he didn't know yet in the side of the head as hard as he could.

Ken Bradley had washed out as a baseball player.

However, he'd learned to box in the Marines. He still had a wicked right hook. He threw his hip into the punch.

Ray hadn't been hit by his father since he was much younger, back when everyone called him Raymond. Ray stumbled backward through the swing set. His knees caught the old wooden seat and he tipped over. His left forearm burned along the chain as he tried to stop himself from going into the dirt.

The ground came up faster than Ray expected and slammed him harder than his father's punch.

The forest's long shadows reached out to Ray with long fingers and sucked away all the light.

13

Day turned to night. A current of air caught Ray's cheek. Water rippled around him. He opened his eyes and, gradually, he discovered he was floating down a river of water so thick and black, it might have been ink.

Caught in the current, Ray was swept forward. Ahead, hanging in a black, starless sky, a bright white light cast its reflection across a shimmering sea. *That's the brightest, closest moon I've ever seen,* Ray thought. *The Man in the Moon is made of white cheese.*

As if hearing his thoughts, the moon turned its face to regard him with a stern and steady gaze. The face had no mouth, only huge, dark craters for eyes, terrifying in their blankness. Whatever the remote thing in the sky was, 'Man in the Moon' made as much sense as anything.

It came closer. The movement was purposeful. Floating wasn't the right word. *It came to look at him.*

Ray did not understand what he witnessed, but he knew this: *It is What It Is. It sees things as they are.*

It's the unexpected glance in a hotel mirror that shows you how fat and ugly you really are. It sees what Is.

He could feel the thing's power. He could not hear thoughts, but he felt small and unimpressive under Its blank gaze. It might be a God inspecting an insect. That face seemed utterly devoid of preference, prejudice or mercy.

Pitiless, Ray thought.

"What are you?"

An old man's voice came to him in a raucous cackle. From nowhere the voice said, "I'm the opposite of true love's first kiss. Is the water fine? Are you glad you came?"

The Man in the Moon, that bright thing in the sky, did not approve of him. Ray felt *shattering* disapproval. He opened his mouth to scream, but his lungs filled with black ink. The liquid burned his eyes and blinded him.

The river's current hastened and Ray dropped, twisted and turned through rapids. The river dragged him down and stretched him out.

The black sea — *C'mon in, the water's deep and terrifying!* — waited ahead.

Ray heard the old man laughing gaily as night turned to day.

14

Ray awoke in a bed. The clock radio on the nightstand flashed: *12:00, 12:00, 12:00.* He had no idea where he was. He felt his forehead but found no wound there. His headache was back. It felt like someone was trying to pry the sutures of his skull open with a crowbar. He moaned in pain.

"Sweetie? Is it time for you to take another Percocet?"

"Huh?"

"Do you need another pain pill?"

"Yes."

"You left them in the bathroom."

Ray looked around the room. It was nicer than the bedroom in his apartment. The dressers weren't made of particle board like his own. A door to his left stood ajar. He could see the bathroom sink.

Ray didn't want to move. Then the music returned. This time his personal soundtrack was an orchestral salvo followed by an energetic thrum that felt encouraging. He pulled himself out of bed. As soon as he stood, he knew something was different. Not wrong, exactly, but *new*. He looked down. He could see his feet. He was not slim, but he'd lost a lot of weight.

Despite his headache, he rushed to the bathroom. Somehow, he knew he'd find a scale in there and he did. He knew it would be on the right, by the bathtub, not on the left, by the toilet.

Muscle memory, Ray thought. *This is like not being able to recall a telephone number you dial often, but without being able to say the number, he could still stab it out on a keypad.*

He stood on the scale. Yesterday he weighed an even 270 pounds. Today he was 223.

But not yesterday. When am I from?

Excellent question.

Ray examined his forearm for evidence of the burn of the swing's chain. It wasn't there. He looked in the bathroom mirror, then stepped back and took a deep breath. His extra chins were gone. He was still a bit doughy, but he had a jawline again. He smiled at himself and was shocked to find he had one gold tooth.

He pulled off his clothes. It was as if, with each moment, a memory of his new life rose up. For instance, he knew the gold tooth was relatively new.

When he was 270 pounds, he didn't have a tattoo of a horned devil's head on his left shoulder. Ray didn't like it. However, it felt familiar the longer he stared at it. "Virginia," Ray said aloud. "I got this tattoo in Virginia. What was I doing in Virginia?"

The answer came immediately: traveling. He also knew that the tattoo artist who had inked him had been a smiling blonde who wore nothing but a skimpy leather outfit that displayed her tattoos. Goblins and dragons had fought across her exposed topography.

Her hair had been styled with straight bangs that hung so low over her eyes Ray had worried she couldn't see what she was doing. As she tattooed him, he stared at her chest, arms and legs where a mural of dragons roasted evil, defiant goblins alive before eating them.

He knew all that with certainty, but he did not know where he was. He frowned and peered out through the bathroom door. A painting hung on the wall above the bed. It was *Cyrano in the Garden at Midnight*. His painting. Ray smiled. Then he closed his eyes and asked the question aloud, "Where exactly do I live?"

The answer came immediately: *Culver City.*

That was a relief. The kid on the swing set hadn't screwed up everything. He'd kept the pounds off and Ray was home. Not the home he knew, but at least close to his other life.

My other time. My other timeline. My other lifeline. How was he supposed to think and talk about this?

But there was a more troubling problem. When he went back in time to Maine, he hadn't become a boy. He met the boy he'd been. Where was the other Ray in this timeline? What if the Ray who owned this apartment in this future showed up?

"Somebody's been sleeping in my bed!" But which Ray would be Goldilocks and which was Papa Bear?

What do I do now? What if the other me wants his life back? I don't want to steal my identity, but if he shows up, we'll have to share it. Or does it work that way at all? Do we have to fight to the death? Then he realized he shouldn't even assume he'd returned to 2014.

Ray pulled a bottle of Percocets from the medicine cabinet. Torment had followed him through time and found him again. Ray put his forehead against the cool glass of the mirror over the sink. Perhaps it was wise that the headache should slow him down. As eager and curious as Ray was, he needed to slip into the hot water of this new existence slowly. He had to give himself time to acclimate. There was an unknown woman in the next room, for instance, and he was naked. He went to the dresser and pulled at drawers, peeking in. They were no women's clothes.

This proves two things, he thought. *I'm not a cross dresser but I'm not married, either. The woman out there (somewhere) is...a girlfriend?*

Andrea? Was that her name? Andrea?

Confused, Ray stared at his face. He looked younger and healthier, but he was almost sure that was because of the weight loss. He was back to his time, but the timeline had been altered.

He found gray dress slacks, freshly pressed, hanging in the closet. He'd always worn blue jeans, black jeans for more formal occasions. He'd never used the services of a dry cleaner in his life.

The reply from nowhere came quickly: *yes, you have. Pickup is every Saturday morning.*

"Oh."

He stood before the dresser, closed his eyes and waited. The socks and underwear are in the top drawers, just like always. That hadn't changed and, as small a detail as that was, stability was a comfort.

He found a blue Oxford shirt and put that on. Ray was relieved to find that his trip into the past hadn't turned him into a fan of tighty-whities.

His preference for black boxers remained intact.

As he pulled his socks on, a pretty woman in a white business suit strode in, head tilted as she fiddled with her earring. "You're going to be late for your appointment, Ray."

Not Andrea. Angela. Her name is Angela.

As soon as he saw her, he knew. She was the ninth floor receptionist at the network. He worked at the network, but Ray was not a writer. He was in sales.

"This is kind of appalling," Ray said.

"What?"

He looked up. "I work in sales. I can't believe I work in Hollywood, but in advertising!"

"Not for much longer if you don't straighten out your attitude. Let's not talk about that again. Besides, if you leave your job, you won't get to see me every day and pretend you don't see me a couple of nights a week." She winked.

Memories flooded in. Rays' eyes widened. "The sex with you is fantastic!"

She paused, then laughed. "Thanks. I know. Are you okay? Headache worse than usual this morning?"

"Yes. Yes, it is."

She nodded. "Did you take a pill?"

"Yeah. I think so."

"You act like you've taken too many already. Go to your appointment. I've got to get going. Your alarm clock didn't go off and a couple of lights were on in the living room. Looks like the power flipped."

"Yeah. I guess it did."

She brushed his cheek with her lips. It was a perfunctory kiss.

We've been going out long enough that the

novelty has worn off, he thought.

The answer came to him. He'd been going out with Angela for a year and four months and he'd been thinking of breaking up with her. She wanted him to keep on doing his job, get promoted and earn more money. She wanted him to ask her to marry so she could have kids and stay home.

She wanted a lot of good things for them both. Angela was a nice person and he liked her a lot. He might have loved her if she didn't want to push him into the corporate coffin, climb in with him, slam the lid shut and live out the ordinary American dream.

"Gotta go," she said. "The freeway is going to be murder and I have to change clothes if I'm to avoid the walk of shame. Love ya, baby!" She walked out and a moment later a door slammed far away.

He'd dated her exclusively for more than a year, but she still didn't have a key. There were no pictures of them together on the dresser. She still kept no change of clothes at his apartment.

He remembered more. Dr. Papua said these were signs he had a problem with commitment. As nice as Angela was, Ray was holding back on hurting her by breaking up. "You're doing more damage now by putting off the inevitable, Ray."

Dr. Circe Papua! Ray's appointment was with Dr. Circe Papua. He was on stress leave from his job and she was still his therapist.

Socks and underwear and Dr. Circe Papua were the constants he could rely on. He strutted out, feeling thinner and stronger, this time accompanied by a disco beat backed by a string section that knew how to pull a man up through the chest and make him feel taller. The music was a constant, too.

For a short time, Ray was relatively happy in his new life. He was free to do something new. He was free of credit card debt. In this life, there was no Marla who taught him yoga and broke his heart. There was no Joe to betray him. Ray's divorce and attempted suicide and all the baggage that went with it was on another time plane.

His old life had disappeared in deep, black water, never to return. The realization hit: There is no other Ray. This time travel is different from that time travel. *I am not Goldilocks. There is no Papa Bear angry about who is sleeping in his bed. I am Papa Bear and this is my bed. This is my life!*

Ray didn't know yet that this was only a test. Of course, all lives are a test.

15

Ray drove a blue Audi. He didn't have to think about where he'd parked it. He just walked to it automatically.

Automagically, Ray thought.

He was worried about getting behind on the car payments, but his job required a certain look. He hated that he needed a certain look, but that was a remnant of the life he knew with Marla.

In that life, the preferred look for game show writers was not to have a special style. It was uncool to care about such things too much. Some guys cultivated a certain air. Grins Well had worn a pinstriped suit for a while, but with bowling shoes or bright white tennis shoes, just to let everyone in on the irony.

Ray missed Joe and wondered where he was. He wondered where Marla had ended up, too. Still teaching yoga? He didn't know, but he doubted they'd found each other without him.

Good, he thought. *Let's start our new lives with a little spite, shall we?*

Dr. Papua's office was where he had left it.

Everything looked the same. Changing the lanes of his life had left the rest of the world untouched. Apparently it took more than changing one life or accidentally stomping on a butterfly to bend the course of the planet toward the apocalyptic.

Life goes on, Ray.

That wasn't his voice giving him an answer. Not that time. It was the old man's voice again.

Ray stomped on the brake. The driver in the car at his rear bumper screeched to a stop and honked his horn long and hard. Ray didn't care. He'd cracked a cold sweat. He gripped the wheel. His body shook. The old man's voice had been close, whispering in his ear, but the back seat was empty.

He remembered the black river and the Man in the Moon. Feeling tiny and insignificant had brought him back to drowning in the River of Time.

The annoying trill of a piccolo pierced his head. It sounded like a terrified bird.

A large sandy-haired man knocked hard on Ray's car window. It was the driver Ray had cut off. Big and beefy, it was clear the man was looking for a fight.

Ray looked up at the man and tried a weak smile.

"What is *wrong* with you?" the man asked.

Ray nodded cordially, opened his door and threw up on the big man's sandals, spattering the stranger's bare feet with what looked like black ink.

The River of Time wasn't done with him. This was just one stop on a journey. Ray didn't know how he knew that. The answers, like the old man's voice, seemed to come from nowhere.

16

Dr. Papua retrieved some ice for the swelling around Ray's eye and leaned down for a closer look. "That's going to turn very black, but I don't think your nose is broken. How is your headache?"

"The headache is fine. It's going strong. It's a beating heart in the middle of my skull." It was a marimba in his head, but Ray held back that information. "Have I had a brain scan?"

"Yes. After your TBI, of course"

Ray sat up straight. "TBI..."

"Traumatic brain injury."

"I know. I...uh, just so I'm clear, this would be a concussion...when, exactly?"

"Two months ago. Are you remembering more about the fall itself?"

Of course, as soon as the right question was asked, the answer appeared in his head. It wasn't The Man in the Moon. It wasn't the old man's voice. It was his own voice providing the answers now. "I fell down a flight of stairs. At work, right?"

"That is correct."

Two concussions, one to a lifetime, lifeline,

timeline...so much for free will. Some things, it seemed, are predestined: socks and underwear go in the top drawer, the kitchen garbage is under the sink and the location of his psychotherapist's office was the same.

Dr. Papua stared at him. She looked concerned.

"I thought so...about the accident, I mean," Ray said. "But I needed to hear it from you."

"*Accident*, Ray? Your fall at work was not an accident. Let's not go backwards. I thought we were making progress." Dr. Papua sat in her chair. He thought of it as her listening chair, in this life and the other one. She watched and waited, saying nothing.

He suspected that technique was a trick to get him to fill in the pregnant pauses. To his annoyance, the trick worked. "Okay, no. My fall at work wasn't an accident."

"Old ground. Let's talk about today. Are you going to tell me about the black eye?"

"That's a story that doesn't start this morning."

"Go ahead."

"Do you have another patient after my appointment?"

"I did have a cancellation, but you know your insurance only covers the usual fifty-minute hour."

"I'll pay myself. When I'm done, you'll want to pay me."

She chuckled. "That is going to have to be quite a story."

"It is. And you won't believe it."

He told her about the divorce papers from a wife he no longer had. He told her about the pothole and how that made him think how easy it would be to leave all his troubles behind. He told her about the palm tree rushing at his windshield and his hospital stay. He divulged the embarrassing details of Marla's list of grievances and his best friend's betrayal.

"That's quite a story," the doctor said. "It conflicts with the history you've given me for years. You know that, right?"

"Here's the part that you really aren't going to believe." Ray related every detail of his trip through the wall of his old, crappy apartment, minus the fact that he'd peed his pajama bottoms.

When he was done, Dr. Papua regarded him for a long moment before asking him to close his eyes. She began to count backwards from one-hundred. At ninety, she told him to release the tension around his eyes. At eighty, Dr. Papua asked Ray to relax his jaw and let his head sink back into the chair. At seventy, she asked Ray to picture a ball of white light, a warm energy, come up through his feet and up into his chest.

Ray was about to protest that he'd tried meditation in Marla's yoga class and it wasn't for him. Instead, when he opened his eyes, the slant of the light told him it was later in the day. Dr. Papua stared at him in a new way. She didn't look bored anymore.

"You must have hypnotized me for quite a while."

"It was quite a story. You hardly changed a detail the second time, except you didn't tell me about urinating in your pajamas from fear the first time."

Ray smiled and found he could breathe a little deeper. Torment was gone. His head felt clear and even his swollen eye had stopped throbbing.

He looked at his therapist and chuckled to the sound of sweet violins playing a soft lullaby.

17

Dr. Papua still sat in her listening chair, her notebook perched in her lap. He'd never seen Papua smoke a cigarette but she did now. Ray guessed he hadn't changed that by going back in time, but hearing his story seemed to trigger his therapist into lighting up. She stared at Ray as if he was a difficult math problem.

He watched the white smoke curl in the air and pile toward the ceiling. Yearning, smoky jazz from a lone saxophone began to fill the room. *Beautiful music, just for me,* Ray thought.

He sighed deeply. It was good to get the secret off his chest. He felt less crazy now that he'd revealed what he had been through. "So?" Ray said. "Do you believe me now?"

"I cannot determine if anything supernormal happened to you through hypnosis, Ray."

"Oh. But...do you believe me?"

"I am convinced that you believe this time travel story."

"But *you* don't believe me."

"Let us put that aside for the moment. What

matters is that you believe it. We should explore that."

"Okay."

"You had an experience. You went back to 1996 by means unknown."

"My wall attacked me."

"Yes, well, that is unusual. Have any other objects attacked you in the past? Was this the first time?"

"You've got to be shitting me."

"Very well. Put that aside for now. You've been under a great deal of emotional stress. Something happened or seemed to happen. You spoke to your younger self."

"Yeah. I wasn't prepared for this 'experience,' as you call it. If I were, I suppose the thing to do would be to go farther back in time and kill Hitler."

"Heh. Yes. That is the expected cliche. I am curious about several things. I wonder why you are not curious about some things?"

"I haven't had a lot of time to process this." Ray shrugged. "I uh...this is my first day."

Papua blew more smoke straight up. "Your memory of your present life is sketchy, yes?"

"Yes and no."

"Explain that, please, because I am very curious how it is that one can exchange lives or skip across time, yet you remember the events of both your lives. You say you were a comedian in your other life?"

"Television writer. I started out in stand-up like a lot of people do, but got tired of doing the road, crisscrossing the Dakotas for lousy gigs and sleeping in the back of an old car half the time. I came back to Hollywood to be close to the business and try to find a way in. I was delivering chicken and ribs until a buddy got me the job writing for *What's My Rhyme?*"

"And you remember this clearly?"

"My old life, sure. It's this new one that is coming to me in bits and pieces."

"Yet you have not mentioned it to me until now."

"The lines between the original me and the new me didn't cross until this morning when I woke up. I just got here!"

She took a long drag on her cigarette and the smoke came out in puffs as she spoke. "I do not want to alarm you, Ray, but your experience could as easily describe a dissociative disorder and a psychotic break from reality. I want you to try to take your emotion out of the experience. I know it all seems very real, but step back a moment and observe yourself logically. Given all you know, time travel versus psychological break, which eventuality strikes you as more likely?"

"Not playing, Doc. I broke away from your reality." He watched her steadily, wondering if he should run for the door. She could use his swelling black eye as evidence that he needed to be protected from himself. Ray began to sweat.

"You have been attending my office for how long, Ray?"

Ray hardly had to think about the question at all. "Soon after I got my job. The insurance kicked in at six months, so...about five years."

"How is it that you remember that if you just arrived in this life this morning?"

"I don't know how it works. I know that if I ask a question and it's the right one, the answer comes to me. It feels like my head is an empty jar. When I need something, it appears in the jar. It isn't there one minute and the next minute, the information pours in."

"Since you're so clear on your other life, let's talk about that. I was your therapist in the other life, too?"

"Yes. For a shorter time."

"Does that not strike you as a strange coincidence?"

"Maybe not as much as it sounds. I work for the same company. You'd be on the list of approved service providers. Your office is on my way to work on the right hand side of the road with free parking. Makes sense. And there's only one Hollywood. I was destined to end up here, one way or another."

"I see."

"It's strange, but it's far from an impossible occurrence. People have experiences all the time that they can't explain, like they think of someone they haven't spoken to in years and, in the next moment, that person calls them on the telephone. People get all excited about that sort of thing. They call it synchronicity and start thinking they're a little psychic. Given what I've seen, that's a small happenstance."

"Yes. I would call that a coincidence," she said.

"Me, too. I'm just saying, with all the little variables lining up, maybe you're my psychotherapist across quite a few time streams, don't you think? People say they want original stories, but there are only so many, right?"

She shrugged. "You think there are many 'time streams', as you put it?"

"C'mon. I don't know shit about that."

"Odd, isn't it? That so little is explained by your experience? Why do you think that magic jar of answers is empty now?"

"If I had all the answers, you'd say it was too pat. Me knowing everything would be grounds for believing me less, not more."

"Do you have a persecution complex, Ray? Can you admit it is possible you're experiencing delusions of grandeur?"

"I only started feeling persecuted when you asked that question, Doctor."

"Don't be defensive."

"Don't be offensive."

"You're deflecting."

"I'm reflecting." Ray took a deep breath and looked at the ceiling. He spoke as if he were reading a teleprompter, trying to sound calm. "People don't believe in long odds and coincidences, but I remember one. A meeting was scheduled at the World Trade Center for the morning of September 11, 2001. It was supposed to be about contingency plans in case of a terrorist attack on the Twin Towers. Someone couldn't make it, so they held the meeting the night before the attack instead. Or what about the fact that, on 9/11, many of the military who could have responded were already training elsewhere for a terrorist attack?"

"Which proves what? You're a conspiracy theorist, too?"

"No. Um, not exactly. I'm saying that whoever's in charge of irony is brutal or careless or doesn't care that we see the awkward seams. Maybe this is just one simulation of a life and some of the programming is glitchy."

"Glitchy?"

"Yeah, bad coding in the program tells you it's a program. Do you read any science fiction?"

She didn't return his smile. "Romantic comedies and textbooks."

"Okay, well, I understand this all sounds fantastical, but weird things happen all the time. How about the congressman who gets caught in a scandal for sending out pics of his wiener and his name is Wiener? Weird, ironic stuff. Maybe those are hints."

"Hints at what?"

"That there are larger forces at work. That there's something about our lives that is artificial and constructed. The emperor has no clothes and the reality we believe is just one possibility. Like, uh... we're in *The Matrix*. You must have seen that."

Papua smiled. "And you are the television ad man who, in your scenario, is the messiah played by Keanu Reeves?"

"I never said — "

"Ray, someone once said something along the lines that fiction has to sound true. Reality does not have to be tied up with that silly constraint."

The old man's voice broke in. *It's no wonder that truth is stranger than fiction. Fiction has to make sense. Mark Twain said that, among others.*

Dr. Papua's eyes narrowed. "Did I say something wrong? You look uncomfortable."

"No," Ray said. "Please continue."

"What I'm observing is that, in both your lifetimes, you were destined to have a concussion. That is ironic, too, no? Both events were recent. Don't you think these hallucinations or false memories could be related to your recent fall down the stairs? Brain injuries are — ”

“I'm only singing the song,” Ray said. “I didn't write it.”

“We should talk of that. What do you think the humming is about? Even under deepest hypnosis, you were humming a little tune.”

“What was it? I was a Motown fan in my other life. Since the concussion, that all changed somehow. I don't feel the need to just listen to the Four Tops or Marvin Gaye or Smokey Robinson anymore. I want to listen to *everything*...I used to *hate* classical.”

“Symphonies. You hummed the most glorious symphony. I could imagine it with a full orchestra. It reminded me of Haydn, actually. You must have listened to a lot of Haydn, yes?”

“Haydn, no. It's not my thing. Well, it wasn't. It might be now.”

“Tell me about changing your other life, Ray. Why did you want to do that?”

“It sucked. I wasn't making enough money. My wife left me.”

“And your situation in *this* life, with Angela, has not changed?”

“No. I haven't broken up with her yet.”

“And you did not share your amazing experience with her this morning, either?”

“No. I was afraid of sounding crazy.”

“Do not say, ‘crazy.’ You came to me for help and I will help you. But you must be honest with me.”

“I am.”

“You have not been honest with me, Ray. In this other life, you claim you had a traumatic brain injury. At work, in this life, you fell down a staircase and experienced the same injury. You admit you drove your car into a tree in a suicide attempt. The fall down the stairs was a suicide attempt, as well. You have admitted that to me already."

The answer came to Ray, clear as a death knell. "Yes. Sorry."

"Do not apologize. I want you to be healthy, not sorry."

A knock came at the door.

Dr. Papua stubbed out her cigarette and waved the smoke away. "Come in!"

Two orderlies in white uniforms opened the door and leaned in. "Are we in the right place?"

Ray turned to Dr. Papua. "You *bitch*."

"I called while you were under hypnosis, Ray. I want you evaluated. It is only a seventy-two hour hold for observation and consultation.

"Shit! Shit! Shit!"

"For your safety, Ray. You have had a break from reality and you are suicidal."

"I wasn't very. I'm more so now. Maybe a touch homicidal, too."

"Ray —"

"C'mon! That was a joke! This whole thing is a cosmic joke."

"It is not funny."

"No," he said. "I guess it's not."

Dr. Papua rose from her listening chair, though Ray wondered if she'd really heard him at all. "Gentlemen, this is Mr. Ray Bradley. He needs a ride. He's 5150."

"What's 5150?"

"I am concerned that you're a danger to yourself, Ray."

The larger of the two orderlies stepped forward and smiled. "You'll be evaluated by a mental health professional at the Abbott Institute for Mental Health in Sherman Oaks. It's not bad. It's Tuesday so it's spaghetti night. How's that sound, Mr. Bradley?"

"Is there garlic toast?"

"Sure. We can get you some garlic toast."

"That toast come with a knife?"

"Not even a plastic one, sir, no."

Ray sighed. "Raymond, you little bastard. You screwed me over. I sure wish I'd had those lottery numbers on me."

18

"This is the common room," the nurse said. "Some of the residents get a wicked game of ping pong going after dinner, if you'd like."

"No."

"Okay. Up to you. Ordinarily we'd have you evaluated right away or participate in group on your first night. However, you've arrived late." The nurse shot a glance at Ray as if that was his fault.

"Next time I'll get started on going crazy earlier in the day. Alarm clock broke. I'm off my time."

"I was about to say, before you interrupted me, that the doctors are in a staff meeting. We'll get you settled in and you can talk to someone in the morning."

"I was about to say, as you were interrupting me," Ray replied, "to screw off."

"Are we going to have a problem, Mr. Bradley?"

"No, Nurse Ratchet. If we were going to have a problem, I would have gone whole hog and told you to kindly fuck off."

"Why so hostile?"

"Hostile? This isn't hostility. Not toward you. This

is seething anger. I've got a massive headache and it's a race to see which blocks out the sun first, Torment or Rage."

"Block out the sun?" she said.

"Turning the sky black around the Earth, yeah."

"Well, it is night."

"Everywhere." He leaned closer, pointed at the space between his eyes. "*Everywhere!*"

"That's just fine, Mr. Bradley, but if you want to get out of here sooner than later, stop acting out."

He was about to shout and scream. They'd taken away his belt and shoe laces. He wore a tracker on his wrist again. Rage seemed perfectly reasonable. He wanted to break something. Something ceramic would be good. Ceramic and glass make a very satisfying noise as they shatter and he was sure they wouldn't make him clean up the sharp shards.

The need for petty violence went away when he spotted the old piano in a corner of the common room.

The nurse was still speaking. He didn't care. He felt a pull from his belly button to the piano as if there was a line attached, reeling him in. She was still talking as he walked away.

He sat on the bench and put his hands on the keys. Ray had never played piano, not in this life or the old one. He could play now. He didn't read music. Just as the right question made the right answer appear in his head, the notes came to him as easily as humming.

All activity in the common room stopped. Every face turned to Ray. The ping pong tournament across the room halted, too. Ray was oblivious to it all. He closed his eyes and saw every note. His hands made the music happen. He played a classical composition on the piano no one on Earth had ever heard. The piano was slightly out of tune, but the music was still unearthly and beautiful.

Ray opened his eyes and watched his hands. His fingers flew across the keys with confidence, hitting every note. He'd never played a musical instrument, but it occurred to him the act was analogous to typing at high speed without committing a single typo. He hit no false notes. He played his headache away.

At the piano, he was not a traumatic brain injury patient. He was a virtuoso. Ray's hands knew what to do. He ran up scales to a crescendo and finished the piece, created in the moment, with a flourish.

The hospital's common room was silent for a moment. The residents and staff stood frozen and stunned. Finally, the patients burst into applause.

The nurse approached Ray and put her hands on his before he could launch into another piece. "Slow down, cowboy!"

"B-but...this is the first time I've ever played piano."

"The first time? Really?"

"Really. I swear."

The nurse gave a lopsided smile and turned to call to an orderly. "Hey, Johnny! We got another one. He should meet the Wizard!"

19

In the morning, a red-haired, freckle-faced doctor named Dickens interviewed Ray. The doctor looked improbably young for his position. Ray told the whole story again, beginning with, "I know this sounds crazy but..."

The doctor didn't look up from typing on his iPad. When Ray was done, he finally looked Ray in the eyes. "Time travel is your mind's metaphor, Mr. Bradley."

"What?"

"It's so obvious. Simplistic, even. You want a new life."

"Well, yeah. Doesn't everybody?"

The doctor spared him a smug smile. "I don't."

Ray sighed. "That's because you're the one holding the clipboard."

"It's an iPad."

"Your iPad is a metaphorical clipboard. It's obvious. Simplistic, even. You enjoy the power it confers. Too much."

"Shall I add passive-aggressive to your file?"

"You're proving my point, Doc."

The doctor added another note to Ray's file.

"Ahem. Doctor? This morning I ate cold oatmeal next to a drooling guy convinced that we're all being watched by a malevolent entity from behind the walls."

The doctor hit him with that smug smile again. "And that drooling patient sat next to a concussed man with suicidal ideation and delusions of grandeur who is scared of walls."

"You think I made up the other life where I was a television game show writer and weighed 270 pounds? I don't think you're clear on what the word 'grandeur' means."

"Our fears and desires shape our hallucinations, Mr. Bradley. The life you describe would have less responsibility and less responsibility is what you want. It's a common ill. Your mind has gone to great lengths to construct a new reality. You are conflicted about the life you've created as a television advertising man versus the life you might have led. Everyone wonders about the road less traveled and you're aching for something different."

And I have auditory hallucinations, Ray thought. *But I'll keep that to myself and hope you don't have a drug for it. That soft samba music is all that's keeping me from punching you in the throat, Doctor.*

Dickens had heard all about his performance last night in the common room. "So...you claim you've never played the piano?"

"I fiddled with the keys at a friend's house once, when I was a kid. Tinkled some high and low notes and left it at that. I'm not claiming it. I'm saying it."

"You're sure?" The doctor's grin revealed uneven

teeth. It was a redheaded doll's cruel smile. "You didn't play piano in either life?"

"No. And now you're being condescending," Ray said. "I'll add that to *your* file."

The doctor put down the iPad. "It's a rare occurrence, but there is precedence. I'm diagnosing you with something worthy of a case study for a journal."

Ray stared at the man, wondering if he was waiting for applause. "Well?"

"Acquired Savant Syndrome!" the doctor announced.

"Savant? Like idiot savant?"

"The term idiot savant has fallen out of favor. In fact, Mr. Bradley, genius savant would be more accurate. You are rare but not unique. There's a young man in Minnesota who dove into a friend's pool and hit his head. He'd never touched a piano, either, but after his TBI, he discovered he could play. Quite compulsively, I understand. Lost his job. Plays piano all day."

"What happened to him?"

"Still playing."

"This...this is a real thing?"

"Of course."

"Acquired...what?"

"Acquired Savant Syndrome."

"I've got ASS? The name for the thing I've got is ASS?"

The doctor chuckled. "I honestly hadn't noticed that."

"I used to be a comedian. It was my job to notice the stupid and ridiculous stuff. Talking about it without irony is how I ended up here. More irony."

"That is...interesting," the doctor admitted.

"What about the river?" Ray asked. "What was that about? I don't think my subconscious is smart enough to come up with something that weird on its own."

"What do you think it means?"

"That's all you've got, Doc? Really? Answering a question with a question?"

Dickens shrugged. "Fine. Tell me again about the river in your hallucination."

"In the *experience*, I was in a river and I saw a huge light in the sky. I thought it was the moon at first. Then..." A tear slipped down Ray's cheek. "I don't want to tell it again. Just...what does it mean?"

The doctor stared into Ray's eyes. "Ray. I suspect this is why you didn't become a writer. It's all in front of you. The river is Time. You say you almost drowned so it is a reminder of mortality. It's too late to pursue the dreams of another life where you are free of responsibility. It is harsh, but it is also true."

"Too late? I'm not that old! Lots of people are late bloomers. What about the guy in his fifties who decides to start climbing mountains or the little old lady who runs marathons?"

"Outliers, mostly."

"That's dismissive."

"A precious few switch horses in midstream, it's true. But what I see is a culture full of Peter Pans, just like you, who don't want to grow up."

"Growing up is overrated."

"That is a funnier thing to say than it is to live. Growing up means accepting that you won't be a firefighter or a cowboy or an astronaut. It means balancing your checkbook and recording receipts for your taxes on spreadsheets and dealing with real life responsibly. I understand why you don't want to face all the boring stuff, but I'm here to help you accept your fate and integrate back into society."

"Geniuses don't integrate, doctor. They watch from the sidelines, appalled. Or try to change things."

The doctor chuckled. "More self-aggrandizement, as a child might do."

Ray decided to stop wasting time and started to hate Dr. Dickens in earnest. He would eventually, so why not start now?

"We only have so many chances," Dr. Dickens said. "Past a certain point, those choices are narrowed considerably."

"Said the dream killer. I can't believe that. It's never too late."

"Never too late is a slogan, Ray. Do you really think you can solve all your problems with wisdom that can be crammed on a bumper sticker?"

"What's your solution, Doctor?"

"Anxiolytics. Talk therapy. Play the piano if you like, during free time. We'll observe and see how you feel about ending your life. We'll take it slow. We want to be sure you stay safe."

"Safe? If it's safe, is it really life? Life is dangerous."

"I can see how you'd feel that way at the moment, but that's what anxiolytics are for."

"Numb us to the truth of reality that the grave awaits and time is running out?"

"I'm a doctor, Mr. Bradley, not a philosophy major." Dickens picked up his iPad and stood, inviting Ray to do the same with a slick maneuver that began as a handshake but ended with pulling Ray up to stand. He took Ray by the arm and guided him toward the office door.

Ray stopped and shook him off. "Wait a minute! What about the light in the sky? What's your explanation of that? What's that mean?"

His doctor pursed his lips for a moment and then went back to his cruel doll smile. "Well, it's your hallucination so you have to find the meaning in the drama you've created. That said, if you were to press me on it — "

Ray was thinking again of punching Dickens in the throat. "I'm pressing you. Tell me."

"I suspect it's your cynosure."

"You want to touch my *what* now?"

"*Cynosure.* It's something brilliant that gets your attention and serves as a guide. You're desperate for stability in your life. I'm sure you'll find it once you get past the concussion. We also have to monitor your testosterone levels. The male hormone can drop drastically as a result of traumatic brain injury."

But Ray wasn't listening. He was thinking of the Man in the Moon again. The fear made his knees weak and his breathing shallow.

Dickens patted Ray's shoulder. "Let me be your cynosure. It'll work out, given time."

"Time."

Dr. Dickens put a hand on the doorknob. "You will need to continue resting your brain. Stare at the walls until you are out of your mind with boredom."

"What about the piano?"

"You can get back to it later. Let's hold off on the piano for now. Stimulation is not conducive to resting the brain."

Ray's heart sank.

"You are very concerned with time. Let's talk about the meantime."

Ray knew what he said, but he heard *Mean Time*.

"Why don't you meet our other genius savant? I think you'll find you are much better off than he. That might give you some degree of solace."

It sounded to Ray like a nasty premise, as if the bitter taste of someone else's lemon made your own shit sandwich taste great. The curly haired Honduran nurse in the first hospital had scolded him for that very thing.

Dickens guided Ray out the door with a gentle push. "Go meet the Wizard."

20

The Wizard's room smelled of fish. Ray detected the odor even before he stepped in the room. The stench wafted out of the open door. The man looked right at home in a mental hospital, as if sent over from Central Casting for a remake of *One Flew Over the Cuckoo's Nest*.

The old man stood with his back to him, a wheelchair behind his knees ready to catch him should he fall back. He wore a white sheet as a short toga that very nearly exposed his bare ass. He wore his hair in a thick white braid that reached his waist.

He appeared to be drawing on the wall. The beige wall was spotted with hand prints and grease stains.

"1.61803398874989484820…" the Wizard said.

"Hello?"

The man whirled. He looked at Ray for only a moment. His blue eyes were piercing. He turned back to the wall. "Who are you?"

"Ray Bradley."

"Did *they* send you, Mr. Bradley?" The Wizard's voice was weak, thin as paper. "Is it time to go?"

"It's time for *me* to get out of here. Soon, I hope.

About you? I dunno."

"Fifty-fifty among the 5150s, eh? How much longer have I got? Quantify!"

"I don't know. Dr. Dickens said I should say hello."

The Wizard turned to him again and looked him up and down. "Hello? Or help? The way you say hello sounds like you need help."

Ray shifted back and forth on the balls of his feet. He could feel his headache coming back. The painkillers were wearing off. He'd told the nurses the Tylenol 3s were nothing more than a water pistol against a charging bull elephant on fire.

"You're in a lot of pain. You should sit and rest, Mr. Bradley."

"Yeah, my head's pounding. How'd you know?"

"I know pain."

"Dr. Dickens called you the Wizard. Why?"

The old man gestured at the blank wall and grinned. "Isn't it obvious?"

"Not really."

The Wizard sighed. Then he took a deep breath and spit out a string of numbers. "1.61803398874989484820."

"What's that? Is that, like, pi or something?"

"Are you, like, an idiot, or something?"

"Opinions vary."

"Pi. 3.14. That's all they teach you in school, or would have, had you been paying attention. 3.1415926535897. Pi. The sixteenth letter of the Greek alphabet. It's one of those numbers that describes us."

"How's that?"

"It's irrational. Just like you and I and our doctor."

Ray didn't know what to say to that so he said,

"Ah."

"Indeed. Pi. 3.1415926535897932384626 4. You can go on forever and it can never be expressed as a fraction. It never settles into a repeating pattern. It just goes on and on, always changing yet always the same. Like people. We think we're so evolved yet we're no different from the Romans who lived more than 2,000 years ago and threw Christians to the lions in the Colosseum."

Ray sat on the old man's bunk. Either he was getting used to the fish smell or he was too tired to care. The Wizard's voice sounded louder in the small space, causing the headache to come faster. "You're a nut," Ray muttered, "so I guess we're both in the right place."

The old man looked him sharply. "I am a member of an ancient cult."

"You follow Tom Cruise?"

"No, you little bonehead. I...am among the *mathematikoi!*"

"The who?"

The old man rattled out words in machine gun bursts. "They sent me a low primate who doesn't know who mastered the lyre, learned the secrets of Egyptian priests and proved the world was round. The master of geometry who developed the theory of color! Philosopher and saint!"

Ray shrugged and held his aching head.

"You've no doubt heard, out in the jungle eating bananas, of the Pythagorean theorem."

"Triangles and stuff."

A moment passed.

"Stop looking at me like I pooped on your bed," Ray said.

"I am a Pythagorean, Mr. Bradley. It's the only cult that ever made any sense. Pythagoras was the Father of Numbers. He and I...we see them everywhere... note the gap between your IQ and mine, for instance."

"According to the boy doctor downstairs, I'm a genius savant."

The old man turned to regard him more closely, as if genius was something visible. "How is your genius expressed?"

"Music."

"I have you there, too! Pythagoras invented music!"

"Bull."

"No, sir! He saw the math of it. He created the scale. He quantified harmony and disharmony. He invented the tuning of musical frequencies based on the 3:2 ratio! Everyone these days is all over Tesla. Tesla! Tesla! *Tesla!* Tesla had a romantic relationship with a pigeon in the park. Pythagoras was treating women as equals in the sixth century before Christ!"

"Okay," Ray said.

The Wizard looked tired. He turned to sink into his wheelchair and stared up at the blank wall. "What were we talking about?"

"You were talking about pi and I was wondering, does the cafeteria serve lemon meringue pie?"

"Pi? Yes! Pi is beautiful and irrational. It's used throughout science yet we do not truly know it."

"What do you mean we don't know it? You seem well-acquainted."

The wizard spun the chair to face Ray. His face creased into a grin that showed long, yellow teeth beneath receding gums. "Pi is the number which, when expressed with a decimal, stretches out forever. No one is sure, but the distribution of digits appears *random!*"

"That's...uh...very interesting."

The old man turned back to the wall, pointing to a specific spot. It was the same spot he'd been tracing with a long, dirty fingernail when Ray walked in. "But you asked about the Golden Ratio!"

"I did?"

"The number I was experiencing when you walked in."

"Experiencing?"

"The Golden Ratio, also known as the Golden Mean, the Golden Section and the Divine Proportion. From flowers to architecture, it's everywhere in nature. It's the ratio that defines beauty." He drew with his finger, his hand not quite touching the wall. "Take any line and divide it. See? A smaller line! Divide the longer by the smaller. The longer divided by the smaller so the whole length...1.618033988 and so on. See?"

"Uh-huh," Ray said.

"Every time I look at that wall, I feel like I'm close to something. I feel like, if I could just concentrate long enough, the digits would coalesce. Time is short. I must make sense of it."

The old man tugged harshly at his long braid. Ray had never seen anyone pull their own hair. It looked painful. It almost made the Wizard look like he was trying to start his brain the way people pull a cord to start a lawn mower. Ray fought the urge to pull the old man's braid for him.

"There's nothing new here!" the old man said. "I've

been trying to see the relationships for ages. I was a young man when I understood the beauty of the Fibonacci Sequence. I saw it in flowers, at first, then in the shape of a full breast."

"What's this Fibonini sequence?"

"Fibonacci, ape man! It's 0, 1, 1, 2, 3, 5, 8, 13, 21, 34...you see? The next number in the sequence is found by adding the previous two. Precious. Previous. Precious. Previous. So close, you see? And the Fibonacci numbers are so close to the Golden Ratio! So close, but not the same!"

Ray held his head. The ache was a pounding bass drum. "Why do they call you Wizard? You sound like a babbling idiot to me."

The old man spun his wheelchair around and laughed. "If I am, it's because I'm an irrational number. Everything can be described in numbers. Mathematics is the science that unveils the art of existence, Mr. Bradley."

"I don't see it. Numbers can't describe...friendship, for example."

"We form bonds based on proximity. Friends are geographical side effects. I could measure your capacity for friendship in feet, or meters, miles or kilometers."

"I don't buy that."

"You don't, but you should. Consider Dunbar's Number! It's the limit of people with whom you can form social relationships. Dunbar says 100 to 200 people. Usually 150 is the default."

"So it's variable. Doesn't sound very exact and scientific."

"The variability depends on the size of your neocortex. I could open up your skull and measure your capacity for friendship in millimeters or nanometers, if you like."

Ray looked at him warily. "I already know my capacity for friendship. It's zero." He thought of Joe sleeping with his wife. Then he remembered that was his other life. He was fatter in that one, but he'd had a friend...at least for a while.

Ray could barely hear the crazed man over the drum in his head. Without conscious thought, he tapped his fingers to the beat, antsy to leave and feeling like he might throw up.

The Wizard watched him tap out a beat. "Music. Music is math. It's a code. It's the number of beats to the bar. It's amplitude... it's — "

Ray stood. "My head hurts! I hit my head and now I've got music and headaches all the time and will you please stop shouting?"

Ray turned to leave.

The old man cleared his throat. "I'm sorry. You must be in a lot of pain because I wasn't shouting. At least, I don't think I was shouting."

"Fine."

Ray was almost out the door when the Wizard asked, "Did the wall get you, too, Mr. Bradley?"

Ray turned back.

21

"**D**id the wall make you obsessed with the Golden Ratio?" Ray asked.

The old man giggled. "I was always fascinated with mathematics, but what I didn't see before my injury was the *music* of numbers. Pseudomathematics tries the impossible, squaring circles and that nonsense. Deep mathematics describes the world. It's the language that quantifies relationships. One is in relationship to two and two is in relationship to one and three. Numbers describe the intersection between what is and understanding what's not. If I had to do it all again, I'd be a theoretical physicist. Stephen Hawking's formula for Imaginary Time, for instance. It's so simple and elegant. I could have done that but he got to it first."

"What's Imaginary Time?"

"Simple. You go out the door, you turn left or right. In Hawking's theory, Time has geography, too, allowing us to get off our linear timeline and move about in time. Go forward and back, or hang a right or a left instead."

"Where are you...or when are you if you hang a

right at lunchtime? What does that mean?"

"It's a good question. I hope to find out."

If he felt better, or if he was smarter, Ray might have been intrigued. Instead, he held his head and thought of the Wizard's phrase, "If I had to do it all again."

I've been steered here, Ray thought.

Yes.

That was not his voice that answered. The old man was watching, possibly from behind the wall. The crazy, drooling guy at breakfast might have been right, after all.

"How did you get injured? What was that about a wall?" Ray asked.

The old man turned back to his dirty beige wall as if he was looking out of a bay window upon a grand vista. "When I was younger than you, I tried to teach mathematics but all my students could manage was simple arithmetic. I had no patience. I lost my teaching job after a year and I went from McJob to joe job. Imagine me behind the counter at a 7-11. Ha!"

"What's the matter? Couldn't make accurate change?"

"Ha! Oh, I could make change...but I became obsessed with tracking the frequency of the year of my birth on coins. I hoarded them...well, okay...I stole them from the till. I'm a little OCD."

"A little, huh? Why the year of your birth?"

"Because I was stuck in a life I didn't enjoy. Obsession is a fine distraction from dealing with real problems."

"That sounds like something Dr. Dickens would say."

The old man winced. "Then I retract that statement. I could be very wrong. Anyway, all I could think about was the coin that marked the year of my birth. Then I started wondering what year my death would come. I got more paranoid, sure that my death was imminent. Then I started collecting as many coins as I could."

"From the cash register."

"Yes."

"And that didn't go over well at 7/11?"

"Or a dozen other jobs. I was homeless. Years later, some college boys attacked me. One of them was a boy I'd once taught in elementary school. He recognized me. He and his friends went into a bar and drank and drank and got their courage from a bottle. I shouldn't have been on the street when they came out of that bar. "

A piccolo and a guitar began to accompany the drum. It was the beginning of a tune. Ray didn't care for this song. It was a soundtrack to an old man's sad life. "What happened?" Ray asked, not really wanting to know.

"Young men times three plus alcohol over time equals a balance of predictable probabilities."

"They beat you up."

"They beat me *down*. I begged for my life. I'd been rude when I taught the boy."

"I can't imagine."

"They threw me head first into a wall, again and again and again. Before they were done, I didn't want to live anymore. I wanted to go through the wall and shatter my skull in the process."

"I'm so sorry."

The Wizard shrugged. "I have not lived on the

streets since. In a few months, I learned to walk again, but I can't walk for long. My stamina was gone after that. The State takes care of me and that suits me fine. I stare at my wall. I'll go through the wall. I'll be the Buddha. I am close to that achievement. I can feel it."

"The Buddha?"

"Surely you've heard of him. Buddhism? Ring a bell?"

"Yeah, but, what's the part about a wall?"

"Our walls define us. The more area we have, for instance, defines our success. Rich celebrities own mansions — "

"And you and I are in tiny rooms with narrow beds."

The Wizard smiled. "Our dimensions restrict us and tell us our worth. We have preset notions of what we can and can't do, what's possible and what's not, what we won't and what we will. Adjust those expectations of what we assume we know even slightly? Then we can all achieve great things. We can open The Gates of Perception and walk through the Walls of Illusion."

"Oh, sweet Jesus. Skip the self-help seminar. What about the Buddha?"

The Wizard sighed. "Before the Buddha was the Buddha, he was a prince. His father, the king, surrounded his son with young musicians and dancers. No one old or sick was allowed inside the palace. The prince was surrounded by walls to keep him from knowing the truth of the world. One day, the prince became curious and he ventured beyond the walls. He saw the old and the sick and the dead for the first time. That's how he discovered his fate, all our fates."

"And?"

"After my mugging, I was suicidal and you know, when you hit your head really hard, they tell you to stare at a wall."

"Oh, I know. Me, too."

"I stared and I stared and eventually, I went beyond the wall."

"What did you see?"

"Imaginary Time." The old man blew out a long, fishy breath. "It's only *called* Imaginary time. I know that firsthand. I moved around the Mindfield and the Timescape of my life. Do you understand?"

"Time travel. I've done it. Day before yesterday I was a comedian and television writer whose wife had just left him for his best friend. Today, I'm an ad man who was supposed to be a comedian."

The Wizard shrugged. "Nah. Maybe you're just crazy."

"What?"

"Look where we are. I know I'm smart enough to go through the wall, but you look like a soft, pale guy with a wicked headache. How do I know you're telling the truth?"

Ray reddened. "Because it was real. Because I didn't call you crazy or stupid."

The Wizard's laugh was a cruel cackle. "Ah. So, like Socrates, let's put all my objections aside and assume you've been through the wall. You're suffering from entitlement, then."

"What?"

"You're thinking you were supposed to be something else. You're trying to change the variables of your equation. You're trying to solve for x."

"I changed my life. You're saying I shouldn't have tried?"

"On this side of the wall, we always end up dividing by one."

"Speak English."

"Are you any happier after your suicide attempt?"

"How'd you know — "

"I got my first glimpse beyond the wall when those college boys were ramming my head into it. I wanted to go beyond the wall and stay there. That's welcoming death and it's a key part of the equation. To near enlightenment, add suicidal intent and you subtract ego from the equation."

"Enough bullshit. What's really beyond the wall?"

"The Beyond is beyond the wall, for those who can unlock the gates. We've known the Beyond is there for a long time, but we didn't know how to get there."

"We know how?"

"The Penrose Diagram."

"The who?"

"It's a mathematical abstraction that extracts the truth. It describes the limits of space-time. We know there is a Beyond, but we can't say for sure what it is. If we could, it wouldn't be very beyond space-time, would it?"

"I guess."

"The irony is that the Beyond is everywhere."

"Like God?"

"Don't get bogged down in semantic structures that don't mean anything understandable. Black holes, white holes, dark matter, all that vast space amid our atoms...it's hiding in plain sight, within everything. It's within us, so we can access it. So, I ask you, what do you know about time travel, Mr.

Bradley?"

"All I know is time is subjective. Whenever I've had sex, time slows down when it's good and speeds up when it's bad."

"Heh. Yes. I suppose. It's been a while since I conducted that experiment. Consider, before the universe was formed, there was no Time. Nothing happened, and it occurred all at once. The Big Bang, happening over and over, shrinking and expanding the universe in and out, like a heart beating. That explosion gave us Time. Time gives structure to matter and events so our tiny brains don't get confused."

"You've lost me again."

"I'm saying there really is no such thing as premature ejaculation...or a climax that takes too long, for that matter. Many would disagree, mostly women, but their perceptions are all arbitrary preconceptions. That's the math of Sex Time."

"That sounds suspiciously like math made up by an old guy to suit his purposes, but as long as you're being scientific about how bad you are at satisfying women...."

The Wizard smiled. "I've got better experiments to conduct, like going back in time and staying there. Drop the illusion and go through the wall and you can erase a lot of problems. You won't, though."

Ray frowned. "Why can't I?"

"Because you're the problem."

Ray frowned and crossed his arms as if he was suddenly cold and trying to hug himself.

"You go back, you're still you, trapped in one set of ideas of what's good and what's bad, what you won't and what you will. Divide by one and you're still stuck with you."

"I can see why they bashed your head in on that wall, Wiz."

22

"You're planning on going through that wall?" Ray asked.

"Of course. Any minute now. Or soon. Or it's already happened. When you step outside the structure, the rules you know aren't there anymore. That's why, if there is a deity, he can't be wrong. He's not within the realm of right or wrong. A true deity would be outside our rules and understanding."

"You're saying God's in international waters so it's all cockfights and gambling beyond the Andromeda Nebula and that's cool?"

"You're amusing, Mr. Bradley, if simple."

"Thanks. I once thought I could be amusing professionally."

"You aren't that funny."

"To you. Everything's subjective, at least until you get through the wall, maybe. What will you do, beyond the wall?"

"When I step into the Beyond, I want to go back to high school. I lived in New Mexico. I had a Mexican girlfriend. If she hadn't been deported, I might have spent the rest of my life with her and things would have been much different."

"How would you change all that?"

The Wizard smiled. "When the conditions are just right, the opportunity arises on quantum waves. Vibrations of thought patterns form very specific harmonies." The Wizard turned back to his greasy wall and added an invisible note in the air.

"Harmonies. As in music."

"Music is one way to change and organize thought patterns, yes. That's a ticket to ride the quantum waves through the wall, I suppose. People are so used to time flowing from past to the future, they think that's the only way. But we know anti-matter is simply matter whose time is working in reverse. Like water, time can flow, forward and back. We can disrupt the time stream."

"'Simply', huh? If it's that close, why do you and I have to work so hard to get there?

"Because we are each stuck in our own little perception traps. We are in love with our technology, so sure machines will solve our problems and, in the future, answer all our questions."

"We do that now," Ray said. "Cell phones are auxiliary brains, keeping all our telephone numbers and remembering the names of actors in sitcoms we can't remember on our own."

The Wizard made a disgusted sound in the back of his throat. "Trivia! The answer isn't in our machines. It's in our consciousness. We can change the world when we get out of these ruts we call thinking. Society works — barely — on inertia. People eat and work and believe the ways they do because their fathers and mothers ate and slaved and thought the same way. It takes a radical paradigm shift to think outside of the way we usually think. The Gates of Perception don't open until you're suicidal and usually not even then. It has to be something...less selfish. When people die, I suspect they might go through the same gate. I peeked through to the Beyond because of violence done to me. You did it through...?"

"Injury and self-loathing."

"That's one way to go. I think the monks who stare at walls until they achieve enlightenment get through out of sheer boredom and desperation to make their lives mean something. Ironic since they often profess that the origin of all human suffering is desire."

"Enlightenment would qualify as a pretty big desire, wouldn't it?"

"Yes. But all the humility and begging and abstinence and need for understanding drives those monks crazy. I think the key to the lock is wanting to understand. The light respects the darkness in us a little, I think. It understands the need to understand and experience."

"It? A light?"

"The light. It's big and...hard to explain. You wouldn't believe me."

The Man in the Moon, Ray thought. Ray shook his head and instantly regretted it. The bass drum in his skull quickened its beat. "What's your point?"

"Haven't you been listening? It all goes back to Pythagoras. He believed that if we were pure, we could escape the cycle of birth. Our souls could transmigrate! Metempsychosis. Life after death."

"Death like real death or Buddha death, like death of the ego, being a crazy monk and never getting laid again, you mean?"

The Wizard sighed a long, fishy breath. "Pythagoras lived in a cave in southern Italy. I think he discovered more than words to live by and startling theories of astronomy in that cave. I think he stared at that cave wall and entered the boundless."

"The boundless?"

"Pythagoras was very big on the boundless." The Wizard tilted his head at his wall. "What waits for us beyond the walls that define us is the Beyond and the Boundless."

"That's awesome, Wiz." Ray said. "I should go."

The old man seized Ray's arm with one gnarled hand and with the other cocked a dirty thumb at the blank wall over his shoulder. "The Gates of Perception wait to be opened, behind every wall. All you have to do is want it bad enough, use your mind and be pure."

"Pure. Do I have to eat only salads? Because I'm not down with that."

"The Father of Numbers himself was convinced that, with contemplation, music was a grand purifier."

"I don't get it."

"What a surprise. You're just a chimp in an astronaut suit, aren't you, Mr. Bradley?"

"Careful. Isn't that attitude how you got thrown into a wall in the first place?"

The Wizard gave him a slow nod. "The Buddha said we fear the end, not for bodily death, but the death of ego. All that weeping at funerals and hospital beds is narcissism. We worry we will lose our selves. The trick is, there is no self to lose. That's the cosmic joke. We're fooling ourselves."

"I get it. I saw *The Matrix.* I was just telling my therapist that and — "

"Turn left or right in Imaginary Time, it's all funhouse mirrors. Change the variables but you still come back here, dividing by one. You're the one. You don't change. Not enough."

"I lost seventy pounds overnight."

"You'll gain it back. If you want to change your life, do something different here, Mr. Bradley. You don't need time travel. You need Weight Watchers."

"Go to hell."

"I'm on my way. I'm not out to escape the wheel of incarnation. I'll ride it to the end of time. You think you're the first to go down the Black River? Reincarnation. Low primates think they know what reincarnation means, but it is literally to enter the flesh again. The way you did, Mr. Bradley."

"You were a teacher?"

"I suppose."

"Then speak plain. You're good at chucking numbers at me. Give me a slow and easy underhand toss of words."

"Very well. Anything I can tell you in words is oversimplified. We are caterpillars crawling through a vast labyrinth. We see the world and miss what's really going on."

"What's really going on?"

"We're only seeing the broad strokes of the painting at a distance. But if we were to go past the red velvet rope at the art gallery and look closely, we'd see the artist's individual brushstrokes."

"Sounds like we're back to God."

"That term is just another broad brushstroke. It conveys no more meaning than the word infinity or a trillion dollars. You can't visualize and work with that. It's beyond human understanding. The universe exhibits design and chaos at the same time, Mr. Bradley."

"But it's got to be one or the other."

"No. No, it doesn't. We are in a multiverse. With such complexity, how do you imagine you can begin to apply one set of rules or begin to understand? How do you stand in one place at all with the sand shifting under your feet as the world spins and the Earth is a rock hurling through space?"

"I'm a writer and you're...some sort of scientist, I suppose. As a writer, I'll let you in on a bit of expertise from my world. Your metaphors suck."

The Wizard rolled his eyes. "Get used to complexity and let go of singular expectations. Contradictions abound. For instance, Newtonian physics — equal and opposite reactions, inertia, blah-de-blah — applies at the macro level. But quantum physics — which opens the door to teleportation, for one tiny instance — applies at the micro level. Each set of ways of understanding the world are contrary, yet both views describe the universe."

"Great. Can I go home now?"

The Wizard sighed. "You have to see the big picture to understand the little pictures. You're looking at little pixels, but there's so much more. When I saw a picture of all the galaxies, the primitive and the new, I began to see...the galaxies, when seen together, look like a vast spiderweb. Time is like that. Each string of the web is a string but, with Time, the strings converge as the potentials become probabilities, maybe even imperatives."

"Um..." Ray said.

"Potentials to probabilities! Think of Roger Bannister! All the experts said no man could run a mile in less than four minutes. Then Bannister did. Suddenly, across the globe, lots of people managed it. Once it was done once, repetition became a certainty. It even became easier. We're at near the beginning now, but the more times we press our limits and go through that wall, the easier it will be... not just here but in all dimensions. Imagine, there's an army of me out there. There's even a bunch of you, Mr. Bradley, God help us."

"I wonder how many of those other versions of me understand this conversation...and how many can rock a goatee? I can't seem to manage it."

"I feel sad for you, Mr. Bradley. You happened across a door to the beyond, but it's a little like sending a naked man to Mars. I doubt you're equipped to deal with the demands of the road less traveled."

Ray frowned. "And yet, Mr. Wizard, you and I are in the same place. Maybe I'm Newton and you're quantum, but neither of us is better off. We're both in an insane asylum."

"Touché! But I'm not staying much longer..." The old man laughed and laughed until it appeared to hurt him. Then he began to cough. Then wheeze.

The old man's musical soundtrack became more frantic and erratic as his eyes rolled up.

"Mr. Wizard? Are you alright?"

The old man's cough turned to a choke and a burble. Ray called for a nurse. Hearing no reply, he yelled for a doctor as he took the old man's pulse at his wrist. He had a hard time finding it. When he did find it, the pulse was weak and thready.

Ray grabbed the wheelchair's handles and spun the man toward the corridor. "Help! We need help over here!"

Two nurses emerged from behind the high desk at their station and hurried down the hall. The Wizard coughed hard, lurched forward and fell out of the chair to the linoleum floor.

Ray knelt beside him and gripped his forearm. "Hold on. Help is on the way."

The old man turned to him and Ray was hit in the face with the thin stream of his exhalation. Ray tasted raw fish guts.

The Wizard's eyes were still the same piercing blue, but Ray was sure the old man couldn't see him. He was shocked at the Wizard's strength when he shook Ray's arm.

The old man pointed back in the direction of his room. He whispered three numbers in Ray's ear before he fell back, smacking his head on the floor hard.

Incongruously, a calm woman's voice came over the public address system. "Code 4. Room 222. Code 4. Dr. Dickens to the second floor, please. Dr. Dickens."

Ray stood back and watched the nurses work as they called for a crash cart.

Code 4, for whatever tragic variety of medical emergency this is, Ray thought. *Room 222 for location. Blood pressure. Pulse rate. Respiratory rate. The Wizard had a point. Life all came down to numbers.*

One of the nurses looked up at Ray, frowning. "He was supposed to be transferred this afternoon!" She said it as though he had done something wrong.

Two orderlies arrived with a gurney and lifted the old man onto it. Dr. Dickens strode up the hallway. "What happened?"

"I think he went to see where the Black River runs," Ray said.

"What?"

"Sadly, I don't think he went through the Gates of Perception. I didn't see it, anyway. He'll never be a Buddha."

"Return to your room, please, Mr. Bradley."

Ray backed down the corridor. "Hey, I'm just a chimp in an astronaut suit. Don't mind me, but at least he tried to be a good Pythagorean Buddhist."

"Go! Get out of here."

Ray watched them disappear around a corner. After the Wizard's last words, he wasn't ready to return to his room just yet. Traveling sideways through Time was more on his mind.

That, and whatever he'd find in Room 348.

23

Ray walked up an emergency stairwell to find Room 348. In his head, cellos played a low, angry tempo. A staccato flourish of violins and oboes occasionally punctuated the beat. That made Ray think of small, terrified animals scrambling unseen, rattling through dry autumn leaves.

Each metal door he passed flaked paint the color of mustard and every door was closed. No faces peered out at him through the tiny windows of glass and wire mesh. Ray would have preferred more mental patients, some noise and even some crying. Instead, the third floor felt like what he imagined the world would be after everything died.

The first and second floors had been renovated in some recent decade, but the third floor's faded green linoleum looked dingy under weak, dead and dying fluorescent tubes. Ray saw no dirt, but the musty air made him think of mold growing and stretching behind the walls, reaching through old asbestos insulation, cracking it and releasing a fine black and deadly dust, perhaps even now caught in his lungs and killing him slowly. Walking down the corridor, haunted by a history of broken minds, it was difficult *not* to ascribe malicious intent to these walls.

Room 348 was not marked. He passed it twice, deducing its location because Room 347 was across the dim hallway. Because it wasn't marked, he'd assumed it was a closet. He knocked anyway.

Nothing.

He opened the door and found he stood at the entrance to a long room. It was a small library. It appeared empty of people and disorganized. The shelves were sparsely populated but long tables were piled high with old dog-eared books.

The hospital had been built on a hill so the long, narrow windows, each guarded with a steel grid locked in place with a heavy padlock, offered a great view of the city.

"Hello?" Ray said. "Anybody here?"

"Take what you came for and get out!"

The voice was deep and mean and bounced with a shine off the walls.

"The Wizard sent me," Ray said.

"Yeah? What does that old maniac want now?"

"Nothing, I guess."

"You guess?"

"I don't know. I think he's dead."

Ray heard the thump of a heavy book on a wooden table and the creak of metal.

An emaciated, swarthy man in a wheelchair rolled out from behind a high pile of old paperbacks. "Well? Come in, then. How'd he go?"

"He collapsed and the nurses were working on him when I left, but the way they were working on him... his lips were really blue. The way the nurses were working on him...I don't know."

"Like their hearts weren't really in it?"

Ray nodded.

"It was bound to happen any day. Not a shock but, somehow, always a surprise. You shouldn't call him Wizard. He had a name. It was Arnold. Arnold Martin."

"Sorry. I didn't know his name."

The man shrugged. "As my mama used to say, 'It don't make no never mind now.' Besides, I think Arnold secretly liked being called the Wizard. He would have kicked up more of a fuss if it really got to him. He was honest about the things that bothered him."

"Honest. That's one way to put it."

"Cranky ass is another."

"Why was he called Wizard at all, then?"

"Dickens names us."

"The red-haired baby-faced doctor. Yeah, that guy seems like a dick. Maybe he's living up to the family name. Dr. Dickens."

The man smiled. "All of us long-term guests get nicknames. Dickens calls me Wheels."

Ray glanced at the big man's wheelchair. "Well, that's...linear." He offered his hand. Ray's hand disappeared into the big man's palm and they shook. "I'm Ray Bradley, no nickname yet."

Ray moved to pull his hand back but Wheels held tight and squeezed hard enough to make Ray wince in pain. "Cut the shit. Did Arnold go through the wall or not?"

"I don't think so."

Wheels pushed Ray's hand away and made a rumbling growl of disgust in the back of his throat. "Still in the trap." He hit the arm of his wheelchair with his right fist. His grimace collapsed his once-handsome face into a bunched collection of horizontal lines. "Still stuck in the goddamn trap."

Ray wanted to leave, but the music changed with the big man's first teardrop. The song, which started with violins, was beautiful and it was not a composition of his making. He recognized the angelic voice that had an odd register, somewhere between male and female. It was *Feeling Good*, as sung by Nina Simone.

Ray stood pinned to the spot. Then he pulled up a chair to listen to the music. Beside him, the big man wept. That took a long time.

Eventually, Ray began to hum along with the song repeating through his concussed brain. He felt no trace of a headache and none waited to swoop in from the horizon. Outside, through tall, suicide-proofed windows, he watched the sky turn black as a bolt of lightning cracked the clouds. It was as if his pain had been displaced. Torment had to go somewhere, so it went to the sky.

Ray hoped death was like that. He hoped the old man who smelled like fish hadn't died a pointless death after a life of pain. He hoped Arnold Martin had somehow found his metempsychosis. Ray hoped it, but he didn't believe it.

After a while, Wheels stopped crying. Then he listened and, finally, the big man joined him in the music and sang the song, too.

Nina Simone sang of freedom while Ray and Wheels sat imprisoned on the top floor of an old mental hospital. Hers was a cracked joy that only knew freedom after many years of captivity. Each syllable of every note was haunted, a butterfly remembering the lowliness of being a caterpillar and the claustrophobia of the chrysalis.

Wheels couldn't hear her song. Though deaf to the duet partner only Ray could hear, the crippled man's song was an ironic echo and a yearning plea. He didn't sing it as sweetly as Nina Simone, but he sang with earnest hope.

24

"My real name is Cenk Duman. My mother was African American and my father was a Turk. I loved my father but I hated his music. Nina Simone... and Aretha and uh, Ella Fitzgerald? Heh. *That* was my *mother's* music. I thought I wanted to be a singer when I was little. Then I went to the movies and I wanted to be an actor. Instead," he threw a glance at his chair, "...shit happens."

"Cenk? I'm sorry about your friend."

Cenk backed up his chair and wheeled behind a table. The old paperbacks, Ray noticed, formed a wall that blocked his view of the door. A spray of magazines and books lay spread before him.

"We probably wouldn't have been friends elsewhere. Arnold was a hard man to love, but underneath it all, he was good. You had to look hard, but it was there."

"Newtonian physics on top, contrary quantum underneath," Ray said.

Wheels smiled. "You must have talked a long time."

"Not really, but he made it seem that way."

"Like I said, hard man to be a friend to. However, people under similar and difficult circumstances take on allies they wouldn't cross the street for out in the world. Still, Arnold and I had common interests. I guess that made us friends. A lot of people in here are hard to talk to. I found Arnold's ideas stimulating."

A crack of thunder rolled above them and the rain began. Ray drew his chair closer. Nina Simone had faded away. Now all Ray heard was marching drums, far off. With the drumming rain, the beats harmonized and soothed him. If Torment waited for him outside this library, he might gladly stay in this fortress of old books forever.

"The Wiz — uh, Arnold talked to you about the Gates of Perception? About going through the wall?"

"He talked to everybody about what's beyond the walls. The boundless, blah-de-blah. Couldn't shut up about it. He talked to everyone about it but I'm the only one who took him seriously. Dickens thought the Beyond was some kind of metaphor for getting out of this place. Dr. Dickens doesn't have enough imagination to take things literally. Arnold didn't mind this place so much. It was Time he was trying to escape, not geography.

"You got enough imagination or," — Cenk gestured at the array of books in front of him — "if you live in a library like me, you can make it tolerable."

"You like it here?"

"No, but some hells are preferable to others."

"And you don't think Arnold wanted out of here? Out of the cage?"

"Well, sure...yes and no. It's his ribcage he wanted to ditch."

146

"I don't understand."

Cenk shrugged. "Dr. Dickens wrote a paper on Arnold. He focused on Arnold's talent for math. Dickens is interested in all that genius savant stuff, but he focuses more on the mechanism of how it happens and less on what a genius savant has to say."

"Kind of weird, isn't it?"

"Not really. Dumb is glorified everywhere and genius is suspect. There's a guy in Australia who woke up from a coma who suddenly became fluent in Chinese. Dickens wants to examine the brain of that dude, not hear him speak Chinese."

"So no prizes in mathematics for Arnold Martin, huh?"

"Nah, man," Cenk said. "Arnold said his diagnosis was Obsessive Compulsive Disorder plus math equations equals living for free indoors."

"That how he got the nickname the Wizard? Being a math whiz?"

Cenk nodded. "Sure. Doctor Dickens thinks he's the shit, but his thinking is pretty — what'd you call it? Linear. To be fair to the doc, when Arnold first got here screaming about high math, he did have a very long beard that made everybody think of Dumbledore."

"Dickens says he wants to be my guide. I hope I'm not here that long."

"What are you in for?"

"I'm here on a 5150."

"So many people come through here on a 5150. Many start out that way but some of us get lost in the cracks and holes. Me and Arnold, for instance. I once asked Arnold if we'd ever get out of here. When he was feeling up he'd say he'd find a way out. When he was feeling down he said Time ends in black holes and every galaxy has a black hole at the center of it that contains another universe."

"I don't get it."

"Me, neither. He was always trying to connect the universal to the daily mundane, man. If you were up to play, he was good company. Sometimes he'd go down the rabbit hole so deep he was a lousy conversationalist and I'd tell him, 'Go play with Alice, Mad Hatter.' But he wasn't really crazy. He was obsessed."

"Is there a difference?"

"Sure. Dickens isn't near as smart as he thinks he is. Sometimes, as in Arnold's case, really smart people look like really crazy people to really dumb people. Arnold was smarter than he was crazy. If anything, it was being sick that made him look crazy and irritable. When I first met him, he wasn't so cranky all the time. You didn't see him at his best."

"Tell me something that does make sense, Cenk. How is it you got stuck here if you came in on a 5150?"

"Didn't they do the breakdown when they brought you in? They're supposed to."

"I wasn't paying attention. I was listening to some music. It makes me less suicidal."

Cenk gave a wide smile. "Ha! Well, places like this used to suck harder than they do now. It's still prison, but it's better than jail. President Reagan, Ronny Ray-gun, we used to call him...he closed down a lot of mental hospitals. It's shit on his legacy now, though people forget how terrible these places were. Lotta people were glad to be out on the streets, actually."

"How so?"

"Convulsive shock therapy was standard for too many people back then. They still use that hammer on a lot of nails, but they use way less voltage now. My mother was a nurse. She had some stories, man. She used to sit on patients while they got their brains zapped."

"And now?"

"They talk about talk therapy. Hospitals officials are high on group therapy since that's most cost efficient. These days it's mostly about the drugs, though. The drugs haven't got that much better, but they shoved all these mental patients out on the streets and expected that if they took their medication they'd be able to take care of themselves and stay out of trouble."

"How's that work out?"

"How do you think? You been out in any city in America? It resulted in lots of hopeless, homeless people who can't get their meds. Or they take the pills for a while, start feeling better and then figure they can stop. They figure wrong, but why wouldn't they? That's why they are who they are."

"Figuring wrong is why we all are what we are." Ray looked away, pretending to watch the storm beat at the city. "Seems like our lowest points define us."

Cenk stared at him for a moment. "Hey, man. Don't tell that to Dr. Dickens. That's the sort of negativity that gets 5150s extended. For a minute there, you sounded like Arnold on a bad day."

"I'd call it honesty."

"If you want to get out of this dead end, being honest with your doctors is not the way to go.

Pretend every fart that comes out of Dickens is an awesome pearl of wisdom."

"Is that how you ended up here? Honesty?"

"You could say that. I honestly thought I should be left alone to do my gig."

"What do you mean?"

Cenk glanced down at his wheelchair. "Bad things happened. It wasn't all my fault."

"What happened? How'd you end up here?"

"We just met. Don't you think you should buy me dinner first and let me meet your parents?"

Ray chuckled and stood to leave. "If you don't want to talk, it's cool. I'll let you get back to your reading. I just thought, since the Wizard sent me up here with his dying words…"

"Siddown, man."

"You sure?"

Cenk waved Ray back into his seat. "Sure. You had me at 'dying words.'"

25

"**I** had a job working behind the bar at Heavy's downtown, but I had dreams of being famous," Cenk said. "A waiter waiting for his big break. Same old Hollywood cliche."

"I was a comedian and a television writer," Ray said. "Everybody comes here with the same dream, don't they?"

"I guess. I always felt like I was almost in the door. I went on every audition I could squeeze into. I had a couple of near misses. I thought I might get a small part in an Eddie Murphy movie once. The casting directors never actually said I was too swarthy, but I know that's what was holding me back. I was good. Did some stage work but I really wanted to get a movie role. Best I got was Bad Guy #2. But, like you said, everybody has the same dream here. Even the plumbers write screenplays in LA."

"What happened to your dream?"

"Oh, one day I was doing my thing, delivering drinks and keeping one eye on the World Cup. In honor of my Dad, I cheered for Turkey, of course. Two Dutch tourists didn't agree that I should be happy about a goal."

"How'd that get you here?"

"Killed one of them. Didn't mean to. He hit his head on the curb when they dragged me outside."

Ray sat back in his chair. "Wow. Sounds like self-defense to me."

"The Dutch guys' lawyer had a different version of events. They were both white and I wasn't quite white enough. I pled down to manslaughter. I thought I could do the time with the sweet deal I was offered, but then the judge screwed me over and gave me the maximum, anyway. That wasn't the deal I agreed to when I signed their papers."

"They can do that?"

"It happens. Every citizen trying to live their lives and be left alone to work on the pursuit of happiness is one accident and a shit lawyer away from places like this, and worse. This place is much better than where I've been, actually. I've got a room and a bed down the hall, but I live in the library."

"How'd you end up here instead of jail exactly?"

"Jail's temporary. I was in prison, but I'm an actor. I acted crazy to get out."

"So you started acting crazy even though you're not?"

"Oh, I'm a little crazy. Crazy as a shithouse rat. That expression gave me the idea. I put on quite a show. I ate my own shit to get out of federal prison."

"Jesus!"

"Something like that really freaks people out, even hardcore guards and hard time inmates. The real trick is to smile and laugh maniacally while you do it." Cenk patted his thin abdomen. "Just the memory plays hell with the appetite."

"I would have thought they'd just throw you in a hole and forget about you."

"They did. But my little cousin is a woman named Sher. When she graduated from law school, she got to work on my case and looked for cracks and holes I could slip through. She got a friendly judge to get me a fresh psych evaluation and I got here on a cruel and unusual objection."

"Cruel and unusual?"

"It was a dodge, but the system bought it. Federal prison is cruel but it's not unusual for it to be cruel. When California brought in a new statute saying you can't put inmates in solitary forever, that was our opening. Sher made good things happen for me. If you're ever in Chicago and need a great lawyer, she's your best choice. She does some kind of corporate law now."

Ray looked around the dim library. Lightning strobed them and, under rolling thunder, he thought of Frankenstein's castle. "This place is a good thing for you?"

"People like you typically come here for short visits," Cenk said. "The doctors are under orders not to fill the place up again like it's pre-Reagan days. Lots of us start as 5150s. Arnold was here because he was too sick. You're here because you're a danger to yourself. I'm here because I'm a danger to others. For some of us, 5150 bleeds into forever."

Ray looked at the man. Sitting in his wheelchair behind his fortress of books, he didn't look dangerous.

"There's a weird little unwritten rule at Polanso, the prison they sent me to. If you smear yourself in feces, they'll hose you down with a fire hose. 500 psi.

It hurts a naked man hard. Feels like they're peeling your skin right off. If you throw shit like a monkey at the zoo, they do more than hold back the bananas. They beat you. Sometimes they beat you so hard they snap your spine and your legs don't work anymore. But if you can take all that and still have enough gumption to reach up and pull a guard's ears off... well, then they call you crazy."

"Are you crazy, Cenk?"

"Pullin' that bull's ears off was the most sane thing I've ever done. He got my legs. At least they could sew his ears back on."

"So this place is great by comparison."

"Better than federal prison, yeah. Polanso put us in triple bunks. They filled up the gymnasium, they were so tight for space for inmates. A man needs more than breathing room. He needs elbow room. A prison that tight is a pressure cooker. Here? I take the meds they give me and Dr. Dickens...." Cenk gestured at the paperbacks. "He leaves me to my sci-fi therapy." Cenk leaned forward. "Don't tell anybody, Ray, but I would never hurt anybody who wasn't hurting me hard first."

Ray realized he'd been holding his breath and he let it out in a slow sigh. "Your secret's safe with me."

Thunder rolled louder and the downpour intensified. The fluorescents winked out and buzzed as they came back on.

Ray stared at the man's emaciated frame. "You really ate your own shit?"

"Lots of people eat shit every day. They get it from their bosses. They go buy it cheap at fast food restaurants. Don't act like you don't know what it tastes like."

Ray broke into a full-throated laugh. Cenk joined him. When their laughter ebbed and ended, Cenk looked Ray in the eye. "You know my secret. It's about time we talked about yours, isn't it? You got something on me and I need something on you."

"I guess," Ray said, "it's about Time."

"Arnold never sent anybody up to see me before. You've been through the wall, haven't you?"

26

"I think you already know as much as I can tell you, Cenk."

"The Wizard was right about his magic spells, huh?"

Ray nodded. "I've been beyond the wall. A couple of days ago I went back and talked to myself when I was a kid. He made changes, but not enough."

Cenk gestured at the room. "Apparently."

"Yeah. I went back in time but it didn't go right. Now what?"

"Arnold said the chances of time travel going right were slim. He'd tried it several times."

"How many times?"

Cenk shrugged. "Several. But he couldn't control it. He tried to teach me how to do it, but either I don't have the knack or somebody up there doesn't like me. We were hoping Arnold would slip through before he died. The Gates of Perception...heh. It all boiled down to meditating your way out of this plane and back to where you mattered, *if* you could get Arnold to shut up about his bromance with Pythagoras. Pythagoras went through his cave wall and Arnold died waiting to go back through his."

"Where...er...when did he want to go to? He did tell me about a Mexican girl — "

"He didn't plan on coming back to the now, man. He wanted to stay in the loop and never die. He figured that if you stay in the loop, repeating and repeating...that's one kind of immortality, right?"

"Could be boring."

"Better than getting old and getting stuck in MRI machines and bending over for proctologists. I'd take a bit of boredom any day over rounds of appointments with doctors that don't seem to end. That's one boring merry-go-round."

"Why is it so hard to get it right?"

Cenk shrugged. "If it were easy, everybody would be doing it. That would make for a very unstable universe, wouldn't it? Still, you ask me, Arnold had a great plan. The Time Worm just didn't feel like obliging him."

"Slow down. I feel like I've come into a movie in the second reel."

"Just like everything else all the time, then, isn't it?"

"Tell me about Arnold. Start from the beginning. Minus Pythagoras, please."

Cenk smiled. "Yeah. I didn't care for that stuff, either."

"Arnold knew he was going to die."

"Oh, everybody knew that. Didn't you smell him? 'Course you did. Nobody could miss that smell. When he annoyed me I called him the Wizard of Halibut. The weird thing was, he knew before his doctors did. One day I brought him an old *Omni* magazine. We both loved *Omni*. That's how we started talking. Bringing around books and magazines is what I do. It's part of the rehabilitation I don't need."

"And Arnold got sick."

"He says to me, you smell that? And I tell him yes, I sure do. And he says you can tell a diabetic by their fruity breath. Typhus smells sweet. Liver cancer smells like fish. It oozed from his pores. He knew he was a goner long before the scans came back."

"Back up. When he talked about time travel, you believed him?"

"Hell, no."

"So what changed?"

"He started talking about metempsychosis. Fancy word for reincarnation, far as I can see."

"Then you believed him."

"No. I'm not that easy. But I wanted to believe. If I could go back, I'm sure you can imagine, I'd make some changes. I wouldn't be in this chair. I was into it. Then Arnold started talking about Kepler and that little niggle of an idea wheedled a needle into my brain."

"Still feel like I'm on the second reel. Arnold said I was a chimp in an astronaut suit."

"Take it as a compliment. He called most everyone a low primate."

"Did he call you that?"

Cenk shook his head. "People with his history are careful around people with my history. You'll run into lots of people, especially in here, who say they can't control their impulses. But put them in a room with a guy with my rep? Wheelchair or not, they act like their mommas taught them to behave in church." Cenk sat up straight and put his hands on the table, fingers interlaced. For a moment he looked like a scolded student. Then he winked and smiled. Watching Cenk mime his impression of a cowed schoolboy made Ray think Cenk would make an excellent actor.

"I'll be as polite as a Canadian so you don't rip my ears off," Ray said. "Just tell me everything Arnold told you, slow as a strip tease so I get it all."

"I started to believe Arnold after I read a story in *Omni* magazine about Johannes Kepler."

"Who?"

"Mathematician. Astronomer. Discovered three major laws of planetary motion. Kepler claimed to be the reincarnation of Pythagoras."

"Sounds like he didn't suffer the death of the ego."

"Heh. Well, that's kind of the point. Maybe Pythagoras managed to survive death, travel through time to 17th century Germany and carry on his work. Arnold said the men had a lot in common. Metempsychosis is deja vu all over again."

"You're bending my mind, man. Are we talking time travel or reincarnation?"

"I said the same thing to Arnold. He said reincarnation was just another form of time travel."

This time travel is not that time travel. The old man from nowhere had taught Ray that. Apparently there were more ways than one to move around in Imaginary time. "This sounds...slippery," Ray said.

Cenk shrugged. "Me, I love science fiction. I'm no mathematician. If I understood anything of Arnold's ravings, it was through fiction's filter. Every time travel story I've ever read looked at the problems and paradoxes of Time as one way or another. You go back and you can change the world or maybe you can't. Paradoxes bend your brain and you get a fun little story that's easy to digest. Arnold's point was that the rules of reality are more flexible than fiction allows."

"Like Newtonian physics versus quantum physics? Contradictory rules, but both right?"

"S'pose so. A lot of what Arnold told me didn't make sense to me. He said if he went back in time, he didn't necessarily meet himself. He said he might not 'share the same plane.' It was inconsistent, but Arnold said that must be part of the design. I told him if he was going back in time, he had to meet his old self. He told me I was still caught up in binary thinking. The universe is more complex than that. Said I was limiting myself, seeing in 2D when the reality was 3D."

Ray gave a slow nod. "Imaginary Time — "

"I don't get that shit at all."

"I've read some sci-fi, too, or at least seen a lot of movies. *Back to the Future* worked by rules. You go back, you'll see yourself," Ray said. "But...what if you start a new timeline every time you go back?"

"Like in Stephen King's book about the Kennedy assassination?"

"Didn't read it."

"Sacrilege! You gotta read The King!"

"Sorry. My point is, maybe the universe isn't so complex. Just too complex for us. I'm a monkey man."

Cenk made a sour face. "I like more science in my fiction, but Arnold said that once you go through the wall, nothing is impossible. It's just that there are a lot of things that are improbable. Improbable does not equal impossible."

"I don't think I'm smart enough for this conversation. Or you're bullshitting me. I just spoke to a dying man who called me a chimp. Am I going to have to go through that again?"

"Not from me," Cenk said. He picked up several books and magazines from the table to show Ray the covers: *Popular Mechanics, Popular Science, Omni, Stranger in a Strange Land.* "This sort of stuff is more my speed."

Ray brightened. "*Stranger in a Strange Land.* I grok that!"

Cenk chuckled. "I prefer Robert Heinlein's juveniles. There's something so hopeful and optimistic about his spaceman stuff for kids. And these old magazines always made me feel like the future was just around the corner."

"No jetpacks and sexbots yet."

"Exactly. But it was the intersection of Arnold's Pythagoras obsessions and science fiction that got him and me talking about Time. We talked a lot about who might have already gone through the wall but stayed in this world. My argument is, time travelers should be easy to spot. Look for the people who are ahead of their time. The geniuses who seem to have more experience than their age would suggest."

"That's interesting. Who's on your list? "

"As a sculptor, Michelangelo spent a lot of time staring at stone to see what to take away. He strikes me as a likely candidate."

"And Da Vinci," Ray suggested. "He was too prolific not to be a time traveler. But what's the sci-fi connection?"

"Think early SF. Mark Twain."

"I don't — "

"Think about it."

"Oh. *A Connecticut Yankee in King Arthur's Court.*"

"Yeah! You ever read it?"

"Everybody read it in school."

"Do you remember how the Yankee's time travel journey begins?"

"No."

"He gets hit on the head."

"So...uh...what?"

"Maybe Twain was leaving clues. His wife, Olivia, had a nickname for Samuel Clemens. She called him Youth. If someone is brilliant at age seventeen, a writer in full voice, already, he could be a time traveler. It's suspicious, at least."

"That's awfully thin, Cenk."

"There's more. In an age when many men thought all that was going to be invented had already been invented, Twain invested in technology. He lost his shirt, but maybe he was a visitor from the *past* then."

"I brain hurts, but not in the usual way of a headache," Ray complained.

Cenk went on. "Mark Twain passed on the telephone, but he was enthusiastic about the typewriter and new developments in the printing press. Twain was most forward thinking when he traveled up and down the Mississippi. Later in life, he took a trip and was appalled by how people lived, especially the black folk. He wrote and spoke about that injustice. School boards across the country have misunderstood his message and banned him ever since. He was a man out of his time."

"I'm not impressed," Ray said. "So he wrote about

time travel. He was fascinated with technology. But you said he *lost* money on investments in technology. A time traveler should make great investments."

Cenk laughed. "He turned down Alexander Graham Bell. Mark Twain could have been the richest writer who ever lived."

"Richer than Stephen King?"

Cenk nodded. "King and JK Rowling and Stephanie Meyer combined."

"Then...that was a stupid move. He *couldn't* have been a time traveler."

Cenk shook his head. "Twain was a humanist, Ray. Only an idiot or a man with a larger plan would have given up getting rich off the telephone."

"What larger plan?"

"Dude! Didn't Arnold give you the permutations, combinations and variables speech?"

"I guess he didn't live that long."

"The trick to time travel is you can open the Gates of Perception, slip through the wall and escape the boundary to the Boundless where nothing is impossible but lots is improbable. That's step one."

"Got it."

"Twain was trying to *change* the future. That hardly ever works out well. Odds are against. It's a gamble."

"Trying to change the future didn't entirely work out for me. The wall is a gamble and the Man in the Moon wins."

"What's the Man in the Moon?"

"Never mind. Something I saw. Tell me more about Twain."

"One day he hit his head and had to recover in a

quiet room. Away from everyone, suffering headaches with only his thoughts for company, he stared at a wall. That's what Arnold thought, anyway."

Ray shook his head. "Doesn't exactly stand up to scientific analysis, does it? Why would he think that?"

"Arnold believed, as I believe, that Twain stepped into the Beyond. He traveled through time, came back and wrote about it. He did not escape Pythagoras's Wheel of Birth, but he escaped the Wheel of Death."

Ray gave Cenk a blank stare.

"He lived again, Ray. Who knows how many times he went back in time to try to fix his old life? Maybe he went back and invested in Ma Bell and something else went wrong, like Bell had a heart attack before he signed the contracts. Or Bell killed him. Or someone else invented the telephone. Or Twain made a mint on his investment in the telephone, but made all that loot on another Earth in the multiverse. There is actually some debate about who invented the telephone, you know, so that made me suspicious of echoes of time loops, too. You read enough sci-fi, you can see how time paradoxes and the Law of Unintended Consequences are real bitches. You could go back a hundred times and never get things fixed quite right. In fact, it might make more sense to escape to the future instead of trying to get the past just how you think you want it. Maybe that's what happened to Mark Twain. In fact, through metempsychosis, I think the man born Sam Clemens who became Mark Twain escaped to the future and got famous again."

"You think Twain lived again? Really?"

"Yes, I do. Really."

"Who?"

"If you think about it, it makes perfect sense."

"For the love of God, *who*, Cenk?"

"He came back as another science fiction writer, of course. Kurt Vonnegut."

"Oh, for the love of Christ."

"For the love of people, maybe."

27

Cenk gave Ray a moment to digest his hypothesis. Then he said, "Let me ask you a question, Ray. You ever study Latin?"

"Do I look like I'm a thousand years old?"

"So, no. You have not studied Latin. Neither did Kurt Vonnegut."

"I sure hope there's a point coming fast."

"Vonnegut never studied Latin, but *he could read it*. Any time anybody does anything well that they shouldn't be able to do? That's a cat you gotta look closer at. Child prodigies, for instance? Every one of them is a potential time traveler."

"I'm unclear — "

"Metempsychosis, dude! Reincarnation! Time travelers can go back in time through the wall. Reincarnators come forward, through death. I think Vonnegut could have been either, or both."

"Kurt Vonnegut?"

"You heard me. Kurt fucking Vonnegut! There are so many parallels in the life trajectories of Twain and Vonnegut, the more you look, the more sense it makes."

"Lots of conspiracy theories make sense as long as it's only conspiracy theorists talking to each other. Most conspiracy theories are loony and way wrong when normal people look at them."

Cenk seemed undeterred. "Twain and Vonnegut. It's the same guy in two different times, man. Two humanists, separated by time but not different in thought. They both went on speaking tours. Both were hit hard by family tragedy. Arnold called that phenomena, 'Time's echo.' Patterns tend to repeat."

"Yeah. He told me I'd gain back all the weight I've lost."

Cenk shrugged. "Arnold says the Time Worm — the thing in charge of the time streams — is resistant to change. I think it punishes us for stepping out of our time cages."

"What do you mean?"

"It's something Arnold said. Trying to change sequences of events is like trying to change a progression of numbers. He said pi isn't pi if you put one right number in the wrong place."

"Why would there be resistance, though?"

"I don't know, man. Sequences of events are stubborn. Think of it like putting a rock in a stream. Makes no difference to the stream. The current keeps going and the water flows around it, nothing really changed. Stephen King wrote about Time's resistance to change, too, in his Kennedy assassination book. The explanation doesn't have to be fancy. Personally? I think it's about homeostasis. Nature leans toward stability. We don't want the planet flying apart. Events and technology can evolve, but Arnold would say we revolve. He said we're essentially the same primates who cheered lions eating Christians. In the big scheme of things, we're very new to the planet and just came down from the trees a few seconds ago. If not for a random asteroid strike killing off the dinosaurs, mammals wouldn't have risen at all. It's all very...tenuous. Arnold speculated that there are probably innumerable Earths in the multiverse where evolved lizards are wearing fedoras on the subway and complaining about the weight of their briefcases on their little arms."

"Heh. Let me stew on that," Ray said. "Tell me more about Twain and Vonnegut."

Cenk tipped his head back and watched the lightning strobe the room. "Twain left behind writing that he insisted shouldn't be published until one hundred years after his death. Vonnegut published several things posthumously, but I think his last non-fiction book ties him to Twain irrevocably. Vonnegut wrote *Man Without a Country*. He said some things that weren't all that popular at the time, still too close to 9/11. People lost their shit and forgot we were supposed to be the Home of the Brave, not the chickenshits who gave up all our freedoms because we were terrified of a small and weak terrorist organization."

"I remember."

"Do you know what the *New York Times Book Review* said about *Man Without A Country*?"

"Obviously I have no idea."

"'Like his literary ancestor Mark Twain, Kurt Vonnegut's crankiness is good-humored and sharp-witted.'"

"Hm."

"Yeah! Hm. You're good goddamn right, *hm!* Once

again, Vonnegut was a man out of his time. They were both humanists who saw the potential of the human race but they were both disappointed in how we ended up. I'd argue they were both great writers and terrible businessmen. Vonnegut's Saab dealership went out of business in less than a year."

"How is that possible?"

"Saab was a great idea, but Vonnegut got in too early, before the brand caught on in the States. Typical time traveler mistake. Twain went seriously broke, too, by the way. They're so alike because they were the same man."

Ray stood. "This whole thing is too crazy— "

"You gotta hear me out, Ray! Vonnegut named his son Mark. He named him after *Mark Twain*. Vonnegut called Twain an American saint. Both Vonnegut and Twain had the same sense of humor. Vonnegut was letting us know with a wink and a nod. It was a signal. Code and clues to the truth!"

"Meaningless synchronicities."

"I think they add up to something more than coincidence, if you look at all the evidence."

"Really?"

"Two words: *Slaughterhouse Five*."

Ray sat and stared at Cenk as the storm lashed the building. The music in Ray's head was a comical take on *Battle Hymn of the Republic* played on kazoos. Kazoos... Ray didn't believe, or want to believe. Not yet. But the buzz of those kazoos made Ray think Vonnegut might approve.

28

Ray listened to the rain. Violins swelled and an oboe wound out a note that set him on edge. "If I hadn't gone through the wall...I...I dunno. I don't think I could sit still for this wild speculation. But... *Slaughterhouse Five*? I read that book in high school. Saw the movie."

Cenk pounded the table once with a heavy fist. "Good goddamn *right, Slaughterhouse Five!* The story of a man who goes back and forth in time, reliving the events of his life. That's how Arnold finally convinced me...and, Ray? I'm a smart guy who was convinced *without* going through the wall."

Ray sat back and thought how impossible it was... except maybe it was merely highly improbable. Like all insane plots, the more he thought about it, the more attractive it was. "Conspiracy theories are seductive," Ray said. "But I need more. Are you saying Vonnegut was Twain or that Twain was Vonnegut?"

"I asked Arnold the same thing."

"What did the Wizard say?"

"He looked me in the eye and said, 'That is a

meaningless question.' Could be either. For all I know, it could be both. Temporal paradoxes are such a bitch. Most time travel stories are stuck in what Arnold called 2D thinking. They deal with one time stream. Arnold factored in the complexity of the multiverse. He said that amps up the possibilities and dampens the improbabilities."

"Lost me again."

"Think of it as one consciousness in two points at the same time. There's a scientific basis for this shit. I don't understand it, but Arnold says it's on Google."

"The *Slaughterhouse Five* parallel is haunting... bouncing around his lifetime. I've done that much once. I went back to a Christian summer camp in Maine. You're saying Vonnegut was writing more non-fiction than anyone suspected?"

"Dude! *Timequake* is even more telling. Vonnegut left clues about the futility of time travel."

"Never read it, but this makes me want to go through the wall again to prove to myself I'm not crazy. Could be we both are."

Cenk shook his head. "Things are crazy everywhere. Genius savants are a thing. A couple of months ago a huge hole opened up in the ground in Siberia in a place that's called, 'The End of the World.' For real."

"That's ironic. The more I look, the more irony I see."

Cenk leaned forward in his chair, excited. "Nobody knows for sure why this big hole happened. The world's full of crazy shit and people pretend not to notice this so-called reality's weirdness."

"Maybe we are seeing the seams of an imperfect fabric sewn by a drunk god," Ray suggested.

"Weirdness is a clue to the true nature of the universe," Cenk said. "I mean, take a look at the vast number of really strange species of animals and fish there are. You can google all day and you'll see shit you'd swear belongs on an alien planet out of a movie. The more you think about our existence, the more you realize, weird isn't the exception. Weird is the rule. Think of all the stuff we accept as normal."

"Example?"

"Arnold broke it down by the numbers."

"Of course, he would."

"One hundred and one Americans die in car crashes every day. We don't run to robot cars or hang tires off the sides of our cars like tugboats to save our lives. We don't even wear a helmet to go get the groceries. Instead, we ignore those hundred or so deaths a day and, if we think about it, we call it the cost of doing business. You go out for ice cream and a drunk driver kills you and you just died for a scoop of mocha almond fudge."

"I guess I hadn't thought of it that way."

"Nobody does. We think it's normal, but only because we live here. Arnold called it the alien test. What would an alien think if he or she or it landed on Earth and saw how we have millions of empty houses and homeless children stuck on the street? Or competitive eating contests here while children starve elsewhere? It takes a guy in a mental asylum to sit back, take a breath and see how far short we've fallen from where we could be. Every politician should be reading more Heinlein and Bradbury, man. They need a little science fiction to open up to new possibilities."

"That much is true," Ray conceded.

"If you can see that, then think about it a moment more. Amid all that craziness, Ray, you wound up in a mental hospital with two guys who share your obsession. What are the odds of that?"

Listen to him, Ray. It was the old man's voice again. Ray looked behind him, but of course, no one was there.

Cenk, who apparently hadn't heard the voice, continued. "In *Timequake*, Vonnegut said people are doomed to repeat the same losses, fail at the same endeavors, suffer the same pain over and over. Even when they were finally free from repeating a decade of history in every detail, they didn't know what to do with their freedom."

"I do want to go back through the wall and fix things," Ray said.

Cenk looked Ray up and down. "You should really read *Timequake*, man. Vonnegut was a tough soldier who knew suffering. You're a doughy ad guy. You think you can change the future where Vonnegut could not?"

"I don't know. But if I don't try, I'm stuck. My sudden weight loss is nice, but like they say uptown, if I walk away now, I leave money on the table. Talk to me about getting through the wall, Cenk. Show me the hidden doorknob. I need an instruction manual."

Cenk shrugged. "I don't have much for your to-do list. Assuming Vonnegut did what Arnold couldn't do and went through the wall? I'd guess Vonnegut was more pure. Pythagoras said you had to be pure to do it and God knows everyone agrees Vonnegut was a hell of a good man. Did you know he was a volunteer firefighter? He adopted a bunch of kids because of deaths in his family, too. How many people would take all that on? But you know the weird thing?"

Ray made a sour face. "What *isn't* weird?"

"Yeah, yeah. Get over it, go with it and strap in for the ride. Vonnegut's brother-in-law was killed in a bizarre train disaster. A commuter train went right off a bridge into Newark Bay. Forty-eight people died. No certain cause was ever determined. Vonnegut was a saint, Ray. If he could travel back in time to save his brother-in-law and forty-seven other people, don't you think he would?"

"Maybe he didn't have enough stones to dam up that time stream. I know now that it's possible to go back in time, but changing the future is obviously hard. Why wouldn't it be? We wouldn't expect going to Mars would be a breeze."

"If you read through Vonnegut's work," Cenk said, "that's your instruction manual."

"I just remember it was mostly a bunch of dark jokes. What do you think happened with Vonnegut?"

"I think he escaped the Wheel of Birth. Or maybe he went back to pilot steamboats again. In *Breakfast of Champions*, an old science fiction writer named Trout yells to his creator, 'Make me young!' Who wouldn't want that? But the author refuses to grant the wish." Cenk glanced down at his useless legs. "We all need to change something. His son, Mark Vonnegut, wrote a sweet goodbye to his father. He said Kurt 'broke his egg.'"

"Meaning?"

"Kurt Vonnegut died of head trauma."

"I feel for him. I scrambled my egg."

"Vonnegut lingered a bit, then slipped away. I'm betting he planned it that way."

"Oh, c'mon!"

"Through the wall, man. Through the wall and leaving only his body behind in 2007 so he could start again in a new timeline, tripping through the thin membranes of the multiverse."

"*Hmph.* Accepting his death the same way Billy does in *Slaughterhouse Five.*" Ray shook his head. "That's a fun theory, dude, but it's still more likely I'm in a hospital in a coma somewhere from an overdose of painkillers."

"Maybe we're all dreaming because we've got an overdose of dumb and crazy. But you prefer Arnold's version of dumb and crazy, right?" Cenk asked.

"Well, yeah. I guess I do."

"You know why?"

"Because Arnold's crazy theory is my only hope to stop being a suicidal guy stuck in a job in advertising?"

"My only hope, too," Cenk said. "Arnold's death... well...I wasn't just crying for him, Ray." He slapped the armrest of his wheelchair. "I was cryin' for me." He started to cry again.

"To do it," Cenk said, "you gotta be pure. I believe that's why I can't do it myself. Arnold coached me. Always remember, Ray, to travel through time, you have to be pure. The universe doesn't care about us, but whoever's in charge expects us to be pure or at least to try. I can't go back and fix it. That's the bitch of it. Who needs to go back in time more than me? Whatever you do, you've got to try to change the past for the greatest good in the future. Understand? Promise me you'll remember." Cenk seized Ray's hand. "Promise!"

"For the greatest good. I'll remember."

Cenk pulled Ray close and hugged him and cried

into Ray's shoulder. The wheelchair-bound man wept a long time before he let go. "Arnold's dead. Now you're my only hope. Dude? Please. Go back."

29

"Cenk. I've got to get out of here."

"For you, the escape hatch might be as close as the nearest blank wall. All you gotta do is watch and wait and meditate, right?"

"It didn't seem to work out for Arnold."

"Wall therapy. You gotta do it anyway. May as well be open to improbabilities."

"How long will I have to wait?"

"This isn't the sort of time travel with buttons and dials and a souped up Delorean, man. You don't set the flux capacitor for the time you want and stomp on the gas pedal."

"What kind of time travel is it, then? What did the Wizard say?"

"On our end? Besides being pure? We have to really want it so it's an act of will, too. Concentrated will, Arnold would say."

"And for some reason, a bit of brain damage helps," Ray added. "What does it take for the Gates of Perception to get unlocked?" An image of the Man in the Moon turning its mouthless face toward him made a shiver run up Ray's spine. His heart went cold, as if he'd swallowed ice.

Cenk looked at him with tears still glistening on his face. "There's a force in the Beyond. Arnold saw it."

"God?"

"I don't think so. Maybe. I don't know. Arnold insisted he wouldn't talk about it in terms that stood for the word *mystery*. Time travel has to be rare," Cenk said. "Nobody seems to be popping over to the deck of the Titanic to tell them to steer a little to the left."

"As you point out, whatever is in charge of the time stream," — *the Man in the Moon,* a voice whispered the answer through the music of the storm. *The Man in the Moon.*

Ray stared, unblinking and lost to the memory of the face in the sky. The music in his head turned to *Stormy Weather* as sung by Lena Horne.

Rain drummed on the roof and the wind picked up. Through the tall windows, Ray saw shingles fly from desiccated roofs. Lights blinked out across the city and, a moment later, blinked back on. The library's fluorescent lights went out and angry thunder soon filled the sudden silence. The power outage triggered a lone emergency light by the door. The light it cast made more shadows, emphasizing the depth of the library's darkness.

Emergency, Ray thought. And, *trigger.* He sensed time had slowed for a moment. He wished he could have seen a clock from where he sat. How many of his heartbeats would have passed before a clock's lazy second hand ticked over once?

The voice in Ray's head (that was not Ray's voice) spoke again: *Look out at the city. It is a damaged brain, just like yours. Every city is a damaged brain with arteries and nerves and electrical signals shooting back and forth. Possibilities wink in and out at every crosswalk and cross street and with every cross word. Time streams are about infinite choices and you, Ray, are a guy who gets stymied if a restaurant menu has too many options.*

This came to him in a voice that was gentle yet strong, but it was definitely the old man's voice again.

Ray closed his eyes. Drums and woodwinds formed the music of the storm. The old man's presence was stronger when he closed his eyes.

The Man in the Moon watched him, too, he was almost sure. He was being watched in the way a boy might peer at ants in a jar, a garden hose ready in one hand, ready to drown an entire colony not from malice, but out of curiosity.

The Man in the Moon was curious, but it did not care about him. This feeling of insignificance made Ray's heart race. He felt claustrophobic, as if his skin was too tight and hot. Being seen by the Man in the Moon was as disquieting as an unexpected breath on the nape of the neck, hot and threatening, a monster's fetid wheeze from out of the darkness.

A new, stern voice sifted into his mind like sand: *Take what you've got, Ray. This is your new home. Stay. Don't try to come through the Gates of Perception again. There are too many variables, too many wrong buttons to push for a chimp in an astronaut suit.*

That wasn't the old man's voice. That was The Man in the Moon warning him to stay away.

"Ray?" Cenk voice was soft and far away.

For a second, just before be could open his eyes and break the spell, Ray glimpsed the great, white light hanging in a starless sky. He stood in a cold desert made of obsidian. He'd seen the Black River to his right. To his left, he'd seen a crowd of men. Each sad man wore his face.

"*Ray!*" Cenk called.

Ray opened his eyes and was a little surprised to find himself still in the library with his new friend.

"What?"

Cenk frowned. "You blanked out, man."

"Lost time," Ray said. It wasn't Ray's answer, though. He was only reporting what the storm in his head told him.

"What did you see?"

"It's more what I heard. At least, the auditory hallucinations are easier to understand. I prefer the music to the voice...and what I think I saw. I'm being told to stay here."

Cenk looked grim. "Go on."

"Whatever it is, it doesn't really care about us. But you know what it is. It's the thing in charge."

"What's that tell you?"

"That we shouldn't do as it says. I'm going through the wall again, as soon as I can."

Cenk shook his head. "That's not how it works according to Arnold. He'd crossed the membrane from this world into the Beyond and Boundless, but it was never a scheduled flight. One timeline is an elastic band that can snap you forward and back. There are infinite elastic bands in all directions."

"Translate to monkey, please."

"I'm not sure. Arnold would start going on about pi and he lost me again."

"You don't think I can do it again? I'm lousy at math, but I have the desire. If I stay, I'm in a mental hospital. And even if I get out of here, I work in advertising."

"Oh, sweet Jesus! *No!*"

"Exactly."

Both men chuckled.

"It's obviously not that I don't want you to try, Ray. It's that Arnold said the wall comes to you, not the other way around."

Ray shook his head. "The Man in the Moon wants me to come through, though."

"You just said it doesn't."

"It warned me, yeah, but this *feels* like a dare."

"But you said — "

"I said what Arnold said. It's not binary. Everything is too complex to be binary. Not everything is either, which is why moral relativism isn't as bad as people usually think. No wonder the Wizard preferred math. Words get loaded down with too much baggage."

Cenk gave a slow nod. "Arnold did say that the way through is not all quantum math and dizzy formulas...actually, he said, 'formulae.' Anyway, he said you go back to where your heart leads you."

"That sounds nice."

"Not to Arnold. He'd prefer we all follow our monkey brains. He says the heart is stupid as monkey shit."

"That sounds like the Wizard, but I don't really know what it means."

"It means you go back when whatever's in charge allows it. If you're pure and mentally prepared, Arnold called that, 'the confluence of the aspirational human and the mildly interested divine.' We go where and when the heart leads us through Imaginary Time. It's unclear to me. Arnold did the math. I just read the sci-fi."

Ray laughed. "I think I picked up something from the Man in the Moon. When it talked, I got more from the open channel than what it was telling me."

"What did you hear?"

"That it's not all yes or no. It's both and...and...I don't know! I lost that part. It was a fuzzy whisper through the static and clarinets. An old man was talking through the static. Usually it's so clear but...I don't know. Walking through a desert, no landmarks. Just sand."

Cenk stared at him for a moment. "I don't like my wheelchair, but it seems a little easier than that riot you got going on in your broken melon."

The lights came back on and the PA system crackled. "All residents, return to your rooms, please. Would Mr. Bradley please report to the nurses' station on his floor? Ray Bradley, report to the nurses' station near your room, please. You have a visitor."

Ray hurried to leave, but he paused at the door. "Hey, Cenk?"

"Yeah?"

"How long did you have to wait?"

"Huh?"

"After you ate shit in prison, how long before you got your appetite back?"

Cenk wheeled out of sight behind his fortress of books, but Ray heard his dry cackle. "There's not enough mouthwash and breath mints in the world, man! I can still taste it. I still can't eat mashed potatoes! Similar consistency!"

30

Ray's father, Ken Bradley, waited outside of Ray's room. Whether Ray was a suicidal comedian writing for a game show or a suicidal ad man working in TV, his father looked the same. His temples had gone gray and he was thin, but he didn't look very different from the man who had popped him in the jaw by the swing set in Maine. He looked angry and made no move to shake Ray's hand or give him a hug.

Ray stood awkwardly, not knowing what to do with his hands. "Um, hi, Dad. How'd you find out I was here?"

"The hospital called me."

"You uh...wanna see my room?"

"I saw your room. I talked to your bunk buddy."

"Bill something, yeah. He's not much of a talker."

"He talked a little to me. Wouldn't stop picking his nose. Says he's got a nosebleed that won't stop. Two knuckles deep and complaining about his bleeding nose like that was some huge mystery. I left him in there to go about his business. I've been standing here twenty minutes waiting for you."

"Sorry. If I'd have known you were coming...I wouldn't be wearing hospital pajamas."

"I talked to the nurse. She said we could talk down the hall in the family room. C'mon."

Ray followed his father to the far end of the hallway. Ken did not walk beside his son. He led the way.

"Dad? Do you plan to *spank* me?"

"Maybe that's what you missed out on. A little more discipline wouldn't hurt. Your mother and I were too soft on you."

"I don't think mental illness works like that."

"You aren't mentally ill. None of that runs in the family. You might be sick in the head, but if you don't have to put a bandage on it, you can get past it if you just try hard enough."

"Dad! You're a diabetic. Do you power through that with sheer force of will or do you take your insulin every day?"

Ken did not answer. He opened the door to what looked like a small conference room. A dead coffee machine without a coffee pot sat in one corner on a battered metal desk. The rest of the space was nothing more than a round table surrounded by plastic chairs.

"I drove through a storm to get here, Ray."

"I appreciate that. Thanks."

"They tell me you tried to commit suicide. They say you threw yourself downstairs at work!"

"The way you say that, I'm not sure if you're more pissed that I tried to kill myself or that I tried it at work."

"Always with the jokes. Even now. Can't you be serious?"

"I gotta be me."

"Well. Doing it at work certainly doesn't help your situation. What were you thinking?"

Ray had been thinking of the suicide attempt where he drove himself into a tree. The fall downstairs at work was much hazier.

No.

Wait.

The answer came as soon as he thought to question it. He hadn't fallen downstairs! He had thrown himself down a stairwell.

Ray's skin went cold. He sat in an orange plastic chair, his head in his hands.

"I talked to a doctor on the phone, Ray. We talked about you and your future."

"I've got some ideas about that," Ray said. "I'm going to try to change that. It's the past that's screwing me up and screwing me over. Like buttoning up a shirt wrong. You get the first button in the wrong hole, you gotta start over."

"This isn't a conversation, Ray. I'm talking. You listen."

"Okay."

"Your mother is very worried about you."

"Aren't you?"

"What concerns me is what the doctor told me... how you ended up in this place. You've got a lot going for you, Ray. I don't understand how the rest of the world can be so messed up but, somehow, *you're* the one who needs anti-depressants. Kids are starving in Zambia, son. And you're an ungrateful brat dissatisfied with his life. Boo-hoo. Do your job and stop whining."

As his father spoke, Ray wished he could hear

186

Nina Simone's calming voice in his head again. Instead, a snare drum struck with each heel strike as his father paced the small room.

"Lots of people are unsatisfied with their lives, Dad. It's kind of setting the bar low to say, 'You're eating so you don't get to complain.'"

His father stepped so close and so suddenly, Ray thought he might lash out with a punch. His father hadn't put on much weight since he'd hit him on the last day of summer camp. Despite reaching deep middle age, his father was still a sinewy man.

"The doctor says he's never heard of anyone trying to kill themselves in the stairwell of an office tower. He says it's one of two things."

"Then he's told you more than he's told me. What's his theory?"

"He says it was probably a pathetic cry for help and an obvious attempt to get out of and stay out of work. If it's help you want, Ray, all you had to do was pick up a phone. How high up were you? What floor?"

"I don't remember."

"They aren't sure, either. They said you hit your head bad and you had some bruises. It couldn't have been too high, could it?"

"What are you? My prosecutor? It happened — " Ray paused. It had been what? Two weeks ago or closer to three? It felt like it happened to someone else. When he thought of his suicide attempt, he didn't see a concrete stairwell. He closed his eyes and saw a fat tree trunk rushing at him through a windshield. The timelines were crossed in his mind.

Ken Bradley grabbed one of the plastic chairs and sat across from his son, their knees almost touching.

"The other possibility is that it was something you did on impulse. Dr. Dickens says impulse control is at the heart of most suicides. A lot of guys wouldn't be dead of a gunshot wound if it took them a few minutes to get to their pistol. Your doctor says people get sad or get in a fight and feel a weak moment and reach into a drawer and *blam!* Their lives are over. He called it, 'the stab of hopelessness.' Is that what you felt, Ray? Dr. Dickens says it's usually because of guilt."

"Guilt? No," Ray said. "I don't think I feel guilt. I feel like a failure."

"That's the problem with a lot of guys your age. You just turned thirty and you don't have the life advertised on TV and movies so you lose sight of what's important. By the time I was your age, I'd already been a Marine, seen the world, had a kid and a wife, owned one house and bought two others to rent out. I felt damned lucky to be around to enjoy my burdens."

"Mom's dad had money and helped you out. It's not fair to — ""I'm still talking and you're not listening, Ray. I've got something to say. You think you deserve happiness. What you should be doing is thinking about what everybody else deserves. The world deserves your usefulness. If you had gone into the Marines or even just joined the Army and served, maybe you'd have that figured out by now. Instead, they tell me you've got music in your head because of the concussion. I took three concussions for my country and I can't carry a tune in a bucket."

"I can play the piano now."

"I play the radio."

"There is music in my head almost all the time,

Dad. Mostly it's stuff I've never heard before. Sometimes it's stuff I know. I can't control it."

"So you're a human iPod and a player piano. Maybe you can figure a way to make money off that after you lose a good job that requires you to wear a suit."

"Maybe. Some big stuff has been happening in my life and I...." When he looked into his father's eyes, he couldn't imagine talking to him about opening the Gates of Perception and going into the Beyond for a do-over. "What I really want out of life — "

"You are not hearing me! I don't *care*, Ray! You've terrified your mother."

"Why didn't she come, then?'"

"You know why, Ray."

"I do?" No answer came in an old man's voice or from The Man in the Moon. Ray guessed he wasn't asking the right question yet. "I don't think I do know, Dad."

"We gotta talk about you being here, son. In this... *place*. We have to talk about your impulse control."

Ray nodded. "Sorry about scaring Mom."

"Oh, you're scaring me, too, Ray. I love you, son, but you have *got* to get your shit together and keep it stowed in one place, under your hat. This isn't just about you."

"Who is it about, Dad?"

Ken leaned forward, his elbows on his knees, and stared up into his son's eyes. "Dr. Dickens says the Golden Gate is the world's suicide bridge. More suicides off that bridge than any other. He says a few survive the drop and they all say the same thing. Each nut who somehow makes it says that they don't even get halfway down and they regret the decision

189

to step into the air."

"So...if they had impulse control, nobody would try suicide?"

"Probably. And you've got poor impulse control. You're in a mental hospital in a dangerous state of mind. You don't have a terminal disease, though. I'd understand suicide if you had pancreatic cancer or something else they can't cure. But you're still a healthy young man who hit his head and hears music. You've got no excuses not to man up. Got a headache? Take a goddamn aspirin and hum yourself to sleep, Ray."

"I'm moving past suicide, Dad. I've got something to live for. I've got stuff to do now. I know that."

"Damn skippy. First thing we have to do is get you out of here."

Ray's eyes narrowed. "Are you worried about something else?"

"Worried? Yeah, I'm worried. I'm worried you're going to get your head shrunk, get yourself some group therapy and confess."

"Confess to what?"

"Don't play dumb. We both know you blame me for being in here. You never call except at Christmas and then you can't wait to get me off the phone so you can talk to your mom. We never get the next call until it's either your mom's birthday or you need money."

"Confess to *what*, Dad?"

Ken Bradley stood and bent to Ray's ear. Ray could smell his father's aftershave and body odor. Ray's stomach curdled as his father whispered, "There's no statute of limitations on murder. I told you that from the beginning."

Ray trembled. "Murder? Who did I murder?"

His father bent closer, his hands on his knees, studying his son's eyes. "Are your brains really that scrambled, boy?"

Ray closed his eyes. He asked the question again, but not of his father.

To his horror, Ray had his answer.

31

On the last day of summer camp in Maine, Raymond kissed a girl. Actually, Emma Seaforth kissed him. He never saw her again. That should have been the worst tragedy of the summer of 1996.

Instead, the boy's father came up the path from Camp Bethany looking for his son. Ken Bradley had not seen his son in five weeks. When he found Raymond, the boy sat on a swing by some fat slob in pajamas.

"What the hell are you doing out in the woods alone with my son in your pajamas?"

"Wow!" the big man on the swing beside Raymond blurted, "You've got *hair!*"

When the fat man's penis flopped out of a gap in the front of his pajama bottoms, his father did not hesitate.

To the boy, the punch seemed to happen in slow motion. The forest turned into a green blur behind his father's fist and the surprised look on the fat man's jowly face.

A popping sound in the fat man's jaw turned the boy's stomach. The way his chin went sideways sickened him even more.

The man twisted sideways from the blow and went through the chain swing. The chain tore the man's bare arm as he fell. He put out one arm to try to stop the ground from slamming him. Instead of stopping his descent, the man's elbow bent backward and broke under his weight.

As soon as the boy saw the big man's elbow snap forward at a crazy angle — elbows aren't supposed to bend that way — young Raymond Bradley threw up, tasting two sloppy joes, Orange Fanta and cake with too-sweet vanilla icing for the second time that day.

The boy fell to his hands and knees. When he was done retching, he looked up to see his father standing over the man, kicking him in the behind and shouting at him. "Get up and fight like a man, you fat shit! C'mon, Chester the Child Molester! Get your fat ass *up!*"

But the man did not move.

Fists held high, Ken Bradley bounced on his toes, smiling. "You see that! That's what you get! That's what you get! One punch! That was just one punch!"

Raymond got up to look into the face of the man who had claimed to be his future self. One of the big man's feet was still hooked by the swing's chain. His pajama top had ridden up over his beer belly exposing white flesh.

His father, still hoping for an excuse to hit the fat man again, danced around the swing set, shadowboxing. His father stopped smiling and let his fists fall. He opened his hands. "Aw, shit."

The man who called himself Ray stared with open eyes at nothing. Blood poured out into the dirt beneath his head.

When Ken Bradley's gaze shifted from the dead man at his feet to his son, Raymond was afraid.

Events went into slow motion again. His father spoke a lot of words, but the boy was in shock, processing little. Raymond stared at his father's mouth. It was like trying to understand hidden messages from machine gun fire.

His father made him help drag the body deeper into the woods, away from the camp. They gathered branches and leaves and covered the corpse.

The boy cried the whole time.

His father swore a lot, but he had a mantra that penetrated Raymond's shock. "If you tell, you'll get in trouble, too. You touched the body. You helped me hide it. It's your neck just as much as it is mine."

Ken Bradley repeated the threats over and over. Then he made his son repeat his oath to never tell. Soon, father and son fled Camp Bethany without a word of thanks or a goodbye to anyone.

Except to gas up, his father didn't stop the car until they reached Lancaster, New Hampshire. Ken bought his son a cone of tiger eye ice cream at a truck stop. As soon as they were on the road again, Raymond vomited the ice cream across the back seat.

His father seemed to yell at him all the way back to Boston. Even when he was speaking normally, it still felt like he was yelling.

32

Once that door to memory opened, it could not be closed. Ray remembered it all.

After witnessing that punch to the jaw, the boy was afraid his father would hit him like that, too. Raymond feared he'd grow up to be the fat man on the swing, on the ground and under the branches and leaves.

He was also sure the police would come for them both. The boy kept his father's secret but he never looked at his dad the same way again. Now the man who had murdered him stared in Ray's eyes.

Loop, Ray thought. *I've got a time loop around my neck.*

"Ray? Answer me. Did you tell the shrinks anything? Did you confess to the pretty nurses? Did you say anything at all to these wack jobs you're in here with?"

"No. I didn't remember it until just now."

His father straightened. "I don't believe that for a second."

"S'truth."

Ken put his fists on his hips and gave his son a

hard look. "You were always such a happy kid before you went away that summer, Ray. That's how I prefer to remember you. My sunny, sonny boy!"

"It wasn't summer camp that changed me."

"You're the kind of guy who never lets things go. You dwell on things you can't control. What good is that?"

"You took a life, Dad. You...took *my* life." He meant it literally, but it worked figuratively, too. One punch whisked away Ray's carefree childhood.

"Don't be so dramatic," Ken said. "I told you the next summer we were free and clear."

That was true. Ray remembered that now, too. His father had picked him up after school. The boy had always walked home in any weather, but that day Ken Bradley picked him up, whistling as he leaned over and pushed the passenger door open.

"Got something to tell you! It's about that accident we never talk about and never will again."

The boy stared at his Reeboks with the bright red laces. "A couple of rabbit hunters found a body in the woods by your old summer camp. Animals musta got at it, because they can't identify who the fat bastard was."

"How do you know?"

"I've been keeping an eye on the situation, checking in at the library each week. I found it in a small item in *The Democrat* from up the road from Camp Bethany in Chester's Mill. Tiny article about a missing man in a tiny paper. No one knows who he is and no one is coming to look for him."

I know who he was and will be, young Raymond thought, *but I can never tell you or anyone else. Who would believe me?*

The boy looked at his hands and pictured the fat man. He liked to think of the living man instead of the dead thing they'd dragged by the feet. The man's hands had trailed behind him, scraping across the forest floor.

Those hands would have had his fingerprints before he'd been left to rot in the woods.

Raymond had suggested they cover the body with rocks. It would be more like a real burial.

"No," his father said. "We want to hide the body, but we don't have time to bury it well. Cover him with leaves and pine needles and moss and let nature take its course."

For all the boy knew, he'd grow up and it would happen again. The next time it happened, he'd be the one whose head slammed too hard into the hard-packed ground beneath the old swing set.

That afternoon after school, his father drove around their neighborhood, giving his son time to take in that they were free. The police would not come knocking. Ken needed to see the boy had absorbed the good news before he brought him home.

"What do you want, Raymond?" his father asked finally. "We can relax now and things can go back to normal. I know this has been tough on you, but it's been tougher on me. I'm not meant for jail, son. I'd die before I'd go to jail."

"You told me."

"So? What do you want?"

"I don't want anything, Dad."

"C'mon. Lighten up. I've made my peace with it. It was an accident and that fat bastard deserved it, anyway. Why can't you just let it go?"

The boy almost told his father he'd killed a time traveler. He almost told Ken that "fat bastard" was his son.

"Let's go get you something. You want KFC? C'mon. You love KFC!"

"No. I want a bike."

"What?"

"I need a new bike. I need...I need to go for a lot of long bike rides. And I'm not eating bad food anymore, either. I'm eating salads and soups and I'll only drink water from now on. No more sugary soda or any of that fried crap."

His father nodded slowly, his eyes never leaving the road.

"Okay. That sounds like a good, healthy idea. If that's what you want, we'll go get you a new bike."

"Now? Today?"

"Okay, son. Now. Then it's all stamped paid in full and put to bed, right?"

"Yeah. Paid in full."

Staring up into his father's eyes in the family room of the psych hospital, Ray knew that nothing ever really goes away. Everything is recorded for later review. If your memory is good enough, everything seems as if it was just yesterday. If you travel through time, it did happen yesterday.

The music in Ray's head was a death metal spike through his brain. The music was no solace now. Torment was back.

33

A hazy figure in white approached Ray as if through a fog made of gauze. He sensed the angel's presence but could not focus on the face hovering above him. He did not know where he was. Everything shone white.

I died, Ray thought. *This is heaven.*

"Mr. Bradley?" the voice boomed.

"Yuh...yaas?"

"Mr. Bradley, we're going to turn down your morphine drip now. It's a little high."

"Oh, fuck."

"Haha! Now, now! *Language!* Would you like me to close the blinds? You're squinting a lot. Is it a little too bright in here for you?"

"Y-yes! Please!"

He felt a device with a button in his palm. His hand moved so stiffly, he deduced that he must be hooked up to an IV bag. Smooth, cool plastic was taped into his palm.

"When you feel you need a little more morphine, click the clicker's button and the machine will deliver a small dose to your needs, okay? Do you understand?"

Click-click-click-click-click-click-click-click-click-click-click-click-click-click-click-click-click-click-click-click!

"Alright, alright! Are you really in that much pain? It won't deliver more than the maximum you get no matter how many times you click it, understand? It takes into account clicks versus allowable dosage."

Click-click!

The woman chuckled. If Ray's head didn't hurt so much, he'd want to hear that soft voice more. His skull felt like it was full of incredibly heavy pushpins.

"D-dad?"

"Your father has gone home, Mr. Bradley. It appears you were overstimulated. Sorry about that. If we hadn't had a couple of new people on the desk, you wouldn't have been able to see your father at all. You were supposed to be in your room staring at your wall, not wandering around the hospital and having visitors at all hours. The storm knocked out our power temporarily and things got busy. We had a lot of agitated residents last night, especially you."

"Wizard?"

"Hm?"

"Where's Arnold? Arnold Martin?"

"Oh, I'm sorry, Mr. Bradley. He's no longer within the hospital, but that's all I can tell you. I don't know more."

That was an odd way to put it, Ray thought. Within the hospital. Not at or even in the hospital? Could that mean Arnold might have escaped to the Beyond after all? Or did that simply mean, The Great Beyond? As in six feet below ground in a pauper's grave, rapidly becoming worm food?

"Can I talk to Cenk?"

"Who?"

"Wheels."

"Oh," She spoke in a low, soothing voice. "Doctors orders are you're not supposed to speak to anyone unless absolutely necessary."

Or was that his father's idea?

"No piano, no common room privileges and no group therapy. You're in a quiet area on the third floor. No one will bother you. Dr. Dickens will be in to check on you, but after your episode last night, your father agreed you should be put in a private room. Bare wall, dim light, drugs for the pain for now. The most important thing you can do to recover from your concussion is stare at the blank wall."

"Wait. What episode? I had an episode?"

"You collapsed in the family room. Dr. Dickens will answer your questions when he's on rounds. We'll get you some breakfast soon and there's ice water with a straw on the tray by the bed. Do you need help with that?"

"No. Thank you."

"Do you need help to the bathroom or would you like a bed pan?"

"Oh, hell, no."

"Okay. I'll take your blood pressure again in a little while."

He wasn't aware she'd checked his blood pressure already. Ray only knew two things: he must have slept very deeply because he went down into the dark where there was no music and no pain. It had been such a relief to feel nothing and, for a while, to be nothing. Now that he was awake, he wanted to be something again.

Ray knew he'd miss that lovely, angelic voice, but he turned on his side toward the wall. His eyes adjusted to the light. He waited for the Gates of Perception to open. He heard a single muted trumpet. It was soon joined by an orchestra. The notes coalesced into an aspirational anthem from an '80s movie, suitable for a training sequence.

"Purify me," he said.

Ray stared. The music's tempo became a determined march to war.

Ray waited for the wall to take him away from this hell of his father's making. He had to break the loop.

"Time to go."

34

The wall did not open to Ray that day. Nor did it come before the nurses changed shifts at eleven o'clock the next day.

By then, he was sweating and exhausted. Ray went over what Arnold and Cenk had told him about breaking out into the Beyond. They'd told him plenty, but little of real use. He had no idea what quantum waves were, for instance.

But he hadn't known what quantum waves were before and the wall had reached out to envelope him in his first wall-staring session. An hour before dawn, Ray gave up and closed his red, irritated eyes. He'd stared until his eyes itched and he thought he would lose his mind to boredom.

As he succumbed to his exhaustion and fell asleep, Ray thought, *Purify*.

He was sure he'd wake up in a strange black desert. The Man in the Moon would be waiting for him. He would have questions and the thing in the sky would finally answer.

Together, Ray and the Man in the Moon would come to an arrangement. How many people had come before him? How many movie stars and celebrities and captains of industry had come to an understanding with the thing in the sky that ruled the Beyond?

He thought of all the inventors and celebrities who had come from humble beginnings but, somehow, had fallen into the right path. What if, for instance, it wasn't merely talent and Hollywood connections through Scientology that made Tom Cruise a star? Maybe he got so much right and didn't seem to age because, most of the time, if he got something wrong he could go back and fix it? Cruise had made a time travel movie about going back to get his actions just right so he could finally win a war and save the world from aliens in *Edge of Tomorrow*.

Anybody involved in time travel projects was especially suspect. And what had *Quantum Leap* been but a television show about fixing mistakes in the time stream? *Groundhog Day* was a genius movie written by Harold Ramis. How many times had Ramis gone through the wall to make it appear he was a genius? Or Judd Apatow or Steve Martin?

Or was Ray simply bored with the view of his wall and naming off all the celebrities he envied? It was difficult to sort out possible time travelers from variables like talent and luck. The Wizard had warned of too many variables. Combinations and permutations created an indefinite number of choices and one wrong choice could throw him from his preferred time trajectory.

Most troubling in his musings was how sure Cenk and the Wizard were that he would fail because of all those treacherous variables.

Michael J. Fox troubled Ray most. He'd been in

three time travel movies. *Back to the Future* had been the most successful time travel movie franchise. Despite all of the actor's amazing talent, success and inspiration, what if Fox went through the wall to fix every misstep in the Beyond and came back to the present every time, still afflicted with Parkinson's Disease?

Ray wept at that thought the night the morphine ran out. The nurses switched him to Tylenol 3s. The music in his head sounded like a Nazi march.

Ray lay in isolation staring at his cracked mint-green wall for two weeks before he detected movement.

Still, another day passed of trying to concentrate on nothing. His headache lessened as he meditated at the wall.

"Be the Buddha, be the Buddha, be the Buddha," became his mantra.

It wasn't until Ray heard the sounds of monks chanting in his head that he began to think he was going somewhere, some*when*. He felt a wave of heat flow over him through the wall.

Purified.

A movement came at the edge of his vision. A stirring in the deep well of his consciousness felt like it was reaching out. It was happening again. When Ray closed his eyes he could see red and blue arcs of electricity meeting at the center of a widening gate. He saw a profound opening, an electrical handshake across dimensions.

For the greatest good, Ray thought. *I'm doing this for the greatest good.*

The monks in his head sang in perfect harmony. They sang the Om.

His eyes watering, Ray said to the wall, "Open Sesame! I'm ready! For the greatest good!"

He felt a hitch in the vibration. Through the harmonic connection, he joined in singing the Om to strengthen the passage between times.

Then...?

Nothing.

"Aw, fuck it. *I give up!*"

The crack in the wall split wide and a torrent of black water surged out. It wrapped around Ray like a giant hand and swept him in, away and beyond his perceived limits. The Gates of Perception yawned open and a wormhole awash in quantum waves swallowed him in a flash of black light.

35

Ray stood on a sunny city street corner in nothing but his johnny shirt stamped with the name of the mental institute.

"*Shit!* I forgot about my clothes!"

The variables of the universe, it seemed, were already out to screw him over.

Ray spotted his destination across the street. Ray had traveled back in time, but he was still in Los Angeles. He didn't know what year it was yet, but the sign hanging above a recessed doorway read: Heavy's.

"For the greater good," he said.

A passerby tossed a couple of quarters on the sidewalk and the coins jingled at his feet. "Get some clothes, freak!"

"Um...thanks."

Ray picked up the coins and wandered forward in a daze. He felt the hot breath from the grill of an old green Barracuda as it screeched to a stop a few inches away from his bare right arm. The car's blaring horn brought him to full alert.

In the time it took him to hurry across the street,

he realized he had no headache, but he still had the music. The tune in his head was an original composition, but not one of his best. It made him think of U2, but without singing and all harpsichord.

Heavy's interior was a long, dim box, as if it had once been a bowling alley with only three lanes. A bar stretched down one wall and he could smell greasy food cooking. Aside from the pot lighting, the bar was lit by two big screens, one at each end of the bar. The FIFA World Cup was playing. Ray didn't have to look closely to know one of the teams would be Turkey. He guessed the other would be the Netherlands.

He scanned the room. Every patron of the bar stared back. Ray pulled his hospital johnny tight around the back to make sure the ties were tight. The last time anything flopped out naked to the world, his father had killed him.

"Hi, folks!" Ray said. "I just got mugged!"

He was met with silence.

"I got this hospital shirt from...from the guy who mugged me!"

Someone coughed. Another cleared his throat. A woman at the rear whom he could not see said, "Aw! Poor guy!" She was immediately shushed by others nearby. They either didn't believe him or they didn't want to get involved. Ray didn't blame them.

"Hey, buddy! You want to call somebody and get some clothes?" The big man behind the bar wore a bright blue vest over a silk shirt unbuttoned to mid-chest, exposing thick hair. It was Cenk, looking younger, taller and heavier. He was still years away from ripping a prison guard's ears off.

Cenk put a phone on top of the bar and the ringer

mechanism within it gave a little ding. Ray looked around. A few people were speaking into cell phones with little antennae, but no one texted. Heavy's patrons had returned to watching the soccer game, drinking, eating and talking to each other.

Ray missed the blue-white glow of illuminated faces bent over tiny screens. He'd hardly be noticed in a dim bar in 2014, especially not in LA.

"Buddy!" Cenk called. "Call somebody or get movin'!"

Ray made his way through a tight labyrinth of tables to the bar. A big burly guy looked away from the television long enough to let out a low wolf whistle. He and his table mate, another husky fellow who could have been his brother, laughed uproariously. They cheered, but their mood changed quickly. They swore when the Netherlands almost scored a point but Turkey's goalie made the save with a long dive.

Cenk cheered the goalie's deft defense of his goal. The pair of Netherlands fans spat out a few phrases in Dutch which Ray guessed had to be more curses.

He knew who the men were. Cenk had said that Time resists change, but the Beyond had delivered him back to a place where he could make a measurable difference. The purpose of Ray's trip here was clear.

Ray slid onto a barstool, careful to avoid exposing himself. The johnny shirt's material was thin and the barstool was cold.

"What number do you want to call?" Cenk asked, ready to dial for him. "If it's the cops, tell them to meet you next door, out front of the flower shop. The boss won't want any cops in here."

"I need to talk to a friend."

"What's the number?"

"What's your number?"

"You're not my type, man. Stop screwing around. Do you want my help or not?"

"I'm here to help you, for the greater good."

"Huh?"

"This is going to sound crazy, but you're going to listen to me, Cenk."

Cenk pulled the phone off the bar. "Out!"

"You should listen to me. I know lots of things. I know your name is Cenk, for instance."

Ray hadn't noticed the name tag on Cenk's vest until he tapped it. "It's right here, David Copperfield. You get one point for pronouncing it right, though."

Ray had known the name Cenk before he'd met the convict in the mental hospital's library. He'd seen the web news show *The Young Turks* many times. The host was a man named Cenk Uygur. However, web shows were still a thing of the future. Looking around, Ray guessed many people still suffered the ridiculously slow connection speeds of dial-up modems.

"We've met before," Ray said.

"Though it's not before. It's...yet. We've met in the yet!"

"Out!"

The burly men swore and told them both to shut up. "We can't hear the game!"

Cenk shook his head. "Enough of this. Leave like a gentleman now. I got customers waiting on food. I've got one cook in the back. We're out of fish for the fish and chips, the regular waitress called in sick and her sub can't be here for another hour. I just want to watch the game, man. Do I gotta throw you out myself or call the cops?"

"You want to be an actor."

"We're in LA. Who doesn't?"

"Your mother loved Nina Simone."

Cenk stared at him for a moment. "I'm calling the cops. If you know what's good for you — "

"Your father loved music from Turkey and you hated it. And you have to listen to me and do as I ask."

Cenk straightened and stared in Ray's eyes.

"My name is Ray and you and I have to get out of here immediately."

Cenk nodded. "Okay."

The two burly Dutchmen appeared, one on either side of Ray. One of them clapped a hand on Ray's shoulder and squeezed hard. One of them asked Cenk, "This has got to be the guy, right?"

Cenk nodded again. His eyes were huge. His lips had gone thin. "This is the guy."

The two men yanked Ray out of the bar roughly. To the right was a flower shop. To the left was an alley. They went left.

Ray yelled for help. They dragged him kicking and screaming. He stopped when one of them balled up a fist and punched him in the solar plexus hard. Ray doubled over and collapsed to his hands and knees, gasping.

When Ray could speak, he managed to ask, "Why?"

Both men bent. He thought they were going to help him up. They started punching.

36

Any delusion Ray might have had that he could fight off two men in a back alley soon evaporated. He was helpless. He tried to gouge their eyes and punch them in the testicles and kick out their knees. However, Ray was already on his knees, barefoot in a johnny shirt. He'd lost his bearings from the first punch to his jaw.

He gave up hope and curled into the fetal position. The Dutchmen started kicking. He didn't think of them as two men anymore. They were not two Dutch men. They'd become the Dutchmen, a snarling, two-headed beast with four arms, four legs and pointy shoes.

Through splayed fingers, Ray looked to the long wall. It was covered with graffiti. Beyond that wall, the patrons of Heavy's bar were watching the World Cup. One compassionate young woman who'd expressed concern for his well-being might be eating sweet potato curly fries with the friends who had shushed her.

Cenk was in there, too, serving beer and stealing glances at the screens. He'd call it football and the customers would call it soccer. Meanwhile, the Dutchmen would, at any moment, split his spleen and break his kidneys. He'd pee in a bag for the rest of his short life, if he survived to have a short life.

No.

No!

What had happened to Cenk was happening to him. Somehow, he was going to kill at least one of the Dutchmen. Somehow, he was going to get up. He'd make them the Flying Dutchmen. He'd crack their heads open on that alley wall.

Then he'd go to jail and be beaten and thrown in solitary and he'd eat his own shit and smile. Then he'd yank the ears off a guard. They'd beat him until he could never walk again. The timeline would continue, with one minor alteration: Cenk would be spared but Ray's miserable life would get more miserable.

Something broke and shifted and went soft in his back. He hoped it was just a rib. The pain was excruciating. It hurt to breathe.

It occurred to Ray he had many more ribs left to break. His bones were the Dutchmen's xylophone. Their fists and feet were hammers. The soundtrack that accompanied Ray's beating was *Flight of the Bumblebee*, on sitar.

"The universe sucks!" Ray screamed.

The Dutchmen paused long enough to roar with laughter. They were both breathing hard. Beating someone to death was heavy labor.

Ray thought again of the compassionate woman behind the wall who had believed his lie about getting mugged. Hers was the only voice that had said, "Aw!" She would have called the police for him.

She would have cared. However, now she was probably ordering a margarita. Ray wanted one but it was beyond that wall.

That wasn't the only thing beyond the wall. Ray stared at the graffiti on the wall, searching for cracks in the concrete.

For a good time, please yourself! read one neatly sprayed message in neon orange.

In blue, another tagger had crossed out the second *e* in *please* and changed the message to read: *For a good time, pleasure yourself.*

Below that, someone had scrawled: *And call yourself Sally.*

For a good time, Ray thought, *escape through the wall.*

His first trip through the wall had taken him to summer camp. That had been some kind of trippy accident. A fluke.

His second attempt had required two weeks of boring meditation and too many hospital meals of stewed tomatoes in a secluded, dark room.

Now, he reasoned, through pure desperation, he'd disappear through the Gates of Perception into wherever the wormhole would take him. "For the greater good," Ray whispered.

"What?" one of his attackers asked.

"For the greater good."

"What's he on, do you suppose?" one asked the other in clipped English.

"It doesn't matter," the other said.

It doesn't matter.

Rage, Ray discovered, can be bigger than pain. The Dutchmen did not care about him. The universe did not care about him. Except to tell her friends she saw a crazy guy in a bar who only wore a hospital gown, even the woman from the bar had already forgotten about him. He was a human being and he didn't matter.

For a good time, please yourself!

"You better let me up and walk away now," Ray said.

The two-headed monster laughed louder and they bantered back and forth in short, telegraphic bursts that Ray did not understand.

"You better let me up or I'll make you regret it."

It wasn't just cruel laughter, anymore. The big men were giggling like schoolgirls, high on their easy victory.

Ray didn't look at them. He stared at the wall, past the graffiti and into the depth of the wall, through the cracks. In a moment, he was sure he'd feel the familiar wash of quantum waves. It would be stunning, but very welcome.

C'mon! Ray thought. *If there is any justice in the world...*

"In a few seconds," Ray said, "I'm going to disappear. Then I'll reappear behind you. I'll be fully dressed, all in black leather and packing all kinds of heat. Guns and retractable batons and grenades and swords and shit."

The Dutchmen howled with laughter. Tears ran down their cheeks. "Maybe you should wear a helmet?" one suggested.

"Or a mask and a cape?" the other added.

They giggled so much they gasped for breath, too. One farted.

Ray's voice was calm and confident. "I'm going to do terrible things to you." His whole body ached. In a moment, that wouldn't matter. When he went back in time, his pain would be erased. He'd find a way back here and extract a terrible vengeance. Ray's tone was so flat and confident, he saw a flicker of self-doubt in the Dutchmen's eyes.

"I am rage," Ray said. "I am vengeance. Do you know why? Because I am a human being. I *matter. I fucking matter*. And I am going to use a shotgun to make you both fly into that wall. I'm going to tear the monster you are in two, then four, then *eight*. You will be The Flying Dutchmen. Flying chunks of Dutch men."

Ray stared at the wall and into and through the wall with all his concentration. *Now*, he thought, *escape! Escape now! Now!*

And, promptly, he didn't.

37

"**A**lright, my droogies! That's enough. We don't want to kill him. That wouldn't be virtuous."

Ray rolled to his back. Above him stood the Wizard himself, Arnold Martin. He wore a long, brown leather coat and a fedora. He looked younger and healthier and Ray smelled no fish.

"You made it!" Ray said.

"Obviously."

"I thought you were dead!"

"Oh, ye of little brain...though technically, I suppose I was deceased. I left the husk with liver cancer behind and emerged in my younger body here! Ha!"

"How? I don't — "

"A flat plane is a flat plane. You wheeled me away from my magic wall, but the floor did just fine! I could see the ceiling and it took me away. That edge of death thing, the desperation. It is motivating, isn't it?"

"How are you now?"

"Feeling better than I have in ages. Got here two days ago."

"You took over your own body?"

The Wizard smiled. "You go through the wall, you don't take your troubles with you. The Time Worm resists change, but the arc of the universe is towards improvement overall. There is some doubt as to what that means for us as a species, but Nature favors the scrappy."

"Um...okay. So, no liver cancer."

The Wizard smiled. "Of course not. It's 2002."

"It's 2002? I wasn't sure..." Ray closed his mouth as Arnold rolled his eyes.

"Anyway," the Wizard continued, "I won't have any detectable cancer of the liver yet, not for another decade. I have approximately 5,250,000 minutes until my liver cancer is discovered. By then it will be too late."

Ray winced as he sat up. "If you know it's coming —"

"Inoperable. It's a terrible variety of cancer. Like a drink of hemlock. There are no treatments. You don't get over my kind of cancer unless you know your way through the thin membranes of the Concurrent Universe."

"I don't — "

"Kepler spoke of the music of the spheres and the organization of solar systems, but the worlds of the multiverse spin and wheel and the times don't all line up perfectly in march step, just as the planets have varying speeds and orbits. It's as if the multiverse is a giant clock, its gears spinning and ratcheting. This time I went back twelve years and cheated death again."

"And here we are," Ray said. "You cut it close."

"The Time Worm is temperamental."

"You...the what?"

"It doesn't matter. Not now. Not in this now."

"What did you tell Cenk? And why did these guys beat the living shit out of me?" Ray held his nose to keep from bleeding more on his hospital gown.

"I told him that you were a crazy person coming to kill him. I said you had inside information that you would try to exploit for some terrible scheme. I said you'd seen his head shots working for a casting agent and you intended him harm."

"He bought all that?"

"I've been friends with Cenk for a long time. I have much more personal information about him than you possibly could."

Ray tried to climb to his feet but his ribs hurt too much.

"Don't get up, my young simian. You could do yourself more damage. My new friends are muscular, aren't they?" The wizard gestured toward Ray's assailants who were now leaning against the wall and smoking. They looked perplexed by the Wizard.

They were no longer one beast in Ray's mind anymore. He still wished he had a shotgun, though. He very much wanted them dead.

"We're missing the Cup!" one of them said. "Pay up, old man!"

The Wizard pulled a pistol from his coat and shot both men. His first shot missed. Every other bullet hit its target and the Wizard did not stop shooting until the gun clicked. It was Ray's dream come true but he shook at what he witnessed.

Arnold Martin tossed the pistol to Ray who instinctively caught it, then immediately dropped it to the pavement as if it was scorching hot.

"Why did you do that?"

"Because Cenk suffered a long time. Beaten and dehumanized in prison, then crippled and sent to a mental hospital to rot. Cenk's the closest I have to a friend. He was nicer to me than most. Besides, these men were evil. For the greater good, they're out of this existence. Maybe they'll do better and get it right next time."

"But why — ?"

"I needed them out in the back alley and..." Martin stared at the dead men, "I'm sorry, Ray. I had to be sure how bad they were and, as they hit you, I suppose I was building up the nerve. I've never killed anyone before."

Ray touched his sore and swelling jaw. "Took you long enough."

"I apologize. I'll be quicker the next time this is necessary. I found it was easy once I got started."

"What happens now?"

"I, for one, am hoping that going through the wall gets easier with practice. Sometime in the next couple of decades I'll have a tumor growing in my belly. Deadlines do focus the mind and I'd very much like to get younger if possible."

Blood seeped out from under the dead men, spreading out and reaching for Ray with crimson fingers. He couldn't tear his gaze from the dead men. Their eyes stared at him.

Martin shook his head. "History is a long list of wars and pain and mistakes and sacrifices. Didn't you ever wonder why?"

"I assumed it was because people are assholes."

"That is a quite dependable variable. But my understanding is that I have to balance the equation." The Wizard walked away.

Haltingly and racked with pain, Ray rose and stepped back from the spreading pool of blood.

The Wizard called over his shoulder. "Cenk, at least in this timeline, will go on with his life. I don't know if we're in the same timeline as before or not. There's no way to tell. I can't solve for x. The equation won't balance precisely. This could be a quantum echo for all I know. However, one Cenk in this sphere, at least, is avenged."

Ray still stared at his assailants. "But this? This is wrong! You could have called the police. These guys are thugs, but you're acting like judge, jury and executioner. They didn't deserve this. I wanted them dead for a while there, too, but...you can't. How could you do this? You could have just stopped them. You had the gun and — "

"My actions reflect the laws of nature."

"What?"

"Nature. My equation is simple: Subtract two and the world is better. Or would you have preferred for me to wait until they killed you? Some people just can't go on living and time, Mr. Bradley, is precious. Those two thugs weren't using their time well. Trust me, I know. They're just like the boys who tortured and battered me. I'll spare them no time nor tears."

"Congratulations. You've lived out your revenge fantasy. But would Cenk have gone for this?"

Arnold Martin shrugged. "Cenk was my friend. He and I shared a fascination with time travel. Cenk is a nice young man with a bright future now. We'll leave him to it. I don't know for sure that he'd approve of cold-bloodedness, but I'm sure he knew jail. He'd understand this."

"I'm not so sure."

Martin shrugged. "Pythagoras dreamed of armonia, universal harmony. I can't control the spheres of the multiverse, but I can do the right thing to nudge the worlds into a finer balance. I err toward the good to get things back on track."

"Isn't that what psychopaths do?"

"Once you accept that there are multiple timelines and multiple potentialities, you'll see my sins are diluted. I've enough math to know the human race is on a path to self-destruction. I think the Time Worm would appreciate my efforts. All gods demand sacrifice. That is their unifying weakness."

"This can't be right. I thought you didn't believe in God."

"My understanding does not require a prime mover," Martin said. "All I said was that the semantics of the divine are opaque and therefore useless to me." The Wizard paused and looked back at Ray. "Think what you want. In a few minutes to a few hours, once you're past the shock of your experience, you're going to start thinking better. My brain works much faster than yours, so I'm going to save you some time. While you're preoccupied with music, I'm preoccupied with potentialities. One potential is you will go back before this event and try to find me. You might want to avoid this unpleasantness."

"Thanks for the suggestion."

"Don't bother. Chances are excellent you'll end up in a completely different timeline. You will not find me but if you do, I'll shoot you, too. I have important work. The multiverse is a fixer upper."

"Martin!"

"My name isn't really Arnold Martin. It never was. And you aren't in any shape to chase me."

The Wizard strode down the alley to an opening between buildings and, possibly, disappeared into history.

38

Ray took the gun with him. He hoped to have the opportunity to ram it up the Wizard's ass sideways until the bastard tasted metal. Also, he had to get out of this alley fast. His attackers' staring eyes made his heart pound. Goosebumps rose on his skin as shivers of cold competed with his pain.

Ray got about ten feet away from the dead men before he turned back. To escape the attention of the LAPD, he'd need clothes. Bloody ones would have to do.

It was a mess and before he was done, he'd be covered in blood. He'd look more guilty but less naked. It was difficult accepting the truth of the Wizard's words. His brain did work slower than the man he knew as Arnold Martin.

Ray guessed that getting a dead man out of his clothes was harder than dressing an uncooperative toddler. In his weakened state, the task was a misery. Worse, he had to do it before someone came down the alley.

That didn't go in his favor, either. If the Wizard told the truth, Time itself was against him.

As Ray tucked in a bloody shirttail into ill-fitting pants, he looked up into a man's fierce, hawk-like eyes. Judging by the shopping cart full of bottles and cans the man pushed, he was homeless. His wild hair almost obscured his face, but he'd spotted Ray well enough.

"This isn't what it looks like," Ray said.

"I can't wait to hear this story. What do you think it looks like, young fella?"

"It looks bad."

"That is so."

The *Theme from Mission Impossible* started up in Ray's head. Ray winced as he shrugged into a leather jacket. He patted the men's pockets down and found wallets and Dutch passports. When he looked up again, the homeless man was a few steps closer and he held a long necked beer bottle at his side, not quite out of sight.

"Don't be a tough guy, man," Ray pleaded. "These guys tried to kill me. I've had it with tough guys for one day. For a lot of days."

"Police!" the man yelled.

"Dude. Don't."

"Police!" he yelled louder. "Murderer! Murder! Murderer!"

Ray pulled the pistol from the back of his waistband and pointed it at the man's head. "You're starting to piss me off. Run away."

The man nodded and Ray relaxed.

The homeless man ran at Ray, teeth gritted as he raised the bottle to break it over Ray's head.

Ray shoved the barrel of the empty pistol into the man's teeth. The man reeled back, cupping his bloody mouth. A moment later, the man stared at two jagged teeth in his palm. "You thonofabith!"

Ray shook the pistol at him. "Don't you know how these work? Get out of here before I shoot you in the dick."

"You wanna shoot me in the dick?"

"More and more, yeah."

The homeless man dropped the bottle and backed away behind his cart. "Poleeth! Murderer!" he screamed up the alley to the busy street.

"Oh, for God's sake!" Ray pointed the gun at the man's crotch and yelled, *"Blam! Blam! Blam! Bang!"*

The man ran away, one hand over his groin and one cupping his bloody mouth.

Ray walked the other way, as fast as he could to where the Wizard had disappeared. Sirens echoed among the surrounding buildings and somewhere nearby, people shouted.

Time, Ray thought, *is of the essence.*

39

Ray's first thought was to find himself a wall and go back to the future. He wished he was a mere television ad man again.

Given what he now knew, living the life of an ad guy with a tattoo and a gold tooth and a girlfriend who wanted to lock him into an ordinary life? That didn't sound so bad now.

However, which future might he arrive in? And, despite the Wizard's bravado, traveling through the wall wasn't so easy. Arnold Martin, or whomever he really was, was still in this stream of time.

With blood soaking through his stolen clothes, Ray might end up in jail. Dead strangers' blood creeped him out. If he got AIDS, Ray didn't think the treatments were all that dependable quite yet.

Ray darted as fast as he could manage down several blocks, mostly through back alleys. He avoided people whenever he could. Where he encountered pedestrians, they turned their heads to stare.

He knew what he was looking for, but he didn't know how far he had to go to find it. He got lucky.

Maybe whoever was in charge of Time couldn't mess up geography to thwart him. Soon he came to the beach. The Pacific Ocean spread out before him.

The pan flute that only he could hear played a sad, vaguely Japanese song. Each note was so long and light, the music was almost tuneless.

He crossed the wide ribbon of sand and marched into the ocean. Ray was relieved to let the waves wash the blood off him. He got out after a few minutes when it occurred to him that all that blood might attract sharks. Sharks, police, a crazed mathematician, dead Dutchmen and scary homeless dudes: there seemed no end to perils in 2002.

He sat with his back against a tree and wondered what to do. What had he been doing in 2002? He'd been twenty, but where was he at twenty? In this time, had he taken over his younger self's body as the Wizard claimed he had done? Or was he stuck with the Goldilocks versus Papa Bear problem again? He'd assumed time travel had fixed rules, but if even reincarnation could count as time travel, apparently not. There was a reason a lot of things didn't make sense. Circumstances reflected how fucked up the universe really was.

Douglas Adams' fiction got reality right, Ray thought. *The answer is 42 and we're no further ahead for all our answers.*

He looked down at himself. He was quite thin, so he surmised that if he was in possession of his younger self, it wasn't the one who ended up as an aspiring comedian writing for a game show. He might still become a TV advertising salesman if he could stay out of jails and insane asylums.

In all the time travel stories Ray could remember,

the hero usually knew what he was doing, where and when. Ray wasn't sure what his goal should be. In this timeline, maybe he wasn't cast as the hero. Maybe Arnold Martin was the man with the mission.

The justice system of the state of California would have no patience for the truth as Ray knew it. They'd call him a liar or insane or both. As bad as he thought writing for a game show had been, it beat eating shit to get out of prison and winding up in Cenk's wheelchair. In the present — a slippery concept if there ever was one — he seemed bound to take Cenk's place.

Was that what the Wizard meant by gods demanding sacrifice? Was there such a thing as free will at all? If he ran away to Texas and became a cowboy, would he still somehow wind up in prison for murders he didn't commit? He thought of the pitilessness of The Man in the Moon. He could see its disinterest as it turned to look at him with a face with huge craters for eyes and no mouth. The memory made him shiver.

Ray suspected something would push him toward Cenk's fate no matter what. People and Nature edged toward symmetry. Why not the Man in the Moon? Ray had to find a way to push back.

Ray remembered dancing in clubs in 2002. The answer came: dancing every night was one of his favorite memories. He'd smoked a lot of weed. Was that the summer he'd worked as a bike courier for a downtown law firm? Or was that the summer he worked half time as a painter in the Valley and delivered pizza at night to help pay for college?

No, he decided. Ten years ago, he was a bike courier. Then he'd painted houses the following summer. He got the job at night delivering pizza because Joe Grins Well knew the manager. The pizza joint couldn't keep dependable drivers and Joe, his college roommate, recommended Ray. But what if the teeth in the gears didn't match? What if nothing was dependable and he was remembering the wrong history?

Ray began to cry. Joe had gotten him that sucky pizza job. A few years later, Joe got him a job again, a much better job, in the writing room. He should have been more grateful. That job was two lifetimes ago.

Then it occurred to Ray that, yes, the Wizard was right again. Ray did indeed think very slowly. So slowly, he might be stupid. He took deep breaths and closed his eyes, quelling the rising panic and loneliness.

Maybe the lifetime he remembered didn't happen. He'd screwed that up when he went back and talked to himself as a kid. Raymond had witnessed Ray's murder at the hands of his father. That could screw up a kid forever, couldn't it?

Ray reasoned that the boy he'd been would either get wilder in the face of craziness or much less averse to risk. Since Ray had ended up an ad man, the kid had probably grown up more conservatively. Ray had grown up watching his weight, but he hadn't ended up on stage at the Comedy Store, either.

Ray huddled against the tree and let the sun warm him, waiting to get a little more dry.

He thought more about the kid he'd been. His father had told him how he'd cut himself off from the family, only calling at Christmas. Why couldn't he have gotten his life right the first time? Why did it all have to be so difficult?

Ray closed his eyes. He waited and breathed deeper and slower. The Man in the Moon appeared in his mind, huge and white and hanging in a starless sky. Its face turned away from him.

Ray's eyes snapped open.

No answer came.

All he had was the Wizard's word. "The Time Worm demands sacrifice," he'd said.

But the Wizard had spoken of infinite complexity, too. If there were no fixed rules of time travel, how could he make sense of it?

The old man's voice came to him. *Contradictions abound, Ray. Remember? Quantum physics works. Newton's scribblings make sense, too. And here we are and so it goes.*

If there were no fixed rules — if it was really all conjecture and guidelines and tendencies — Ray reasoned that maybe he had a chance to change his fate. Success was improbable, but not impossible.

Ray shivered as ocean breezes gathered force and became a stiff wind pushing him away as the sun sank into the black Pacific. Long after dark, Ray pulled himself to his feet and walked back into the broken city under a blood moon.

40

Ray's mother and father lived in a bungalow at the end of a dead end street in Fairfax. He didn't know how he knew, but as he walked a cab appeared. As soon as he saw the yellow taxi, their address appeared in his mind. He had enough money from his attackers to get there.

It was late when the cab dropped him off in front of their home. Wouldn't the summer camp murder have changed where his parents lived? Cenk (when he was Wheels) and the Wizard (when he was Arnold) both warned of too many variables, permutations and combinations. Ray realized he wasn't really sure what a permutation was, but somehow he knew this was his parents' home.

Judging by his weight loss, he had changed. *Seeing your own death changes you,* Ray thought, *but maybe not really much for the better. I don't feel very different, just doomed. Maybe time is like a story: you can change how you tell the story, but you tend to hit the same plot points.*

He searched his memory. He asked questions, but the answers didn't come. The Man in the Moon wasn't cooperating.

"Man in the Moon," Ray muttered. "You are a cheater."

The dice are loaded and the House always wins, Ray.

"Oh, *now* you want to talk, but just to taunt me."

He heard the old man from nowhere chuckling.

The night air was chilly and cooled his sweat uncomfortably. If his parents didn't answer the door, Ray didn't know where to go next. As he was about to knock, the porch light came on and Ray braced himself.

Martha Bradley opened the front door wide and stared at him through the screen door. Her eyes were wide. "Son!"

Ray's shoulders relaxed a little, but instead of opening the screen door he waited a beat, just in case his mother's next words were, "Son! Son! Bring the baseball bat! There's a stranger on the porch who looks just like you!"

Instead, Martha said, "Are you coming in, Raymond, or do you want me to meet you at the coffee shop down the street?"

Ray's jaw went slack. She wasn't kidding. "Um."

"Go around the back and wait for me to open the basement door," she whispered. "Your father's asleep."

She closed the door in his face and Ray stared at it a moment. The taxi's taillights disappeared around a corner.

Too late to change the plot now, Ray.

The old man was still laughing at him.

His mother let him in the back door. It wasn't quite the same basement he remembered. The bicycles had always been stored by the washing machine. Instead of three bicycles, there was one and it was a girl's bike.

Martha embraced him, squeezed hard and didn't want to let go. "It's been too long!"

Ray stared at the bicycle hanging on the wall. "Is that your bike, Mom?"

She broke the embrace. "You haven't been home in three years and you're asking about my bike?"

"Where's mine and Dad's?"

"Don't you remember? You took yours with you," she said. "And Dad hasn't had a bike in years."

"Since when?"

"Since...I don't know. What does it matter? Raymond, are you still on drugs? You look terrible. And your clothes — "

"It matters. Please, tell me."

"We hardly ever hear from you and you show up in the middle of — "

Ray seized his mother's forearms. "When did Dad last ride a bike? Think!"

"Boston," she said. "Not since Boston."

"You, me and Dad used to ride our bikes down to the beach every Sunday morning. That was the ritual. We did it in Boston and we kept it going as soon as we moved out here."

"You are on drugs," she said.

Ray released her arms and she rubbed the places where his fingers had dug in.

"Sorry, Mom."

"What's gotten into you?"

"It's not drugs. Wait — "

Ray brushed past her, farther into the basement. The sunken living room was just as he'd remembered it. *Except....*

Ray surveyed the room. The old plaid chair and matching couch he recognized from Boston were still there. He'd often fallen asleep on that couch as a little kid as his father watched the news each night. It was hard to imagine now, but that ratty old couch had been their good furniture once. Now it had been relegated to the sunken living room, out of sight.

It took Ray a few moments to sort out what was missing. "Where are my soccer trophies?"

"Raymond, you never played soccer."

"Not since Boston when I was ten or so, right?"

"You started at age seven. You used to love it. I guess those trophies are boxed up in storage somewhere. What is this about, Raymond?"

"I never played soccer in California?"

"No."

"And you don't remember me ever riding bikes with you and Dad?"

"For God's sake, Raymond!" When she fell back into the old chair, the springs squeaked.

"Dad and I never got along. Not since summer camp, right? Not since the summer I stayed in Maine."

She stared up at him and nodded. "Sit down and tell me what this is about, son."

"Dad and I don't get along."

"I'm aware."

"We used to."

"A long time ago." She flapped a hand in Ray's direction. "Puberty does that sometimes. Men and sons get competitive. The young man sets out to define himself as different from the father and the father wants a little clone. Reaching for immortality, maybe. That's what my therapist said before I couldn't afford a paid friend, anymore."

"No, Mom. It wasn't just puberty."

His mother fixed him with a steady gaze. "Raymond, if this is another lecture from you about what an asshole your father is, I know. I live with him. He's a moody bugger given to rage. But he's mellowed since you left. I hope you've mellowed, too. God knows, you guys had some awful fights and that wasn't all his doing. Ken may be an asshole sometimes, Raymond, but he's *my* asshole. Uh...that came out wrong. But if you'd give him another chance, you'd see he's not just an asshole. He's a badass. That's what I liked about him when we met. Seems unfair to complain about it now."

"And what if I told you he murdered a man in cold blood on my last day of summer camp, Mom?"

"I'd say that was manslaughter at worst and he was trying to protect you. He was a hero that day and you never once said thank you."

Ray stared at his mother, his jaw slack. "You knew?"

"Of course, I knew. This is all old hat."

"It's still kind of new hat to me, Mom."

Ray sat on the couch. He wanted to sleep and retreat.

"Your father and I have been married a lot of years. How could you think I wouldn't know? You *know* I knew. Honestly, Raymond! Stop trying us and judging us. At least in a real court of law, they can only find you guilty once. For the last time, Ken told me what happened and that knowledge saved our marriage."

"What?"

"We sent you so far away to summer camp so we could work things out. Things were shaky that summer. When you came back, you were a moody little bugger, too, just like your father. You wouldn't have anything to do with him. But he told me the truth. Despite our troubles, he trusted me with the truth and I saw him for the man he is. Your father was only trying to protect you from a predator that day. You felt guilty and pushed us away, I suppose... but it wasn't your fault, Raymond. You must know that by now. Do you?"

The way she said it, Ray wasn't sure that his mother believed he was blameless. Ray stood and paced the small room. He felt like he was at sea — *a black sea,* came a whisper at the back of his mind. He had no light to steer by.

"I'm not guilty of anything."

"Because you were the victim."

"The victim?"

"I've read up on this. Pedophiles befriend their victims. You were just a little boy. Whatever happened between you and that man was not your fault, son. Whatever happened, we love you."

"Pedophile?" If he'd had sex with himself that day, it would have been masturbation. Ray almost let out a laugh, but it would have come out high and giddy and he couldn't share the joke with his mother. Instead, Ray asked, "Did Dad tell you I was molested at camp?"

"No," a voice spoke behind him. Ray turned to find his father standing at the foot of the basement stairs. "You told me that."

And the Man in the Moon opened the door to memory. The thing in charge — It — let Ray remember the lie. The lie was easier than the truth. The truth would have put him in an insane asylum certainly, and possibly put his father in jail.

Ray had protected his father, too. He thought the lies had kept his parents together.

"Are you in trouble, Raymond?" His father looked down at his torn clothes. Not all the blood had washed away. "You seem like you're in deep."

Ray shivered. The shakes took over his body and he began to cry. "Up to my neck, yeah."

"How can we help?" Martha asked. "You know from experience, we'll do whatever we can."

"There's a bad man. He's threatened me and he's stolen my...he's stolen my life, my *identity*. I don't know how to find him, but I can't go to the police and he's got to be stopped. I can't tell you more than that. Not without putting you in danger."

His mother nodded. "History repeats itself." She looked to her husband. "He needs us."

"I have to find this man. He'll tip the police that I did something bad, just to keep me away. But I didn't do it. It's something he did! I have to find him fast before this gets worse! There's just no way to find him."

Ken Bradley shrugged. "I know a guy."

"Who do you know, Dad?"

"Call him Skip."

"A guy named Skip can help me find a bad guy?"

"Sure. Skip is good. His last name is Tracer."

"His name is Skip Tracer? Really?"

"No, Ray," he father said. "Not really. Don't be an idiot."

"I'm a work in progress, Dad."

"Stop screwing around, Ray."

Wallflower

"Okay."

41

Skip Tracer's real name was Victor Morin. Ray's father knew Victor since moving to California. Ken Bradley managed several properties and apartment buildings. Victor had worked for landlords all over Los Angeles. When tenants tried midnight moves to get out of paying rent and damages, Victor tracked them down and got them to pay up. Victor was out of skip tracing deadbeats and into the nightclub business now. However, Ken still had his private number.

When his father handed him the phone, Ray stared at it for a moment. What could he say that wouldn't make him sound insane.

"Hello?" Behind the deep voice on the phone, Ray could hear the thump of a beat. The music wasn't in his head. It was something funky with not enough treble to balance it out. Ray's head only played good music.

"Who am I talking to? Ken? You still there?"

"This is Ray. Ken's son."

"Yeah? Whassup, Ray?"

"I need to find a guy."

"Like I told your dad, mostly I manage nightclubs now. I help guys and girls find each other. And guys and guys. And girls and girls. I do it with techno and lasers." His laugh made Ray feel more miserable.

"I need to find a bad guy."

"Chillax. I can find anybody, kid, especially bad guys. They leave a trail."

Can you find people who drop through trap doors in time?

"Ray? You still there? Who am I looking for?"

"He's an older man. Late 50s, early 60s. Tall, with a long beard."

"Okay. We're narrowing it down. Got a name?"

"Arnold Martin. But I don't think that's his real name."

"Last known address?"

Ray was stumped. His last known address hadn't happened yet. At least he didn't think so. "Not sure. He could have been in and out of mental hospitals, though. Or homeless shelters."

"Okay. Maybe I'll start with Men's missions and work my way up. Last known job?"

"He said he was a teacher for a short time. Taught mathematics. He's really into math. Then a series of short-term, low-paying jobs."

"Drifter?"

"Kind of, yeah." *Time drifter.*

"Any known aliases?"

"The Wizard."

"He into pinball or something?"

"No, like I said. Math. As in math whiz."

"Okay. Weird. Anything else?"

"He might be kind of dangerous."

Victor laughed. "Good. He's probably got a

record."

"I hadn't thought of that."

"It's all about knowing which rocks to turn over. The more people do, the easier it is. That's why I don't do this anymore. It's only going to get easier. I see the writing on the wall. More Internet, connectivity...soon, nobody will need skip tracers. It's like typing teachers. Who needs 'em when you've got Mavis Beacon on the computer showing you how?"

Ray wasn't in the mood to chat. "Can you find him, though? I've got to find him fast."

"I'll call you back when I have something."

Ray hung up and his mother hugged him. Then, to his surprise, his father hugged him, too.

Group hug! Oh, God! "I've got to get out of these clothes," Ray said.

"Your room is just as you left it, Ray," his mother said. "I've got some boxes in there and I've made it into a bit of a sewing room, but just move that stuff aside. Why don't you get some sleep? Things will look better in the morning."

By sunrise, Ray thought, *that bum who wanted to be a hero will have talked to police and my sketch and description will be all over the news.*

"It'll be okay," his father told him. "Victor's good."

"It's almost midnight. How good could he be finding anyone at this hour?"

The phone rang. It was Victor Morin. "I have the information you're looking for. Come get it."

Before Ray left his parents, they both hugged him. Ken held on a little longer and whispered in Ray's ear, "Victor has a temper. Be careful around him. No stupid jokes. Take him seriously. Take everything more seriously."

"It does seem like the universe is pushing me away from life as a comedian," Ray admitted.

"Shoulda been a doctor."

"I would have been a terrible doctor."

"Bad doctors make good money, too."

"Bye, Dad."

* * *

The nightclub was called Burnt for a reason. It was a church that had been destroyed by fire and then minimally repaired. Ray's internal music source was busy composing opera. As he stepped out of the cab, he felt the techno beat in his chest. The fuzzy woofers made Ray crave the opportunity to sit at a piano again and lose himself to his own music.

Ray got boos and cat calls as he walked to the head of the line. The lighting around the frame of the door was nothing more than strings of Christmas lights. Out front, two huge spotlights pointed to the sky, painting the cityscape in a slow, endless figure eight.

A big bouncer dressed in a Clippers jersey stood out front of a red velvet rope. His jersey was almost ample enough to serve Ray as a blanket. Over that he wore a black vest that sparkled. Beneath the vest was the visible bulge of a shoulder harness and handgun. The bouncer looked Ray up and down and frowned.

Ray wore tennis shoes, acid wash jeans and a plaid shirt with pearl buttons. The bouncer did not approve. "Who you supposed to be and what are you doin' out here in front of my place?"

"I'm supposed to be on the list. Ray Bradley."

"I don't care who you are. You coming into my club dressed like you're going to a hootenanny? See this church? It's a club, but it's still *my* church! Look down that line. See these girls in short, silver, yummy dresses lookin' all fine like superheroes? How you gonna come into my club dressed like a rodeo clown?"

"When I moved out I took the clothes I liked with me. This is what was left."

"I don't want your life story, man! I want you to go get yourself a leather jacket, decent shoes and some self-respect!"

"Victor sent for me."

"Victor sent for you?"

"That's what I said."

"Well, alright."

Ray paused a moment as the big man unclipped the velvet rope from its post. The people in line behind him booed louder as Ray leaned in close to the bouncer. "Dude," he said. "I'm thinking about what you said."

"Yeah?"

"Please, don't be a dick. I'm having a rough day and whatever clipboard power trip you got going on —"

The big man grabbed Ray by the collar. "Man, I let you in! What's your problem?"

"I'm seeing about growing a spine," Ray said.

The bouncer hauled him back. That saved Ray's life. He heard the report of the pistol nearby and the whine of the bullet as it ricocheted off stone. A woman in line screamed. The crowd ran.

Ray cowered before the bouncer, confused. The big man's eyes were huge. His mouth dropped open and his body shook as more shots rang out.

The bouncer fell forward on Ray like a tree. Ray squirmed, but the man was dead weight, at least three-hundred pounds. When he looked up, he saw the Wizard reloading a little pistol.

"Arnold! What are you doing?"

The Wizard paused. "I'm trying to kill you, you idiot."

"Why?"

"I went through the wall again! It's getting easier! But when I did, I saw you and I in a hotel room and you were stopping me!"

Ray struggled to push the bouncer off him but it was no use. He squirmed more and managed to work his hand under the big man's vest.

"I can't have you stop me, Ray! My mission is far too important for one man to stop me. I'm very sorry, but I'm going to have to kill you now!"

Ray pushed and pulled and finally yanked the bouncer's pistol free.

The Wizard lined up his shot, aiming for Ray's head.

Ray couldn't aim, but he managed to get the pistol up enough to squeeze the trigger. The black vest ripped open as Ray shot through it. He missed.

The Wizard fled unharmed. For the second time in one day, Ray was bathed in a stranger's blood.

42

People poured out of the club like it was a broken beehive. One of them paused to look down at Ray. He was a lean, muscular man with a gray buzz cut. He pulled the bouncer off Ray and rolled the dead man over to his back.

The man reached to the bouncer's neck to check for a pulse, but changed his mind. The dead man's eyes stared, unblinking, at the sky, into the big spotlight's lazy figure eight.

Lazy eight. The symbol for infinity, Ray thought. *Good luck in the Beyond. I hope you find something out there. And thanks for being my human shield.*

"You Ken's son?"

"How'd you know?"

"You're a younger version of him. And you're late, just like Ken."

"You must be Victor."

Victor nodded and pulled Ray to his feet. "My car's parked around the block. Let's go."

Victor drove a Porsche. He pulled away from the curb slowly, not wanting to get the attention of all the police cruisers converging on his club. Lights and sirens, it seemed, were everywhere.

"The dead man's name was Wayne," Victor said. "He was a pretty funny guy."

"A friend?"

"An employee. We didn't hang out together, but I enjoyed him. Never thought he'd go like that. Our clientele is very uptown. Shouldn't have happened."

"Wayne saved me," Ray said. "He didn't mean to, but he did."

"How did you get mixed up with the nut with the gun?"

"It's a long story."

"Shorten it."

"That was the Wizard."

"I guessed that. How'd he find you?"

Ray guessed that a time traveler that could go back and forth easily would have plenty of opportunities to track down anyone trying to find him. Arnold Martin might have gotten caught once or even twice and then returned through a wall to get Ray instead of the other way around.

This might not have been the first time Wayne had been killed and Ray wouldn't necessarily know it. Time loops and echoes were too tricky for him to be sure. However, Ray was sure of one thing: it seemed the only way to stop Arnold Martin was to kill him. All prisons had walls.

"Ray? I asked you a question. How'd he find you at my club?"

"I don't know. He happened to me."

"Bullshit. People make bad choices. What were yours? How'd you end up anywhere near this guy? You owe him money? Sleep with his wife?"

"I tried to kill myself."

"Do you still want to kill yourself?"

"No. I want to kill the Wizard."

"Good. Me, too," Victor said. "His real name isn't Arnold Martin. It's Martin Arnold."

"That shows a surprising lack of imagination."

"It was enough to fool you. Besides, your Wizard teaches math, not creative writing."

Ray ignored that and turned to watch the street lights of LA flash by as Victor pressed the accelerator harder. The engine growled and broiled under the hood.

"You sure this is the right guy we're going after?" Ray asked.

"Seventy percent sure. We'll look him in the eye before we blow his head off. How's that?"

"What did you find out about him?"

"He's a math professor at UC Davis. Taught in the engineering department."

"What makes you think he's the right guy?"

"He was pinched for uttering death threats to students."

"That does sound like him."

"The charges got dropped but he's on stress leave. He's about to get more stressed."

Ray cradled the bouncer's nickel-plated 38 between his knees, feeling its lethal weight. He still hadn't killed anyone. Not yet. That knowledge and the arias playing in his head made him feel pure. He doubted he'd stay that way much longer.

* * *

The address Victor Morin had on the Wizard was in West Hollywood.

Victor found a parking space after circling the block twice. When he climbed out, he pulled a sledge hammer from the floor behind the driver's seat. He groped under the driver's seat again and came out with a pistol. He checked the clip, worked the slide and slipped it into the waistband of his pants.

"What's the hammer for?"

"That's my master key. Unlocks any door. I thought my skip tracing days were over. I shouldn't have answered the phone tonight. If I had, Wayne would still be trying to pick up girls at the club."

"Sorry."

"You should be."

They found the house, a small dilapidated bungalow on North Harper Avenue. All the windows were dark. By the reach of the yellow streetlights, it was clear the place was in need of a paint job. White paint peeled back to reveal gray.

"I'll go around the back," Victor said. "If he runs out the front, shoot his ass. Think you can manage that?"

"I think so."

"You think so or you know so?"

"Let's find out before the urge for me to go home and pull the covers over my head becomes overwhelming."

"Shoot straight, do not hesitate and do not let him get away, Ray, or I might shoot you myself. I am not happy with you, either, right now!" Victor jogged around the back of the house. Ray stepped to the front porch and listened.

A tinkle of glass.

A sound that might be a door bursting in.

A light came on in the front of the house.

Two gunshots.

Ray ran at the front door and threw all his weight against it and bounced off. His right shoulder ached and burned and buzzed so badly that Ray had to switch the pistol to his left hand to keep from dropping it. His ribs went from dull aching to a sharp pains.

He returned to the front door. He heard something inside the house get knocked over. A struggle was going on inside.

Ray ran around to the back and, too late, entered the dim living room. The room's only illumination was a lamp on the floor. Victor Morin and Martin Arnold each held the handle of the sledge, trying to pull it from the other's grasp.

If not for the fact that Morin bled from the head and side, he would have easily overpowered the old man.

"Shoot him, Ray! Shoot his ass!"

All Ray saw were two silhouettes against the light cast from the fallen lamp.

The Wizard turned his head and the light caught his face. Ray raised the gun, less sure with his left hand.

"Don't do it!" Arnold Martin screamed.

"Stop fighting!" Ray ordered.

The professor stopped pulling at the hammer. Victor Morin didn't. As soon as the math professor let go of the sledge hammer, Morin stepped back, hefting his weapon. He stepped forward in a quick cha-cha and brought the hammer's heavy head down on his opponent's skull.

The professor's head caved in, as if a cereal bowl had materialized in the topography of his skull. The math professor collapsed to the floor. He might not have been dead yet, but before Ray could stop him, Morin brought the hammer down again.

Martin Arnold's skull was a blood and brain piñata.

"No!" Ray cried out. "*No!*" The sudden corpse was not the Wizard. "Th-that was the *wrong man!*"

"What?" Morin's face drained white.

Ray peered at the dead man's face. The beard was shorter. This was a younger version of Martin Arnold.

Right house, wrong timeline. Or was it? The rules of time travel weren't static. Maybe the man who had shot at him and killed Wayne had popped out and back in to commandeer this man's body.

Ray closed his eyes and took a deep breath. "Time travel needs some solid rules."

"What?" Victor turned toward Ray and looked like he might attack him next.

Ray let his breath hiss out between his teeth slowly. His thoughts were so disordered and his panic ran so high, he could hear no music. "Wait... wait. No. This is okay."

"What?" Morin repeated, his voice shaky.

"If this is the younger version of the Wizard from this timeline, then there can be no older version. Kill the younger iteration, the older iteration gets canceled out. Maybe. If so, we're still good here."

"What the actual fuck are you babbling about?"

Ray looked to the skip tracer. "The old man is dead here. Like he never existed. He never got older than when he was this guy. It's going to be okay. You got him, Mr. Morin. Thank you. I hope the Time Worm is happy with the sacrifice it got."

Ray shook his head, bewildered.

"It's over, is what I'm saying. Your friend the bouncer is alive again, I think. Wayne might be alive!"

"What kind of stupid are you, boy?"

"I'm not sure, but, if this is the young version, then...yeah, it must be over. Could be. Must — "

The older version of the Wizard opened the front door, house key in one hand and the little pistol in the other.

43

Time froze for a moment.

The Wizard looked almost as surprised as Victor. The skip tracer looked at the old man and mystification spread across his blood-spattered face. "Loop," the Wizard said.

The Wizard shot Victor once. The skip tracer shouted in pain as he twisted and dove away.

Ray shot at the Wizard as the time traveler charged at him. Ray's shots went wide. Chunks of the door splintered but Ray's attacker was unharmed.

Martin Arnold knocked Ray to the floor as he barreled past and disappeared through a door and downstairs.

Ray pulled himself up using the arm of a chair and ran to the couch. The bullet that almost drilled through Victor Morin's head had creased his scalp instead. There was a lot of blood, but the wound was superficial. He had two holes in his side, however. Blood pooled under him.

Morin stared up into Ray's eyes. "Go get 'em, cowboy. It's your rodeo now." He smiled weakly. "If anybody asks, tell them those were my last words.

That'd be cool."

Sirens sounded in the distance. Ray glanced out the window to see a small crowd had gathered on yards across the street. Red, white and blue strobes pulsed across the neighborhood as the police arrived.

"Somebody reported gunfire, Victor. Help is on the way!"

"Go. I'll wait here," Victor said.

Ray snarled and ran downstairs after the Wizard. He had his pistol out in front of him, holding it in two shaky hands, ready to fire. However, by the time he hit the bottom of the stairs, he realized Martin Arnold must have escaped through a wall.

He checked the whole basement as quickly as he could. His brain, he knew, was slow compared to the Wizard and he couldn't trust it.

In the basement, between a freezer and pool table, Ray found an empty chair pointed at a concrete wall. A square in orange chalk was drawn upon it, just big enough for a crouching man to step through.

Ray tucked the pistol in his pants pocket and sat in the chair.

The police would burst through the doors at any moment. They would find him in a house with a body and a wounded man. He'd have no answers to their questions. The authorities probably had a description of him from the murder scene at Heavy's by now. He had to get out of there, but Ray's experience with going through walls was slight.

The bludgeoned professor was clearly younger than the Wizard Ray knew, and yet the older man remained alive to trip through time. Ray couldn't understand that. Aside from being smarter than Ray, the Wizard had found a way to make the trip through walls faster.

Maybe he had the key to the Gates of Perception. It had taken considerable effort for Ray to come through.

I'm so screwed, he thought, *they're going to have to invent a new word for how screwed I am. If I were a faster thinker, I would have escaped out the back door instead of getting trapped down here.*

He heard the *whomp, whomp, whomp* of a helicopter flying low over the house. There was nowhere to run. He had to make his way through to the Beyond.

Ray closed his eyes. A single, hot tear slipped down his right cheek as he tried to breathe deeper and slower. He should have spent more time meditating in yoga class instead of trying to bang Marla.

"Hello? Anybody in here? LAPD!" They were already in the house. He heard their heavy footfalls as the police officers yelled to each other. He heard the staccato of radio chatter as commands to set up a perimeter were issued.

"I'm going to end up in an insane asylum, just like the Wizard wanted when he cast his magic math spell on me," Ray told the wall. *I wonder if they'll beat me into paralysis here or later?*

He was short on time, but he was desperate. Ray opened his eyes and stared at the wall.

Take me now.

I need to see the Man in the Moon.

I need answers. Please!

Ray guessed if the Man in the Moon was the God of Time, that was the only prayer he had time for.

And, like all prayers in Ray's experience, nothing

happened.

No cracks opened.

No gates unlocked.

No black water reached out to pull him to an audience with the Man in the Moon.

Ray closed his eyes, waited for the police and listened to the beautiful music that only he could hear. The music was soft and light and he could feel it in his chest. It made him sit up straight. The music made him warm and calm. A little smile formed on his lips.

Eyes still closed, Ray raised both arms, his hands open. Ray was far too tired to come up with a story that would make sense to the hard men in uniform.

"Hello, young fella." It was the old man's voice.

"Hm?"

"Young man," the voice came again. "I suggest you come with me if you don't want to get caught."

Ray opened his eyes. The orange square was swirl of energy. An old man with curly hair and dark eyes peered out at him. "Better hurry if you're going to take a trip on the Reality Train, Ray. Ting-a-ling and all aboard!"

"Somebody's downstairs!" a cop yelled.

"Shake a leg, as we used to say."

"Really?"

The old man gave him a friendly smile. He had a kind face. "C'mon in. The water's warm."

The police crept down the basement stairs.

That was okay as far as Ray Bradley was concerned. He'd already disappeared, safely, through the wall and into the Beyond with Kurt Vonnegut.

44

The fine desert sand beneath their feet was red as blood. The orange sun hung low, so bright it seemed the clouds were aflame.

"So? How do you feel?"

"Confused."

"Are you confused normally, or is that the usual fuzz of the quantum wave?"

"Both, probably. And a bit dizzy. This is...wow. It's a real honor to meet you. This is amazing."

"I don't think Wayne and Victor and Professor Arnold would agree."

Ray looked around. They were alone in a desert, but he was neither hot nor cold. He took a deep breath and waited for the dizziness to pass.

The writer stood aside and waited in silence.

"Thanks for getting me out of there."

"Oh, don't thank me yet. The thing in charge...well, it demands sacrifice, you know. No free lunches, as they used to say, though a free lunch now and then is as good for the giver as it is for the receiver."

"I can't believe I'm talking to *the* Kurt Vonnegut!"

"You're not."

Ray stared at him. He had the same kind eyes and the hint of a smile. His guide sure looked like Kurt Vonnegut, if a little younger than when Ray last saw him. Ray had watched Vonnegut on television. He was the only author of fiction Ray could remember appearing on *The Daily Show with Jon Stewart*. It was for the release of *Man Without a Country*, shortly before his death.

"It's occurring to you slowly that you must be talking to a ghost."

"Uh...yeah."

"Now it's occurring to you that this can't be happening to you at all."

"I guess."

"Catch up, Mr. Bradley. Time is short. Everyone on Earth reaches their deathbed and says, 'I can't believe this is happening to me.' As if they're the first person in history to die. Everyone dies surprised. The ride seems to end quickly even though we are warned well ahead that, looking back, life is a quick roller coaster ride that plows into dirt when you hit the sudden stop. That attitude suggests a lack of compassion for the dying, in my opinion." The old man sighed. "No matter how cliche the truth becomes, it seems we can't learn the lesson and value life unless we're dying."

"Sorry. Could you explain how you are not *the* Kurt Vonnegut?"

"Sure. That's the perfect way to phrase that question and you arrived at it by accident, if you believe in accidents." The old man grinned. "I'm not *the* Kurt Vonnegut. No one is. I'm *a* Kurt Vonnegut. I don't suppose you thought to pack a pack of menthols? I haven't smoked since before I died. I would have smoked on my deathbed if they had let me. What did they think they were saving me from?"

"Uh, no...sorry. I don't smoke."

"Just some interdimensional humor, there. I have new hobbies."

"Here? What do you do in the desert?"

"First I thought sandcastles, but you really need moisture for that. Mostly, I think. It's less painful here than I've found it to be elsewhere. This is the Nexus. It's in the Beyond."

"Beyond what?"

"Beyond the gears that turn the multiverse. Beyond the big Xerox machine in the infinite sky. It's really the only quiet spot there is. I opted out of reincarnating. I've chewed all I can swallow. Let's walk as we talk, Ray. Places to know, people to knee."

They walked around a dune and a flat expanse awaited them. Ray could detect no end to the desert, only sifting sands in a stiff wind. "How far do we have to go?"

"Geography is all relative. People fly across the world to climb a mountain and call that an accomplishment. They were higher in altitude on the plane flight over. Where were we?"

"You were going to explain how you aren't Kurt Vonnegut."

"I'm a dilution. You are, too. We all are. Doesn't make you less special, but it does make us numerous."

"I'm confused."

"That's established. Asked and answered, councilor, and so stipulated! Don't repeat yourself. What surprises me is your aspiration to be a writer for television. Too many cooks amplify the sloth. To be honest, son, you don't strike me as all that funny. Meant for other things, maybe. I don't see you as a comedian."

"I wrote for game shows."

"I don't see that, either."

"Are you saying I was supposed to be in advertising?"

"Oh, no, I wouldn't tell anyone a thing so cruel. I worked in advertising. Never believed in cruelty to animals so why be so mean to people with that vocation? Selling stuff to each other is one of those things you get tired of long before you die. No, Ray, I'm talking about your big picture."

"Movies?"

"Bigger."

"Video games?"

"Maybe you better shut up and let me talk, Ray."

"Mm'kay."

"Everything you've ever known is a metaphor for something else. Just like a book. You look deeper, themes emerge. For instance, all around us now? All that shifting sand? That's a metaphor, perhaps so on-the-snout as to be clumsy."

"You better lay it out for me."

"Shifting sands?"

"Does it mean...Time?"

The old man shook his head. "*Buzz.* Try again. Shifting clouds? Suggest anything?"

"Clouds are always changing shapes so... permutations and combinations?"

"Closer, but *buzz!* Still a miss and points off for regurgitation! I'll tell you plain. Lots of tiny little granules rubbing against each other? That's us. All of us. All that ever were and all that ever shall be."

"Humans."

"They aren't all worthy of the name, but yes."

"What about them?"

"You have a common misconception that's throwing a wrench in the gears that turn the world, Ray. You're hooked up on time travel. I'm sympathetic and not judging. I was snagged in that snare myself. I seem to remember one time I got writer's cramp. I'd been writing longhand in my little writing shack. A bit of writer's block would have saved me some pain from my hand to my elbow."

"I don't — "

"Pardon me," the old man said. "I was remembering the wrong life. I wrestled my dogs a lot so I rarely suffered the affliction of writer's cramp. That happened when I was Clemens."

"As in Twain? Mark Twain! Holy shit! You were *the* Mark Twain, too?"

"No. I wasn't. I was *a* Mark Twain. I was *a* Kurt Vonnegut. Generally, we're all supposed to stay in our lanes and not skip across the multiverse. You and your friend are breaking conventions in interesting ways, though."

Ray stopped. He looked back. His tracks were already covered. There was no way to find his way back. The flat expanse offered no measure of progress. It felt like he was walking on a sand treadmill. He turned to his companion.

"You were about to call me a nasty name, Ray."

"I was."

"And now you won't."

"Only because I don't know where I am or how to get out of this place. I'd be happier if you stopped talking in riddles, Mr. Vonnegut."

"Call me Junior."

"Okay. Junior? Eh, I don't know if I can do that, sir. Can you stop talking in riddles, though?"

"Nope. Have to talk in riddles. You wouldn't understand the math. Neither would I, for that matter, and I remember being okay at arithmetic. But this place? This is where the math meets the poetry. You'll have a better shot at understanding using poetry."

"Just tell me what's going on, please."

"You're stuck in the idea of the universe. *Uni* meaning one. Verse, from *versus*, meaning to turn. But everything that is? Think of it as a coy poem. It doesn't reveal itself all at once. Only, it's not one poem, you see. It's many verses within many poems. It's the *multiverse*. All of it, all those permutations and combinations the Wizard told you about? It's all going on at once, more or less."

"How does this relate to time travel?"

"It doesn't. You haven't traveled through time, Ray. You've been hopping dimensions. Imagine this desert, with all its shifting grains of sand, each one a life. Now try to imagine an infinite number of deserts — you can't, no one can, but imagine a lot, anyway. Imagine all those deserts of experience stacked up as far as you can see and beyond. Sometimes one of those grains finds a way from one plane of existence to another. He or she might even think they traveled through time. He or she might be an idiot carried on the quantum winds."

"And I'm one of those little grains of sand."

"You're one of the idiots, yeah. Funny thing about sand," Vonnegut said. "The grains all look alike. It can gum up the works of the gears of a tank or it can polish things. It can even turn into glass...if you burn it."

"Great."

"Part of our misunderstanding is the use of the words 'planes of existence.' It's all wheels within wheels within wheels, ad infinitum. So when you went through the wall and skipped into the space between, you got a glimpse of the Reality Train under a full moon."

The old man smiled. "When you stepped off your wheel, you stepped into another dimensional plane that happened to line up with your heart's desire. You wanted a do-over so you got to go back and try to set your twelve-year-old self on the right path."

"But you're saying it wasn't my twelve-year-old self."

"Your heart was in the right place, son, but no that wasn't you telling you to lay off the donuts. That was you telling another child who looked and sounded exactly like you at that age on another wheel of existence. It only looked like time travel because the other Raymond was from another wheel that lined up with yours."

"I'm going to need a flowchart."

"Nah, it's simple really. Imagine you are revolving on a stage. If you step off the stage at one point in the revolution, you get off and there's a twelve-year-old you sitting in the front row. Suppose you hop back on the stage and wheel around for another turn or two. You get off and you're looking at another you. Maybe the seat is empty and a whole new construct pops into existence and you get to take it over. Maybe not."

"How many seats are there?"

"No one knows. If I were to say an infinite number, I'm not being a smart ass."

"But why are there so many of us? Why so confusing? This isn't very user-friendly."

"To hold a proper experiment, you have to have a lot of subjects, Ray."

"I don't understand."

"You probably won't, so I suggest you just go with it. It's like when your loving sister or mother insists you have more coleslaw, but it's the vinegar kind and you want the creamy kind. Still, it's your sister, so you go with it and smile."

"I'm not happy with that answer."

"Okay," Vonnegut said. "Like the politician said to the voters, if you don't like those convictions, I have others."

"Tell me."

"The experiment is big because...well, you know how it is when you are walking along and you get to a corner and you could turn right or left?"

"Yes."

"You have to choose, so choose."

Ray stammered. "I-I...uh, right. No. Left!"

"Take it easy, Ray. It's just an illustration. You chose left. The experiment is to find out what happens if you turned right."

"I'm still lost."

"You're right here and that's fine. Now imagine the experiment is for every choice we could make. Left? Right? Invest in Coca Cola? Have a Pepsi? Fall in love with her but marry someone else. The experiment goes deep into every permutation and combination."

"But why? What's the experiment out to prove?"

"That gets meta."

"Tell me."

"The point to the experiment is to find out if there's a point to the experiment. We're rats running through an infinite labyrinth and whoever set up the experiment is watching and taking notes."

"God?"

"There you go again. Could be anybody with power. Having the power doesn't make it a deity. Could be a really powerful nerd. That's my bet. All the weirdness of life, I think it's a crap shoot. Often we make life into a load of shit. But the experimenter might be interested in seeing more variables."

"What are you saying?"

"In one short declarative sentence?"

"That would be best."

"Life's not fair, but we're supposed to try to make it that way."

45

"I'm dead, aren't I? This is it." Ray sat in the sand. He put his face in his hands and squeezed, trying to feel something. He felt no headache pain. He hit himself in the face as hard as he could. "Ow. Okay, that hurt."

Vonnegut laughed. "You wanted it to, so yes, if you want to do something stupid, that's up to you. I don't recommend it."

"Is this heaven or hell?"

"Don't get caught up in that poltroonery."

"Meaning?"

"Don't be so pusillanimous."

"You're just fucking with me now, Junior," Ray said miserably. "It's not nice."

The old man laughed harder. "Sorry. It's not my way to be obtuse. I was trying to be acute."

"Oh, *God*."

"Don't be upset, young man. You're worried about heaven and hell, and yet here you are, apparently still enjoying consciousness on some level and having a delightful conversation with one of your favorite writers. You seem to be forgetting I'm adorable. And dead people aren't as confused as you are."

"Sorry. I forget my manners when I'm dead."

"Like Time, Dead is relative. I knew a bunch of guys who worked in advertising and publishing. They were all dead at their desks long before anyone put them in a fancy planter and stuck 'em in the ground."

"Funny."

"Something I'm famous for. Do you know how many graduation speeches I gave?"

"No."

"I forget, but it was a lot. As I remember, I was quite a hit."

"Great."

"You're upset and that's upsetting. Let me set your mind at ease." The old man stuck out a hand. "But, please, let's keep moving. Places to flow, people to sneeze."

Ray allowed the old man to help him to his feet and they set off toward the setting sun again.

"You say you aren't Kurt Vonnegut. Then you say you are."

"Well...on the big scheme of the machine, we are all one. Ego divisions tend to be our iotas of consciousness flattering ourselves. We're dust motes in a sunbeam. We're part of something bigger. However, on the tiny scale, I'm one of many Kurt Vonneguts. There are as many of us as there are choices. Personally, I think the whole free will experiment was ill-conceived when you see some of the choices people make, but there you are. That's people for you. I imagine many of my doppelgangers did not survive the war and never wrote

Slaughterhouse Five. There are probably some Ray Bradleys out on the eternal wheel who are telling jokes at the Playboy Mansion, if *Playboy* is at all relevant in those dimensions. Come to think of it, it was on the wane long before I left. Never mind."

"In all these dimensions, am I rich somewhere?"

"Undoubtedly, in one universe, anyway."

"Maybe I could visit that dimension."

"Possibly, but it could be quite a long search. There are so few really rich people, though television would lead us to believe otherwise. Statistically, you're probably very poor everywhere else. Everyone is a fan of reincarnation, but few think of the risk of coming back as a Third World starving child who dies of First World Neglect."

"I should have gone to a dimension where I was rich."

"If you run into him, you might have to fight the guy who thinks he's you. That could get awkward. Or maybe you'd overshoot the runway and end up in his body but he's got stomach cancer. The whole body snatcher thing is a neat little sub-routine in the experiment to see how dimension hoppers handle the egregious. Ever notice how so many people die in terrible circumstances? That's why. Part of the experiment. The Nerd is watching and taking notes to see if it was all worth it...he's quite a voyeur, isn't he?"

"I don't, uh..."

"Don't dwell on it. Infinity is so common a word, no one thinks about what it really means. Lots of gurus on Earth talk about infinite possibilities but they only limit themselves to tiny imaginations and a few easy answers."

The orange sun seemed closer, but lower in the sky now. Night was coming. The old man picked up his pace again, pumping his arms harder. "The last time I marched, heh...well, I don't have to tell you. We're still all soldiers. Many of us are stuck in the Comfortable Couch Army but we're all still in the service. If we still called it the service instead of the military, maybe we'd think of it differently. Feeding village kids powdered milk has to be a cheaper and more effective war strategy than bombing it flat and making red mash of everybody."

"Kurt...you didn't really answer me about heaven and hell and I want a straight answer. This doesn't seem like heaven to me. We're not on one of those stages...in one of the regular dimensions, I mean."

Speeding up the pace didn't seem to bother the old man. He spoke without losing breath. "Death is change. You get a turn on new wheels. Recycling. Ultimately, death doesn't matter. Each life is another movie. I wish I'd starred in a porno but — "

"This doesn't sound like you."

"I was writing from a human perspective at the time, Ray. Gimme a break."

"But after all you wrote about the bombing of Dresden and the losses every war imposes? In *Blackbeard* — "

"I know, Ray. I wrote it. I was there."

"Sorry."

"The tragedy is not in the death. Like many people, I was opining about the wrong war. The real tragedy is cruelty. There's still lots of it. That's what matters in the big picture. There's a compassion deficit in all the worlds, Ray, across all the dimensions. Death and taxes aren't constants. Cruelty and cancer are."

"*Cancer* is everywhere?"

"All dimensions I know of, yes."

"For God's sake, why?"

"There's a flaw in the experiment. The fuel that allows for healthy biodiversity also allows for a liver cell to go to your lung and start trying to set up shop as a new liver. Cells grow in an organized way and we say, look! A beautiful baby! Some cells grow in a disorganized way and the doctor tells you that you better sit down to hear the bad news."

"Why allow disorganization?"

"Because the experiment has no point without randomness. If anything can happen, that allows free will and bad choices. If we're to understand the ghost in the machine and grease the gears of existence, we have to be open to new possibilities."

"I always thought the world didn't make sense because people are stupid and God was high."

"That's uncharitable. There is plenty of stupid to go around, but a lot of people are just too busy staying alive to pay attention to what's happening behind the scenes."

"What about my idea that Whoever is in Charge is high all the time?"

"I don't know about that. It might explain a lot, wouldn't it? But don't get too caught up in that God stuff. Just because something is powerful and supernatural doesn't make it God. That sort of thinking can get you off track trying to choose between Loki and Thor. Look, there's math to this, but how are you doing keeping up with the theater in the round metaphor?"

"I think I understand. I think you're saying the Nerd in the Sky is powerful enough to set up the experiment — ”

"But needs to *run* the experiment, anyway. Permutations and combinations. When the number of choices are so astronomical, you need to start with one dimension, watch evolution run its course and see where it all ends up. As the people multiply, though, so do all those combinations and permutations. It's a lot of data. And now you're thinking about Professor Arnold talking to you about pi."

"I was."

"Yeah, well, his explanations aren't all wrong, but they can only get you lost in the nitty gritty."

"Because of my simian brain."

"Primate. We're all primates. We like to think of ourselves as more, but that's just because we appear less hairy." The old man looked down and appeared to consider his hand as if he'd never seen it before. "And our thumbs are quite elegant."

They walked into the sun and Ray found he was squinting against the bright light on red sand. "Where are we going, Kurt?"

"Well, if you aren't too busy, Ray, the multiverse does have a mission for you."

"I thought whoever's in charge worked against us making any changes."

Vonnegut smiled and sighed. "No. That's a misunderstanding, son. When the monkeys start to try to run the zoo, they're liable to make a lot of mistakes, pushing buttons they ought not to and chewing on live electrical wires. That doesn't mean the zookeeper is insane."

"It means we're monkeys...er...primates."

"Well, yes," Vonnegut said, "but we are evolving as

Robert Chazz Chute

we revolve."

"What's my mission?"

"Same as the Wizard. We were heading to a better place but got off the compassion track. Time for a revolution."

"So the Nerd...that's the Man in the Moon, isn't it? What the Wizard called the Time Worm. You know... all these names are confusing."

"That's part of the convergence of so many potentials becoming probabilities. Once you visualize all the strings of time as a spiderweb coming together in the middle...well, it does get confusing. As more data floods in, we'll find more ways to travel through time, I'm sure. That's us, achieving our potential."

"Like that guy who ran the four-minute mile for the first time? You said —

"Roger Bannister, yes. Cracking open perceived limits and paving the way for many more runners after him, fulfilling their potentials — "

"Still kind of confused about the different names, though," Ray said.

Vonnegut shrugged. "All worlds and all times are confusing. The complexity is part of the design. Anyway, 'time worm' is a fanciful and confused reference. A time worm is a visualization of where you go through space-time if you left a trail to show the tracking. Here's a hint: we go to the bathroom a lot. I like your word for the Big Nerd. Man in the Moon is descriptive."

"Thanks."

"What exactly does the Man in the Moon want me to do?"

"Introduce more variables. Get fresh data."

272

"How do I do that?"

"You can start by saving the world."

"All of them?"

"Echoes and ripples, Ray. Echoes start with one sound in the right place. Ripples can start with a single stone thrown into the middle of the pond. Or in this case, the interdimensional vortex at the heart of the labyrinth of multi-universal possibility."

"Jesus."

"Funny, you mention him. Your mission is not the first time this has been attempted, but his mission was a highlight."

"Jesus?"

"John Lennon reached a lot of people, too."

"Wow."

"Yeah. Imagine."

46

The sun fell out of sight and the Man in the Moon rose into view. The moonlight lit their upturned faces as the desert turned black.

Vonnegut recited, "The moon was a ghostly galleon tossed upon cloudy seas."

"*The Highwayman*," Ray said. "My mother read that one to me."

"It's a good one. I always think of it here. I call this place the Oasis of Truth."

"Why?"

"Clarity. This is where visitors get clarity. From here, if you concentrate, you can see forever. This is where we watch the workings of the multiverse. And the rats run the maze."

Ray gazed up at the moon and, with the old man nearby to share the view, he wasn't afraid of the Man in the Moon. "Tell me everything and please, speak plain."

"I'll speak as plainly as I can without lying. Lies are easier to understand, though."

"Are you the reincarnation of Mark Twain?"

Vonnegut smiled. "Yes. In the dimension you and I

shared. In other dimensions, the other Kurts are not reincarnations of Samuel Clemens. I like him. He and I are good friends. Sam and I visit sometimes, here in the in-between. All our iterations do. We have a lot in common, as I'm sure you can imagine. The multiverse is very dedicated to biodiversity, so there are many variations. We're all unique in our times and in our existence, playing out our choices on our little stage for an all-seeing audience. Personally, I prefer the dimensions where Sam and I are two different people. Spread us around, I say. Still, scarcity is what makes things valuable, I'm told."

"Yeah, yeah. All life is precious."

"Trite and true, tried and true...but, excuse me," the old man said. "I forgot I was speaking to another who contemplated suicide."

"I didn't just contemplate it. I tried it a couple of times."

"Mm. You need more friends, Ray. A person with more friends will have less inclination to end the ride early."

"I had a best friend, but I didn't choose wisely. He was sleeping with my wife."

"Then you should have made more friends. Eventually you could find some people who would find your wife repulsive, I'm sure." The old man laughed. "No reflection on her. That's just statistics. Some people hated my books, if you can imagine that."

"I wasn't good at making friends."

"No offense, friend, but that sounds lazy. Everyone, *everyone*, can find a friend in this universe. The multiverse is full of too many terrors to face it alone. We're stuck with family, I'll grant you, but everyone gets to go off and make a family of their choosing. Friendship. That's one ship you have to work hard at to sink...unless you're a shit, of course. About your wizard friend — "

"He's not my friend."

"That could change."

"I don't think so. I've seen him do terrible things."

"Soldiers do a few terrible things. I don't care for that sort of math myself, but, hypothetically, what if he were serving a higher purpose to save millions? Billions?"

"I, uh — "

"Never mind. That's for later. I was going to say that your Wizard friend was thinking time rather than geography, clocks instead of maps. Space-time is the fourth dimension, of course, so it takes some doublethink to understand it."

"Of course," Ray said, but he was looking at the stars. Despite the full moon, other galaxies seemed much closer here. The sky was full of flaming galaxies and, the longer he looked, the more he saw.

"Did you know Samuel Clemens and I flirted with suicide?" the old man said. "Sam had a hard time with debt and I...well, sometimes I wondered what the point of everything was."

"The point of everything. That's — "

"The point of the experiment, yes. I'll be interested to see the final results. There may not be a point, you know. Not as far as the experimenter is concerned."

"And what do you think?" Ray asked.

"Best answer I came up with when I was alive was that we're here to fart around."

"And now?"

"Death gives a different perspective. Glad I didn't commit suicide. To find out I was still alive in the afterlife after killing myself would have been a circumstance of some chagrin, to put it mildly."

"First you say the universe is about biodiversity but the multiverse has many of each of us?"

"One per universe. That's one guideline that keeps things a little less crazy complex."

"How do you know when to meet here?"

The old man shrugged his shoulders. "There's a resonance throughout all the planes of existence, Ray. The universe has its own music. That's why many of the variations and combinations are so similar. Most people eat the same few meals every week. We don't expand our choices to meet our full potentials. The epidemiologists might call it homogeneity. The biologists would favor homeostasis. It's all the music of the spheres: harmony. But the multiverse needs some new music to dance to. If the experimenter doesn't get new data, the Big Nerd will shut the experiment down."

"What does that mean?"

"When the Nerd shut down the dinosaur experiment, meteors and climate change were the weapons of choice. There are lots of ways to shut down the experiment, Ray. They're all terrifying. As a race, judging by how we act, I think we're suicidal. The Big Nerd might grant our wish, and soon."

"You're talking about extinction."

"Yep. No more sweet dessert coffees at Starbucks. No more fucking. No more babies. No more fun."

"I'm only one guy. I can't...shouldn't we call in experts or something?"

"I don't think we have time to train Seal Team Six

in suicidal ideation, meditation and the quirky physics of Time."

"But what can I do?"

"Change the equation by adding new data," Vonnegut said. "Do that in one dimension and it echoes and ripples through all the others. Resonance could save the race. We need to keep our rat race running. We're a bio-diverse machine, Ray, but I told you, we're also all one."

"I think I need some drugs to really get this."

"I tried to tell everybody. I'd been through the wall a few times, but...you don't get the big picture until you step back."

"Here? At the Oasis of Truth?"

"That's where it happened for me. Are you getting the signal?"

"All I can think of is the Wizard."

"Yes. The outlier. The world needs outliers. We've always been too obsessed with making everyone normal. Conforming and indoctrination into old ways of thinking isn't going to open us up to new possibilities."

Ray turned to the old man. What had Cenk called him? A disappointed humanist. That's what he looked like now.

"Every system has outliers, Ray. You're one. Martin Arnold is another. Outliers are the point of data that science tries to eliminate, disregard and discard to support a hypothesis. They should spend more time trying to understand the extraordinary rather than negate it."

"The Wizard is my mission, isn't he?"

"No, Ray. He was the test."

"You said people don't travel through time, but he

did! The loop at his house. The Wizard shot Victor. And he tried to kill me!"

"He's a facet of the multiverse, trying to assert homeostasis." Vonnegut put his hand on Ray's arm gently, then squeezed so Ray would tear his gaze away from the rising moon. "The Wizard thinks he's working for the greater good, too, Ray."

"I've seen him shoot four people to death so far. And he tried to sentence me to a wheelchair in an insane asylum."

"To take his friend's place. Friendship. Kinship. Tribalism. Nationalism. You can blind yourself and convince yourself of anything if you think you're doing it for friends, family and country. It gets back to that lack of compassion I was talking about."

"He tried to murder me!"

"You don't know the big picture. He just needs to open up to new possibilities. A lot of people do. That's where you come in."

The Man in the Moon turned and the red desert turned to obsidian. The music Ray thought only he could hear began to play throughout the desert. It was a woman's soprano emerging from the haunting notes of a theremin. A vast orchestra that sounded like wet fingers on wet water glass rims joined in to make the black desert sing.

Vonnegut hummed along and smiled. "That's you, isn't it? I've never heard anything like it. That's beautiful, Ray. Thank you."

Ray looked up to find the face of the Man in the Moon staring back. The massive craters didn't look indifferent or scary anymore. They looked... interested.

You have Our attention, Ray Bradley. Is it time to

tune the machine?

"Yes," Ray said. "I'll try."

What you choose next will resonate through all the realms. We need a new harmonic to adjust the machine.

"Why me?"

Why not you?

Vonnegut patted Ray on the back. "As you know, I'm a free thinker, but there is one biblical poem I like: *To everything there is a season, and a time to every purpose under heaven.* I like the way it ends most: *a time to love, and a time to hate; a time of war, and a time of peace.*"

"What are you saying? Tell me straight."

"I tried to warn people. I said it all so gently in the seventies and eighties. I told stories. I gave people examples of the heroes they could be. I asked people to relax and to be decent. I made a lot of jokes. Sometimes I ranted a bit. But it seemed I was always preaching to the choir. Not enough people read and understood. I told them as much as I could, plainly and sternly, toward the end of my life. Be decent to one another because we've tried everything else. Let's try compassion next. When you lose a thing, it's always in the last place you look."

"That's because when you find it, you stop looking," Ray said.

"Go looking for compassion. Help them find that, Ray. Help the Wizard find it. You need him on your side if this is going to work."

"How do I do that?"

The Man in the Moon answered: *Eliminate fear.*

Ray looked from Vonnegut to the Man in the Moon. "You want me to work *with* Martin Arnold?"

"Reasonable people can disagree and still do great things together."

"The Wiz is not reasonable."

"You caught him at a bad moment," Kurt smiled. "Metastases to the brain and whatnot."

"How can I eliminate fear if I'm terrified of the guy I'm supposed to work with?"

Vonnegut turned to the Man in the Moon. "You allowed an exception for Martin. You'll have to do the same for Ray."

The author nudged Ray and gave him a wink and a grin. "Bureaucracy. One day we'll eliminate all the red tape. We'll open up the Gates of Perception to everyone and fly to the stars with our minds." He paused and turned to give Ray his full attention. "In fact, you might be the one to do it."

Ray wanted to believe him. He wanted to hope again. He wanted to erase the shame of resorting to suicide when he could have done so much more with his life. He wanted to believe in the future.

The deal was struck. The Man in the Moon would allow him to travel on the same wheel as much and as easily as he needed to fulfill his mission. Ray truly became what he thought he already was: a time traveler.

Ray Bradley offered his hand for Kurt Vonnegut to shake. The old man smiled, shook his head, and pulled Ray into a hug.

"I...uh...I don't know what I'm doing."

Vonnegut clapped him on the back and chuckled. "Nobody does. Not really. Explains a lot, doesn't it?"

"But — "

"Be careful down there, Ray. You know what happens to anybody looking to change the prevailing paradigm. Somebody might try to nail you to a tree or something. First there's much resistance to change. Then, when change finally comes, it'll seem like the inevitable arrives all at once, like everybody suddenly wakes up together."

Ray's eyes widened. "Oh! Wait a — "

The River of Time came at him like a flash flood. It swept Ray away in a furious current of black ink under a watchful moon.

47

Ray awoke in a king-sized bed. Nightstands. A desk. A chair. He was in a hotel room that smelled like someone had poured alcohol all over it.

Ray's headache was back, but it wasn't Torment. He was exhausted and disoriented, but compared to a concussion headache, this was nothing. Somehow, he knew that full feeling in his skull was an effect of being carried on quantum waves passing through a portal.

He turned to look at the wall behind him. He remembered now. Sometime in the night, Ray had come through the bare wall beside one of the nightstands. He'd come from Clarity and left Torment behind.

Ray had his music, too. This time it was a jocular marimba beat that occasionally sojourned into a riff and electric guitar sting that reminded him of a James Bond movie soundtrack.

He went to the bathroom mirror first. No tattoos. No gold tooth. Then Ray opened the drapes to bright sunshine.

Before him stretched a city. He could see the Eiffel

Tower, the Sahara, the Sphinx, a massive pyramid, New York City's skyline and the Statue of Liberty. Ray let out a low whistle. "Good Christ! I'm in Vegas!"

The last time he was in Vegas, he'd pledged his undying love and married Marla. "Everything is a gamble," he'd told her. "Let's throw the dice."

Somewhere, in another dimension, Marla had wisely turned him down and saved them both years of heartache. Somewhere in the multiverse, maybe Joe Grins Well was the jilted husband and Ray might be the guy to whisk her away. So many choices and so many wrong paths available. No wonder it's so easy to go wrong.

"It's not that the universe is out to get us," Ray told the empty room. "It's that, as a race, we're suicidal. No wonder. This can be such an unkind, inhospitable planet."

The old man's voice reached him from nowhere. *You're paraphrasing me. What else you got?* Kurt Vonnegut was watching and, Ray was sure, smiling.

Ray answered, more for his own benefit than for the dead writer. "As individuals, we don't have enough data to make better decisions and we're terribly afraid."

Lose the fear. Increase the kindness. The information will come.

It was past noon. Ray blinked at the sunlight that flooded the room's disorder. Bottles of vodka had been knocked over on a low table and they had not been cleaned up. That was not Ray's doing and this was not Ray's room.

A knock came at the door.

"Who is it?"

"Hotel security, sir. There's been a complaint. Can you open up, please?"

Ray opened the door to find he was face to face with Professor Martin Arnold AKA Arnold Martin AKA The Wizard. The Wizard stepped into the room, leading with the muzzle of his little pistol. He looked very pale and Ray smelled fish.

"So! The ape man! It's the primate in the astronaut suit!"

"Hi, Wiz. Do you prefer Arnold or Martin, for a first name? Don't you think running around multiple planes of existence is confusing enough?"

The old man looked unsteady on his feet.

"Are you okay? Do you want to put down the gun and lie on the bed?"

"I was told to come here. I don't know why."

"Who sent you?" Ray asked.

"Samuel Clemens."

"Oh...you overshot the runway, man."

"What?"

"Did you get clarity?"

The old man swayed. "Yes and no. I wasn't satisfied with the answers I got. My calculations didn't work because I was only working with a regular chess board. The multiverse is three-dimensional chess, but worse. It's too complex to understand. Samuel Clemens told me I haven't been traveling through time. He said I've been 'traipsing across dimensions, trying to outrun Death.'"

A tear slid down the old man's cheek. "I knew there would be permutations and combinations, but I couldn't have known there were so many. No one can visualize the infinite. I should have known better. I should have stayed with the Mexican girl when I had the chance."

"Sorry about that. I really am. You made a lot of sense to me, back at the mental hospital." Ray looked down the barrel of the little pistol. "You're a very smart man, but nobody's smart enough to make existence make sense."

The old man dropped into the chair by the desk. He leaned heavily on it, but kept the pistol trained on Ray.

The wall behind Ray shifted. He felt the buzz of quantum waves through his head. Someone was coming through. At the same time, there was another knock on the door. Before Ray could move, the door burst in.

Another Wizard stood in the hall. He had a little pistol, too. He didn't point it at Ray. The new Wiz pointed the weapon at his doppelganger by the desk and fired and fired and fired until the pistol clicked.

The Wizard with the fishy smell didn't even try to get off a shot. He fell to the floor and rolled over to his back.

Ray knelt beside the fallen man as the Wizard stood in the hallway. He watched another version of himself die.

"Clemens told me..." the dying man said weakly. "He told me I couldn't outrun death. He said I'd meet it on the road to Damascus."

"Or in a Vegas hotel room," Ray said.

The dying man smiled. "Clemens also said it doesn't matter. He said I'd get another chance. Maybe I'll find the Mexican girl. Do you think I will?"

The Wizard breathed his last before Ray could answer.

When Ray looked up, he saw another Wizard

coming through the wall. Before the Wizard was all the way through, Ray thrust his hand into his pants pocket. The bouncer's gun was still there.

He pulled it out but the sight caught on his pants and, as Ray struggled to get off a shot in time, the newest intruder pulled back into the Beyond.

"Loop," the Ray said.

The Wizard who had killed his copy stepped into the room and closed the door. "Actually, that one was a skip. It's all skips and loops. Time loops. That's paradox fodder. The one coming through just now was a skip, incoming from another dimension."

Ray was anxious as he watched the Wizard reload. He was equally relieved when the man stuffed the weapon into his overcoat. This one wore far too many layers for Vegas heat.

Ray stuffed his pistol back in his trousers. "The one who came through the wall for a moment...I think he was the one I chased into a basement. He said something about seeing me thwart you...him."

"Sure," the Wizard said. "Take all the credit." He looked down at the dead man and shook his head. "Handsome devil." His mouth was a tight line as he strode to the bed and pulled the bedspread over the corpse on the floor.

"You don't look surprised to see me," Ray said.

"I am not. New orders."

"From whom?"

"Mark Twain."

"There are so many of us," Ray said.

"Yeah, yeah," the Wizard grumbled. "Each a special snowflake and slightly out of phase. No wonder there's so much empty space between atoms and stars. It's Nature trying to achieve balance and homeostasis."

"You're not going to do math are you?" Ray looked worried.

"No time. Get behind the door before the imperatives come back!"

"Were you the one who tried to ruin my life? Did you kill Victor and the bouncer? Big guy named Wayne? Remember that?"

"No," the Wizard said. "I'm the one who took a right on Hollywood Boulevard. The one who just came through the wall was that guy. I told you. Crack open a limit and it gets easier, not just in this dimension, but in all the dimensions. More potentials are becoming probable. We're not the only ones going through walls."

"Are you saying we're going to get a flood of clones from other — "

"Well, they wouldn't be *clones* — "

"You know what I mean!"

"There are so many dimensions and time streams, it's not like our copies will all show up here. There's a whole universe...a *multiverse* to explore, man!"

Ray thought about that for a full minute before he moved. "So you *did* shoot the Dutchmen? Or didn't you?"

"Don't be an infant. *Dutch men*. Yes. I did shoot and kill them. No one is perfect. I'm sorry for what I got wrong, but my mission is still to make as much as I can go right. I'm...er...evolving."

"You weren't working with enough information, maybe," Ray said.

"I pictured a clock with one wheel — "

"But there are infinite gears to the multiverse's clock," Ray said. "Yeah, yeah, I get it. You're revolving. Thanks for not trying to explain that with a math equation."

"Sorry about what I did before. I was doing the best I could at the time for Cenk. I know better now. I was working on faulty intelligence. Common problem. Rationalization is what we do. Fear is the engine. If we understood motivations instead of ascribing them, the engine would run out of gas."

Ray sighed. "We've talked too much. What are we supposed to *do*, though?"

"When the imperatives get here, I'll show you."

"The imperatives?"

"This is one of their hotel rooms. They meet back here soon."

"What's the plan?"

"Newtonian, actually. A balance of forces. For every action, there is an equal and opposite reaction," the Wizard said. "For centuries that's meant force against force. I have a better idea now. Mr. Twain approves."

"I'm still kind of freaked out here," Ray said. "If this doesn't work, I reserve the right to shoot you and start again, Mr. Wizard."

"If this doesn't work," the Wizard said, "I'll thank you as I die. In the meantime, you can call me Martin and, instead of ape man — "

"Call me Ray."

A cranked up, rocking version of the theme from *Mission Impossible* ignited in Ray's head again.

The two men — time loopers and dimensional skippers — shook hands.

48

Ray Bradley and Martin Arnold sat across from each other. Between them sat coffee, croissants and scrambled eggs. Neither man touched his food. For Ray, Nina Simone was back, singing *Feeling Good*. Every note felt sincere.

Martin's beard was shaved short in what Ray playfully referred to as Martin's Tony Stark look. The professor was such a fan, he kept returning to *Iron Man* movie premieres in 2008. Martin said he loved the movies because he identified with Robert Downey Jr.

However, Ray suspected what really excited Martin was seeing a handsome young actor in the background of several scenes. It was Cenk Duman, looking fit, tall and walking.

Ray stopped fidgeting and put his fork down. "I've been thinking about your liver cancer, Martin."

"Thank you, Ray. That's possibly...*considerate*? I try not to think about it much. Road to Damascus and all that."

Ray smiled. "What about seeking treatment elsewhere? Couldn't you do something about it long before you start smelling like trout all the time?"

The Wizard looked around to make sure no one could overhear their conversation. "You mean that I should seek treatment else*when*."

Ray nodded. "I've got a tiny simian brain. Surely, you, with your big ol' brain in a sling, have already given it some consideration. You're going forward in time to watch movies, surely a hospital tour is worth a look. Suppose you were to dip into the future thirty years and see what post-modern medicine has come up with?"

"You mean post-contemporary medicine. I did check into it. Thirty years isn't enough time. Not for my particular brand of cancer, anyway."

"Kurt told me that cancer is a constant, but maybe that's something that can change throughout the big wheel, too."

"The Biodiversity Catch is the problem," Martin declared. "Cells must be mutable but we don't want our own to mutate. It seems inescapable."

"Then go forward fifty years and see what's up in the world's research labs."

"Perhaps we could get cancer to the point where it's manageable, like herpes or AIDS," Martin said. "My prognosis seems rather bleak at the moment but, with some of the changes we have facilitated, perhaps things will become more optimistic. If we work more on cancer funding in *this* now, thirty years might be sufficient when I check back. I still have nine years before the first symptoms. You and I have so much to do before things get dire."

Ray smiled. "If we can switch the world's focus from perma-wars, years from now, conspiracy theorists won't be worrying about the military-industrial complex. They'll be talking about the medical-industrial complex, instead."

"Let's hope so," Martin said. "I know you don't like to look at the numbers. It seems especially strange to say this given where we are today but the chances of death by terrorism are negligible compared to the risks of cancer and heart disease."

Ray leaned forward and whispered. "Have we made the necessary changes in the here and now? For today's events, I mean?"

"If you're asking me if I made all the right phone calls, yes. We got the imperatives. Without their ringleaders, the rest of the organization is a shambles. The imperatives were the key integers to the event cascade."

"If you're wrong, Martin," Ray pointed over the professor's shoulder, "I get to jump through that wall first and we go back to Vegas and do it all over again, no matter how messy it gets. I'm willing to shoot them all in the head if there is a next time."

Martin shrugged. "And you're the one always telling me to relax. To answer your question, this is a start."

"Do you think we should call ourselves something?" Ray asked.

"What do you mean?"

"I don't know. I was thinking, just between you and me, we could call ourselves the Time Regulators."

"No." Martin studied the view of the sky and chewed a thumbnail absently.

"Time Shifters?"

"Absolutely not."

"Multiverse Echo Technicians?"

"God, no."

"Harmonic Convergence?"

"Sounds like a ska band from Portland."

"How about Time Warriors?"

"Shut up."

"Men in Black?"

Martin looked up. "Mm...let me think about that one. Maybe. It's taken, though. Nah. Not on point."

"Do you have any suggestions or are you just going to shoot all mine down?"

"Sometimes I think we're on a grand adventure to save the multiverse from itself," Martin said. "Sometimes I think you and I are still mental patients locked away somewhere."

"Somewhere in the multiverse, Martin, we still are."

"In many locations, Ray, yes."

Ray waved a hand to get their waiter's attention. A moment later, the waiter wearing a short white coat and white gloves set two champagne flutes before them. Both men raised their glasses in a toast.

"Ours is a grand enterprise," Martin said. "Let us hope the echoes and stirrings of this historic day — "

"Of this *non*-historic day," Ray said.

"Yes, let's hope our efforts ring through the multiverse and harmonize."

They drank.

Ray checked his watch. "It's almost time, Martin. You're sure?"

"If my calculations are correct — "

Ray groaned.

Martin cleared his throat and began again. "If we've done our job, we have freed up a lot of money and resources for your pet project, Ray."

"Compassion isn't a pet project, Martin. It's our mission now, straight from Vonnegut and the Man in the Moon."

"I've decided something. I'm going to teach you mathematics before I die."

Ray's face fell. "Oh, God."

"You're going to need to master some math!"

Ray's eyes narrowed. "Did you...?"

"I went forward and back. Clean drinking water and mosquito nets for all areas with malaria. That's a start."

"How?"

Martin placed a Powerball lottery ticket beside Ray's plate. "Also, I checked. Bush and Cheney only serve one, delightfully uneventful term."

"No Iraq or Afghanistan. That will echo through the many realms." Ray smiled wide.

"As long as we pay a visit to Osama while he's still in the construction business."

"I won't forget."

They clinked glasses again and drank.

"We've confined ourselves so far. But what would have happened if Kennedy had lived and Hitler had... let's say 'disappeared'?"

Ray rolled his eyes. "I knew you couldn't leave that old trope alone. I'll bring it up with Kurt on my next trip to Clarity. I'm sure he'll have some thoughts on the matter. We've got our hands full moving forward."

"For now," Martin said. "So, until Powerball night, what do you want to do?"

"I have an idea. Enjoy your champagne without worrying about your liver and guard that lottery ticket. Revel in the clear blue skies on this sunny

Tuesday morning because all is right with the world."
Ray checked his watch again. "You think they're
late?"

Martin smiled. "They aren't late, Ray."

"Then through the interdimensional principle of
harmonic resonance, as I dimly understand it, all is
right with the *worlds*."

"Plural, *ad infinitum*." Martin emptied his
champagne flute down his throat and grinned.

Both men's eyes were wet.

"Three thousand lives, just today," Ray said. "Did
it!"

"And we usher in a new set of happier
repercussions and possibilities," Martin replied.

"All good, except for a bunch of Saudi Nationals
who are, at this moment, getting reeducation
lectures in compassion in a strange desert under a
full moon. If anyone can turn them around, Kurt can.
They have eternity to come around to peaceful
expressions of outrage."

Ray rose from his chair and walked across the
room to seat himself behind the baby grand in the
corner. He didn't need to read music. He had it all in
his head and he couldn't wait to get it out for the
world to hear.

Just as he touched the keys, he looked up. Startled,
he hit a sour note. At the far side of the room by the
windows, Ray spotted four men at a table whom he
hadn't noticed enter the restaurant. Two of them
looked exactly like Ray except one wore a scraggly
and ill-advised goatee. The third man looked like
Kurt Vonnegut. The fourth was a keen-eyed
gentleman in a white suit and vest. The stranger
raised a glass in a toast and nodded at the piano.

295

Mark Twain, or rather, a copy of Mark Twain from another dimension, urged him to begin.

Ray Bradley's first concert had been a small audience in the common room of an insane asylum in 2014. Ray's second performance was for the breakfast crowd at the Windows on the World Restaurant atop the North Tower of the World Trade Center on the morning of September 11, 2001.

Ray began his concert with *America the Beautiful*. He played sweetly. He did not hit one ironic note.

A LOVE LETTER TO KURT VONNEGUT

**For more books by Robert Chazz Chute,
please check out my Amazon page.
To find out when new books are coming
out, sign up for updates, podcasts and more
at
AllThatChazz.com.**

And now...

In addition to reading his books and books about him, I saw Kurt Vonnegut onstage at Dalhousie University twenty-five years ago or so. He obviously made an impression.

Kurt talked about writing and meditation. He felt reading is superior to the meditative experience. His eyes were bright with kind ideas. We don't have enough Kurt Vonneguts in the world. (We need more George Carlins, too.)

And we need more kind ideas. We're getting better and better at killing people. Between missile strikes and Internet trolls, we've cornered the market on making enemies. We should slow down research that promotes collateral damage (an obscene euphemism) and alter the technology that facilitates mean and thoughtless YouTube comments. We're good enough at that stuff. In fact, killing people is too easy. We are experts at killing. But helping isn't really as hard as we often imagine, either.

Vonnegut was a disappointed humanist. He saw our potential as a species, but he was also clear how far short we fell of those lofty possibilities.

It is a troubling theme I come back to in my writing often. What are we really? Are we all about war or cooperation? There are ample examples of both those facets of human nature. Some idealize the ever-spinning wheels of war even as suicide rates and Post Traumatic Stress Disorder savage staggering numbers of soldiers.

We praise "decisive action" and "leadership" that are supposed to protect national interests but often succeed only in killing innocents and lining the pockets of defense contractors and war profiteers.

We never would have made it out of the trees and into the caves and, finally, out of the caves, without cooperation. Helping each other, *really* helping, is in our nature, too.

Solving problems that more of us encounter would make us all happier. I'm hoping for advancements like better treatments for heart disease, cancers and traumatic brain injury. Create a healthy salad that tastes like chocolate fudge. That's my advice. You'll be a billionaire by next Tuesday.

I suspect Mr. Vonnegut would agree about our dual nature, though it's always a dangerous act of hubris to put words in a giant's mouth, even if he's dead.

A couple of weeks before I finished the first draft of this novel, I was in a bookstore. I looked up and Mr. Vonnegut stared at me, life-size, out of a black and white poster. He's sitting in a living room chair, head turned in that picture. His eyes are piercing.

That stare took me back twenty-five years. I was about to graduate from journalism school and I had hope for the future. I want to feel hope again. I'm reading Vonnegut's books again to fuel that aspiration. I wrote *Wallflower* to find hope again.

Cynical people (and I'm often one of them) say hope is for young people with long lives ahead of them. When I come back to reading Kurt Vonnegut, I know three things:

1. Books are time machines. I'd rather Kurt stayed on Earth among the living, of course. I can read his books and read them again and it's not as good as having him here. It's the next best thing, though, and that's something.

2. Books are a meditation that take us out of time and into many dimensions.

3. As long as there are books, Kurt Vonnegut will never die. It's not just about all the books he wrote that are his legacy, but all the writers he mentored and inspired.

In the spirit of kindness, and since we may as well start with doing the easy awesome now, I have a favor to ask all readers of this book.

I know a man named Russell Sawatsky. Russ needs a kidney. This is something a live donor can provide, though Russ isn't fussy. A cadaver would do. Modern medicine can do wonders in the field of changing and saving lives. Organ donation is science fiction made real. We aren't quite ready to harvest the needed organs from test tubes, however. We need you.

Please sign your organ donor card. If more people donate once they don't need their organs anymore, fewer people will die needlessly while they wait for matching organs. It's just the right thing to do.

To find out more, please go to KidneyForRuss.wordpress.com. Follow Russ @RSawatsky on Twitter. Spread his word. Russ isn't just out for himself. He's trying to increase awareness so anyone in need can receive the gift of organ donation.

Far too many of us are capable of giving this gift but we're missing out on doing the easy awesome. The people of Earth are faced with huge challenges. Let's start by taking on the problems we can solve now. Perhaps such certain successes with acts of kindness will inspire us for the greater challenges we face.

Thank you. Much love.

Chazz
June, 2015

ABOUT THE AUTHOR

"That Apocalyptic Guy," Robert Chazz Chute, writes suspense, dark fantasy and SF. Winner of eight writing awards, Chazz's best known book, *This Plague of Days, Omnibus Edition,* won Honorable Mention from *Writers Digest* Self-published Ebook Awards in 2014.

Chazz is a former journalist, frequent podcast guest and independent publisher who practices rehabilitative therapy in Other London. You are invited to join Chazz's Choir for complimentary review copies, exclusive announcements and updates about new books at AllThatChazz.com.

Thank you so much for reading **Wallflower,** I'd certainly appreciate it if you left a happy review.
Cheers!
~ Chazz

DISCOVER MORE TITLES BY ROBERT CHAZZ CHUTE

This Plague of Days Series
Books One, Two and Three
This Plague of Days Omnibus

The Ghosts & Demons Series
The Haunting Lessons
The End of the World As I Know It
Fierce Lessons
We Battle Demons, The Ghosts & Demons Omnibus

The Hit Man Series
Bigger Than Jesus
Higher Than Jesus
Hollywood Jesus
Rise of the Divine Assassin Omnibus

Intense Violence, Bizarre Themes
(My Criminal Autobiography)

Wallflower

* * *

<u>Anthologies</u>
Self-help for Stoners
Murders Among Dead Trees